Wolf Tales VI

Also by Kate Douglas:

Wolf Tales

"Chanku Rising" in *Sexy Beast*

Wolf Tales II

"Camille's Dawn" in *Wild Nights*

Wolf Tales III

"Chanku Fallen" in *Sexy Beast II*

Wolf Tales IV

"Chanku Journey" in *Sexy Beast III*

Wolf Tales V

"Chanku Destiny" in *Sexy Beast IV*

Wolf Tales VI

KATE DOUGLAS

APHRODISIA
KENSINGTON PUBLISHING CORP.

APHRODISIA BOOKS are published by

Kensington Publishing Corp.
850 Third Avenue
New York, NY 10022

All Kensington Titles, Imprints, and Distributed Lines are available at special quantity discounts for bulk purchases for sales promotions, premiums, fund-raising, and educational or institutional use.

Aphrodisia and the A logo Reg. U.S. Pat. & TM Off.

ISBN-13: 978-0-7394-9717-7

Printed in the United States of America

I was recently asked who I feel has helped me most in my career. Of course, I immediately thought of my amazing agent, Jessica Faust of BookEnds, LLC, and my editor, Audrey LaFehr, who chose *Wolf Tales* for the beginning of Kensington's Aphrodisia line and continues to give me such wonderful freedom to write my stories. And of course, there's my husband, an absolutely fantastic guy who has always supported my writing career—literally—even when I wasn't selling diddly-squat.

Then I thought of the ones who have been there from the beginning, when dreams of publishing were just that—dreams. My very first critique partner, author Kathryn North, who patiently explained to me what passive voice and point of view meant, and author Patricia Lucas White, who taught me the concept of paying it forward long before it was a catchphrase. Angela Knight, an angel in the publishing community who writes kick-ass heroines and shares her expertise on how she does it with the world. There's Stephanie Burke, an author with a most amazing imagination who taught me that anything is possible in the world of the paranormal, and Treva Harte and Shelby Morgen who helped me develop a very thick skin when it came to critiques! There are so many others I can't name them all, but I have never found more generous souls than those in the writing community. I feel blessed to count myself among their number, and I will be the first to admit I didn't get here on my own.

Acknowledgments

My very special thanks to the amazing women who are willing to take time from their own very busy schedules to read my stories, tell me where I blew it, and do their best to make me better. Karen Woods, Dakota Cassidy, Ann Jacobs, Camille Anthony, Devyn Quinn, and Sheri Fogarty—all of you talented and smart and so much fun. I am honored to have you as friends, and even more honored you are so generous with your time, your expertise, and your thoughtful comments and observations. The best thing of all? You are utterly unshockable! With this series, that's a definite plus.

I also wish to thank an amazingly talented group of men, the writers who contribute to The Sticky Pen website at www.stickypen.com. The stories you so generously share help me bring my characters to life.

Chapter 1

"You bitch! You're nothing but a cock-teasing bitch."

Eve Reynolds twisted to one side and tried to duck, but the big guy kicked the motel room door shut with his foot and slammed her against the bedroom wall. His buddy stood to one side, watching with a salacious smirk on his face.

She aimed a kick in his direction. The smaller guy jumped out of the way before she could connect. Eve twisted in the bigger man's grasp, felt her T-shirt stretch, heard it tear. The shredded top drooped to her waist, a meaty hand surrounded her exposed breast, thick fingers dug into soft flesh. It hurt, damn it, but not as much as when he shoved his thigh between her legs, lifting her feet off the ground while he groped her other breast.

She twisted, but couldn't break free. He was taller and stronger and totally enraged. Adrenaline poured into her system. Eve's vision blurred and she fought the need to shift. It would be so easy—so utterly satisfying. Just be the wolf long enough to take them out, both of them—the big guy assaulting her and his smarmy buddy, too. She could change in a heartbeat, all slavering teeth and powerful jaws tearing into her attackers. Eve pictured the blood and the rewarding burst of terror. She felt the first frisson of change course through her body.

The man's thigh ground against her sensitive pubes. She tensed, preparing for the wolf. Then Anton Cheval's words of warning leapt into her mind. The leader of the Montana pack had been deadly serious and his warning was branded in her mind.

Our identity as Chanku is a closely guarded secret. Take care no one learns what you are.

These men would know, if she let them live. Eve wasn't ready to kill a man, much less two, which she'd have to do if she shifted. Leaving witnesses wasn't acceptable, damn it all, but she really hated to do the girlie thing. Then a hand snaked down the front of her shorts and rough fingers scraped at tender flesh, forcing entrance. She screamed, loud and long, her voice powered by anger, not fear. Then she bit into the man's thick bicep, the only body part within reach of her teeth. Her human jaws lacked wolven strength and sharpness, but the combination of scream and bite, of nearby doors opening and people yelling, was enough to stop the attack.

The big guy shoved her to the floor, yelled for his buddy, and the two of them raced out the door and climbed into their truck. The shiny red Chevy 4x4 fishtailed out of the parking lot, spewing gravel and dust in its wake. Light from the garish streetlamps turned the dust to gold and the gravel twinkled like precious gems. A perfect example of things not always being as they seemed.

Eve held on to the doorjamb and gasped for air as she watched them leave. Neighbors on either side of her ground-floor room spilled out into the night. She clutched her torn shirt across her breasts, waved off their concern, and apologized for the disturbance. Then she closed the door to her motel room and leaned her head against the warm wood.

Heat and moisture engulfed her. Heart pounding, breath still rasping in her lungs, she concentrated on the thick, humid air and the silence, now that the truck was gone.

And the fact she'd managed not to shift.

Eve rubbed her left arm, well aware she'd have the jerk's fingerprints imprinted in her flesh for the next few days. Her crotch hurt where he'd shoved her with his thigh and violated her with his filthy fingers. Both her breasts were bruised.

Moving on unsteady feet, Eve limped into the bathroom. She glanced only briefly in the mirror before looking away. She didn't need to see the tangled blond hair or the bruise along her left cheek to know she looked like a wild-eyed tramp. Hands shaking, head pounding with the onset of a headache, she stripped out of her clothes, stepped into the shower and turned on the water. All she got was a tepid spray, but it was enough to wash the man's stink off her bruised body.

Eve let her mind go blank as water sluiced over her head and shoulders. When she finally got out and dried off, though, her head still ached. She grabbed a washcloth, rinsed it out, held the damp cloth to her forehead . . . and thought of Montana.

Clear skies and dark, cool forests. Trails leading into magical places where wild things ran and the water tasted clear and fresh against her tongue. Thick grass beneath her paws, the sound and scent of her packmates beside her. The sense of belonging, of being one with nature and the pack.

She'd known that closeness for such a brief time, but the feeling hadn't left her. The sense of brotherhood, of family. Of belonging. Still, she'd had a good enough reason to leave after a mere taste of what her life could be, hadn't she? Discovering she was a shapeshifting Chanku with the ability to switch instantly from woman to wolf had opened her life to freedoms she'd never imagined but always craved. Freedom she would have given up had she stayed with the man who wanted so badly to claim her.

Adam Wolf. Damn, how she missed him.

She brushed the unwelcome sting of tears from her eyes, took a deep breath, and slowly regained control of her shattered emotions. It had to be the adrenaline from the attack. That's all it was. Adrenaline and nerves. Not Adam. Never Adam.

Talk about sucky timing. She'd wanted independence her entire life. When it was finally handed to her, even beyond the amazing power of the wolf, she was every bit as trapped by love as she'd ever been by circumstances. Recognizing her unhappiness, Anton Cheval, the uncontested leader of the Montana pack, had given her a beautiful, cherried out antique Ford pickup to drive, credit cards with unlimited funds, and a pocketful of cash.

The fact the truck was supposed to go to his packmate, Stefan Aragat, as a birthday gift, hadn't seemed to bother Anton a bit. He seemed certain Eve would have it back in time.

So what had she done with his largesse? Driven clear across the country to the town she'd grown up in, parked her butt in a nicer motel that she'd ever been able to afford before in her life, and waited to see what would happen next.

So far, nothing good had come her way, and she had no idea what had drawn her back. No idea what was good enough in Tampa to lure her away from the beauty of Montana and people who loved her.

What kind of fool was she?

Eve freshened the washcloth under the faucet and wrung the excess water out of it. This time she held the cloth against the bruises on her left breast where the flesh had been so cruelly twisted. She had no one to blame but herself for tonight's little episode, but damn, she hurt all over and felt like a fool. A very lonely fool.

She'd had such a short time in Montana with Adam Wolf. The name alone should have warned her, but he'd been everything she'd ever wanted in a man . . . and more. They'd found a connection unlike anything she'd experienced. When he'd brought Oliver, the quiet young man who worked for Anton Cheval, into their bed, the sex had been little short of mind-blowing.

So, what did she do? She ran. Fast and far, afraid of the overwhelming emotions, frightened as much by the changes in her body as she finally embraced her wolven, Chanku heritage, as she'd been by her attraction to Adam.

Unfortunately, she hadn't been able to leave her libido behind. Tonight, she'd lost control, and along with it, what little respect she thought she'd held on to. She'd wanted sex. She'd wanted a repeat of that amazing night with Adam and Oliver. Every night since coming to Tampa, she'd found a quiet place to run as the wolf, to learn more about her new body. The downside of the exhilaration she experienced on four legs was that damned Chanku libido. Desire, hot and potent, streaming like a living entity through her veins, and needs she really couldn't satisfy on her own, no matter how fresh she kept the batteries in her electronic buddy.

Each night she returned to this room aroused beyond belief, her blood racing, sexual desire taking precedence over all other instincts, all sense of caution. How else could she explain what she'd done tonight? She'd gone trolling for a man.

The two men from the bar had seemed nice enough at first. She'd led them on, invited them back to her room. Eve thought she wanted both men and all they promised, but when it came right down to it, she'd not wanted them at all.

She'd wanted her own kind. Her body still thrummed

with the dark cravings, the sexual needs unfulfilled these past three weeks since she'd left Adam. Cravings that intensified each time she shifted, each time she raced through the night on four legs, searching for others of her kind even though she knew there were none here.

Needs she'd thought she might satisfy with the two men she'd brought home with her tonight. Except, once again, it had felt all wrong.

They'd both kissed her, a man on either side in the front seat of the big pickup truck. The larger of the two had been the most aggressive. He'd stroked the warm folds between her legs, rubbing her through the soft cotton of her shorts, and her body had responded. Her breasts tingled, her pussy clenched and creamed and she'd thought it might work. She'd hoped her body would continue to react, but his kisses weren't Adam's. His touch wasn't as loving as Oliver's. He didn't understand the needs of the wolf and his mind was closed to her deepest desires. Would it always be this way? Would she only find satisfaction among other Chanku?

Sighing, Eve stretched out on the bed and held the damp washcloth against her breasts. It didn't do a thing to ease the all-consuming ache between her legs. The constant throbbing, the clenching of muscles too long denied, the desperate need for penetration, for sexual release.

She lay there in the dark, naked and sweating. The little air conditioner hummed and rattled, but it didn't touch the thick Florida heat. She retraced the past month of her life, the three weeks since leaving Montana. So much had happened in those few days after she'd met Keisha Rialto and Alexandria Olanet, when their wonderfully protective mates, Anton and Stefan, had rescued her from an abusive relationship turned deadly.

Why was she always drawn to losers? Probably for the same stupid reason she'd walked away from the finest man she'd ever known. She was an idiot, pure and simple. Too stupid to live . . . wasn't that how the saying went? *TSTL*? It fit her perfectly.

Her life was spinning out of control, twisting pointlessly in a maelstrom of need and arousal, of desperate cravings and unfulfilled desires. And she was lonely. So damned lonely. Eve rolled her hips against the bed, imagining Oliver beneath her and Adam between her legs. The memory brought forth a rush of fluids and a hollow, empty feeling deep inside.

She clutched the bedspread with both hands, accepting her needs, her powerful desires. Accepting, yet wondering how it could happen, how she could take this woman's body and become a wolf?

How she could take a man like Adam Wolf into her bed, into her heart, and find real love? The kind of love in fairy tales. The kind of love she'd always been denied.

Take that love and then stupidly walk away from it.

Once she'd discovered her heritage as a shapeshifter, a member of an ancient race that somehow appeared on the inhospitable Himalayan steppe so many eons ago, everything had changed. It was hard to say what was the biggest thing that had happened—shifting into a wolf, or meeting Adam, a man so tender and loving he made her ache with wanting. A man who claimed his only desire was to fix things.

Eve wondered if it was too late, if now that she'd left him, would he ever be able to fix her? Would he even want to?

Not if you keep running away, you idiot.

Nothing quite so sensitive as an inner critic. Eve moved the washcloth to her right breast. Her nipple tightened almost painfully when she scraped the sensitive tip with the cotton cloth, so she repeated the motion. Again. And again.

She shifted her hips against the wrinkled bedspread and her body felt all itchy and achy. She wanted to run. Wanted to shift and become the wolf and race through the forest. She hadn't run tonight. She wanted the wild and cool forests of Montana, not the hot and humid parks and gardens around Tampa, Florida.

She wanted to hunt for rabbits and deer, not worry about stepping on a cottonmouth snake, or running full tilt into a hungry alligator.

What the hell was she doing here, anyway?

Idly rubbing at her taut nipple, Eve reached between her legs and stroked her clit with her other hand. The tiny nub stood upright, hard and slick with her cream. She bit back a frustrated moan. Her fingers weren't enough. Her needs were too great, her body too desperate, aching for the heat and weight of a man.

She thought of the new vibrator in the table beside the bed. She'd never even used this one. Big and thick and perfectly formed to give her release, according to the advertising. *Crap.* Who was she trying to kid? It would take a lot more than plastic and batteries to ease the ache building inside.

Why had she even come back? When she was eighteen, she hadn't been able to get out of town fast enough. Away from the foster care system, from abuse and emptiness and a sense she was always searching, always looking for something just out of reach. Keisha had referred to it as quiet desperation, that knowledge buried deep in the heart, always calling to those who shared the Chanku genetics. Hinting at more, at something just out of reach, some visceral knowledge yet to be discovered.

She'd found it in Montana with the pack of Chanku shapeshifters. Once she'd started taking the big, ugly brown capsules Anton gave her, once her body had received the nutrients it needed, completed its changes and she'd finally been able to shift, Eve discovered a side of her life she'd never imagined. Never dreamed existed.

She should have been happy there, finally at home. She

could have been happy with Adam and Oliver, if only she'd been able to ignore the tugging sensation deep in her heart. She'd thought it was her need to be her own woman, to succeed entirely on her own. Now that she was here, living alone and feeling lonelier than she ever had in her life, Eve knew that wasn't it at all. There was something more, something still unexplained.

For whatever reason, it had called her back to Tampa. Until she knew what fate held in store for her, Eve knew she couldn't leave.

She sat up on the edge of the bed, her mind filled with thoughts of Adam. She missed him. Damn, she hardly knew the man, yet the image of his tall, rangy body filled her heart and her mind. Made her body anxious and miserable with wanting.

Did he feel the same? Had he missed her over these three long weeks? Would he come to her? *Why should he?* Her shoulders slumped and she sighed. *He's just found his sister and his mother, and a new family in the Montana pack. Why would he come after me?*

She glanced toward the window. Through the slightly parted curtain she saw the cherry '51 Ford pickup parked outside her room. Black and shiny beneath the parking lot lights, it gleamed with lots of chrome and expensive paint. The truck had been a loan from Anton Cheval, but he wanted it back by July 20, in time for his packmate—and lover's—birthday.

Stefan's birthday was just a little over a week away, and Eve still wasn't sure why she was even here. She really didn't want to go back without finding out what had drawn her to Florida in the first place, but she'd promised Anton she'd return the truck.

Unless, of course, she couldn't. Maybe because it wasn't running?

Grinning broadly, Eve grabbed a fresh cotton gown and slipped it over her head. She went outside, lifted the hood on the truck and stared at the myriad bits and parts of whatever made the darned thing run.

She shrugged, looked around to see if anyone was watching her. Then she reached inside and pulled a few wires loose. For added measure, she tugged a couple of unidentifiable things completely free and tossed them inside the cab. Then she went back inside her motel room and placed a call to Montana.

Adam threw an extra pair of clean jeans into the sports bag and zipped it shut just as Oliver walked into the room. He glanced up. "Are you ready, Ollie? Got your bags packed?"

Oliver shrugged and sat on the edge of the bed. Small and dark, yet always meticulous in both dress and action, he took a moment before answering. "Are you certain you want me to come? I invited myself along when you said you were going after Eve. I did it without thinking, but I don't want to intrude."

Adam shook his head, but he couldn't hold back the laugh. Damn, he was going to see Eve again whether she wanted him or not. Of course, if she'd called Keisha to say the truck wasn't running, she must have known who would be sent to fix it.

"You're going with me, bud. We're taking the Jeep and someone needs to drive it home. I'll be traveling back with Eve. I'm not letting her out of my sight once I find her."

"You're certain?" Oliver sat a bit straighter.

"Of course. That is . . . do you think Anton will let you go?"

Oliver smiled. "Unlike my first master, Anton doesn't own me, but I checked to be sure. He said he and the others will manage without me. However, he didn't sound happy about it."

"Who's going to cook?" Adam sat next to Oliver and bumped his shoulder companionably. Oliver quirked one

WOLF TALES VI / 11

perfect eyebrow. Adam grinned, imagining the somewhat pompous magician and his pack dealing with the intricacies of Oliver's household duties. "They're all going to starve."

"I hope not. Stefan volunteered to cook. I'm hoping he knows what he's getting himself into. They can always shift and feed in the forest. The woods are full of game this time of year."

Adam flung his arm over Oliver's shoulders and felt the smaller man stiffen, but he didn't pull away as he might have a couple weeks ago. Adam wondered if Ollie would ever grow used to the touching and closeness that was so much a part of the Chanku pack. Having lived as a eunuch most of his life, Oliver had held himself apart from everyone. The adjustment to his new sexuality, to full status within the Chanku Montana pack, couldn't be an easy one, but of all the things Adam had been able to fix in his lifetime, returning Oliver's manhood had been the most fulfilling. "I want you with me, Ollie. I wouldn't think of going after Eve without you beside me."

Oliver merely nodded. Adam wondered if this wealth of feeling was as hard for Oliver as it was for him. He felt his throat tighten and sucked in a deep breath. A burst of emotion washed over him and he struggled for control. This past few weeks had changed everything Adam had ever known, ever believed, about his life and his own sense of who and what he was.

It had also given him the first true friend he'd ever known. A friend and a lover. Not only had Oliver brought him into the pack, he'd been the one to recognize that Adam was the missing son of one of the newest Chanku, Millie West.

From life on the streets to this beautiful, palatial Montana home, from a solitary existence without family or loved ones, to an emotional reunion with a mother and twin sister he'd never known. A sister whose existence he had sensed for most of his adult life. Sometimes, when he thought of all that had happened over the past few weeks, Adam was overwhelmed by the wealth and complexity of change.

And then there was Eve. A strong, beautiful woman who fulfilled him in ways he'd never imagined. For a few short days their relationship had been intense and satisfying, almost frightening with the power of their connection. She'd loved him, linked minds with him, but not bonded. Even so, she'd given Oliver his first sexual experience. She'd given Adam even more.

A sense of the future, of possibilities and promises, without ever saying the words. Then she'd moved on to deal with her own inner demons. The wolf was only a small part of Eve Reynolds. She still had to come to terms with the woman.

The very complicated woman.

And so she'd gone. She'd taken Adam's heart with her, but he'd known he would find her again. Still, the connection now seemed almost dreamlike, too amazing to be real. Sometimes it was almost too much to comprehend.

Oliver made it real. For all the pain in his life, Oliver was a survivor. Castrated when he was still very young, sold into slavery, denied his rights not only as a man, but as Chanku, he'd still maintained an unwavering optimism, a hope for the future that Adam envied. When Adam managed to find a way to help Oliver gain the manhood he'd never known, it had seemed only right the two of them would feel a special bond, but it went beyond the fact Adam had been able to fix what was wrong in Oliver's life.

Oliver, in some inexplicable way, completed him. Adam couldn't explain the feeling, but he needed it. Needed Oliver, almost as much as he needed Eve.

When Oliver turned, almost shyly, and pressed his lips against Adam's throat, there was no hesitation. They weren't planning to leave until morning. There was no reason not to share a bit of passion tonight, especially after running.

Shifting definitely had an amazing affect on a man's libido. Arousal thrummed in Adam's veins. It was always this way after racing through the forest, two wolves on the hunt, sharing a kill. A connection unlike anything else, that sharing of warm meat and fresh blood.

It would be so much more powerful with Eve, once they bonded. He was sure of it, though they'd never even run together as wolves. She'd made the change a day ahead of Adam, shifted and run with the others, and then she'd packed her bags and run away. He thought he understood. He'd certainly wanted to believe Anton when the wizard said it wasn't Adam that Eve was running from.

It was her own life she was running to.

Whatever it was that left Eve incomplete would have to be fixed before she could give herself over to another. Anton had cautioned patience. He'd given Eve the vehicle, the money, and the blessing to figure out what she needed, and he'd given her a reason to return.

There had been no doubt in Anton's mind that Eve would come back to Montana. Until she did, until she was able to bond freely to him, Adam wouldn't experience the mind and body connection of two wolves as one, their every move and thought in sync. He wanted that feeling, that connection. He wanted it with Eve. Sighing, thinking longingly of the woman he already thought of as his, Adam kissed Oliver and lowered him gently to the bed.

The second day after her assault, she was still every bit as sore as she'd expected, but at least the bruises were fading, thanks to her Chanku genetics. Eve crawled out of bed before seven and showered before throwing on shorts and a tank top. She stepped out of her motel room into the suffocating heat, and stared at the truck. Then she walked across the parking lot and headed to the closest store. She couldn't take the truck. No way was it going to work after she'd stripped so many wires out from under the hood.

There was a little convenience store half a block from her motel and the coffee was good. She'd even grown accustomed to the egg and sausage sandwiches she could stick in the small microwave she'd bought for her motel room.

The clerk behind the counter waved and smiled, proof Eve had been staying in the same place much too long. She grabbed a newspaper and poured a cup of coffee, then studied the various sandwiches wrapped in plastic.

Staring at the selection of croissants and bagels and rolls, she let her mind wander west to Montana and the sun-dappled forest she never realized she'd miss so terribly. What she wouldn't give for a nice, juicy rabbit!

A frisson of awareness skittered across her neck and down her spine. Little goose bumps prickled over her arms and Eve blinked herself back to the present. She glanced toward the cold case where the beer, soft drinks, and lunch meats were kept. A young woman stood in front of the frosted doors. Her long, coal-black hair swung past her hips like a curtain of silk. She was tall and slender, her jeans torn and dirty. They hung low on her slim hips and her skintight, pale blue cropped tank was badly faded and stained.

Something about her caught Eve's attention. Maybe it was the cocky tilt to one hip, the way she glanced toward the clerk then quickly looked away. Maybe it was the sensual sway of her hair or something deeper, more profound. At the moment Eve couldn't put her finger on whatever it was that made her watch. Made her concentrate on the woman while pretending to check over the choices on the morning take-out menu.

Had she not been watching, she might not have noticed when the girl slipped a package of sliced turkey into her purse. Might have missed the two candy bars that followed, and the small carton of orange juice.

If the girl had just left it at that, she might have made it out the door with no one but Eve the wiser, but she got greedy. Or maybe she was just so hungry she forgot about caution. About survival. She fingered a perfect orange on top of a stack of fruit on a table near the door, rolled it into her palm and quickly headed for the door.

"Hey you! Lady! Stop now! Ya gotta pay for that orange!" The clerk vaulted over the counter and reached for her arm. The girl spun around and grabbed the door handle, but the clerk, a young man with a long reach, barred the way.

Eve stood unmoving, watching to see what would happen next. The girl twisted and tried to pull free of the young man's grasp, but he held on tight and pulled her back toward the counter, cursing her each step of the way. The girl struggled, obviously panic-stricken, but so far she hadn't said a word. Then she curled her lip and snarled.

That was the only way Eve could describe the sound. It startled her into action. "Wait," she said, reaching out to touch the young man's shoulder. "I'll pay for whatever she took."

The clerk stopped and stared at Eve. "Why? You with her?"

Eve shook her head. "No, but I've been hungry enough to steal." She looked at the girl, who held herself as far from the clerk as she could with him still hanging on to her arm. "Is that okay with you? I'll pay for the things you took."

The girl didn't speak, but she jerked her head, a short, sharp nod of agreement. The clerk turned her loose and stepped around behind the counter.

"That orange'll be a buck fifty."

Twice what the sign said. Eve bit back a grin and set her

own items on the counter, a couple of breakfast sandwiches and a cup of coffee. Without looking at the thief, she asked, "Okay, now what about the things in your purse?" She turned and stared at the young woman who at least had the grace to blush. The girl pulled the other items out of her bag and lined them up on the counter. The clerk glared at her while he rang them up. Eve pulled some bills out of her pocket and peeled off twice the amount of the total. "Keep the change. I appreciate your not calling the cops."

"Thanks, lady." He stared at the young woman. "Don't ever come back here again, got it?"

She nodded. Eve took the bag from the clerk and turned to the girl. "You got anywhere to go?"

"No."

"Ah. So you can talk. Come with me. I'm not staying all that far from here." She held the door open and the young woman stepped out ahead of her. For whatever reason, Eve felt relaxed for the first time in weeks. She wasn't sure how or why, but the little thief with the silky black hair seemed to hold answers.

Answers to questions Eve hadn't even thought to ask. Smiling, clutching the bag of groceries against her chest, she headed back to the motel with her young charge in tow.

The microwave dinged. Eve pulled out the little round table from the corner of the room and set out napkins as place mats, put a warmed breakfast croissant filled with ham, cheese, and eggs on each one, then set the orange juice in front of the girl and the steaming coffee by her own. "Go ahead," Eve said, when the young woman hesitated.

That was all it took. She practically inhaled her food, shoving big bites into her mouth and swallowing huge gulps. Eve ate at a much slower pace and studied her guest. Something about the young woman intrigued her. She wasn't sure of her age—the girl could be anywhere from twelve to thirty—but for some strange reason, Eve felt as if she knew her. Could she be Chanku? That growl certainly hadn't sounded human.

"What's your name? I'm Eve Reynolds."

The girl swallowed. "I know. I remember you."

"What?" Eve sat back in her chair, shocked. "How?"

"The Bostick place. You lived there when I was real little." She took another big bite and washed it down with a swallow of juice. "You kept the big kids from picking on me. By the time you left, I was big enough to take care of myself."

Eve blinked, remembering. "Mei? You're little Mei?"

The girl nodded, smiling. "Mei Chen. Yes. That's me. I was about four, you must have been eight or nine. Sheesh, that's over twenty years ago! I missed you so much when you left." She took another bite of her meal, chewed and swallowed. "Why did you go?"

Eve shook her head, remembering things she'd tried so hard to forget. "I don't know. It always seemed as soon as I got comfortable in a home, I'd get moved to a new one, have to prove myself all over again." She rolled her shoulders, put the memories back where they belonged. "Mei. Wow . . . I can't believe this. It's good to see you. How have you been?"

Mei looked down at her napkin. "I wish I could say I was great, but . . . not good. Homeless for the past few months. I got my GED for high school, but no college. I really wanted to go to college, but . . ." She shook her head. "No training for anything. It's tough, ya know?" She raised her chin defiantly and stared at Eve for a moment. "I worked in a couple of fast food places." She smiled crookedly. "Jobs were okay, managers had too many ideas and too many hands."

Eve could understand that. Mei practically pulsed with

sensuality. Her clothing might be torn and ragged, but her hair was shiny and clean, her skin clear, her tall, lean body absolutely gorgeous. She moved with a sinuous grace, an innate passion that spilled over onto Eve. Aroused her even beyond the frustrated desire she felt night after night.

Eve squeezed her legs together and felt an answering shiver race along her spine before it arrowed directly to her clit. She took a deep breath. For the first time, Eve noticed Mei's eyes. Dark lashes surrounded perfect, almond-shaped, green eyes. Eyes the color of summer grass with specks of amber scattered throughout. Eyes almost like the other Chanku shapeshifters Eve knew.

Almost, but not exactly. She took another bite of her sandwich and concentrated on Mei. Concentrated on her thoughts and tried to find an answer to her sense of the almost familiar.

The frisson of awareness intensified. It was there, just beyond reach. Alien, unfamiliar, suffused with sensual needs almost completely overwhelmed by fear and loneliness. Still, she felt the connection to another mind, to another's desire. Mei raised her head. Looked long and hard into Eve's eyes. Brushed her hand across her forehead and blinked.

"What are you doing?" Mei's whisper radiated confusion and desire. "I feel you." She tapped her temple lightly with her forefinger. "Here. I feel you here. And here, as well." She swept her hand along her torso, paused at her small breasts, then roughly grabbed herself between the legs. "Here, most of all. What the fuck are you doing in my head?"

Chapter 2

"I wondered if you could feel my thoughts. My arousal." Eve slowly gathered up the papers and crumbs from her meal to give herself time to think.

"You a lesbian?"

Eve smiled at the challenge in Mei's voice. "When the company suits me." She stood up and walked across the room, dumped her garbage in the small trash can and grabbed the bottle of brown capsules Anton had given her. She sat down again and smiled at Mei, pushing gently with her mind. Sharing her growing arousal. "What about you?"

"Sometimes I like women. Mostly I dig guys, 'cept when there's not one around." She was watching Eve now with more than a little interest shining in her green eyes. Watching the pill bottle Eve had set on the table in front of her.

Somehow, Eve had to get Mei to take Anton's pills. The big, ugly capsules were filled with a mix of dried grasses specific to the Tibetan steppe, the Chanku ancestral home. The nutrients in the pills activated a small gland lying dormant near the hypothalamus of a latent Chanku. It was the only way, she knew, to find out if Mei shared the same genes.

If Mei was merely human, the pills would have absolutely no effect on her. If she was Chanku, she would have the ability to shift from woman to wolf within a week.

Eve took a capsule out of the bottle, popped it in her mouth and downed it with a swallow of coffee. "They're vitamins," she said, holding the bottle out to Mei. "Nutrients and stuff to keep me healthy. I get them from a good friend. Do you want one?"

Mei eyed the ugly pills suspiciously. "I don't do drugs." She took one out of the bottle and sniffed it. She raised her head and frowned. "Smells like weed. Really expensive stuff."

Eve laughed. "I don't do drugs either, and these are most definitely not marijuana. Never mind. I don't have all that many of them anyway. I just figured your diet's probably not been all that healthy. These are a good supplement."

Mei gave her a crooked grin. Instead of replacing the capsule back in the bottle, she popped it into her mouth and swallowed it down with a gulp of orange juice. "Last night's dinner came out of a dumpster near that hamburger joint on the corner. I'll take your pills."

Eve grinned broadly as she took another sip of her rapidly cooling coffee. "You need to find better quality dumpsters. That place has lousy hamburgers and really greasy fries."

Mei laughed out loud this time. "Yeah, well . . . when you're on the streets, you don't always have much of a choice." She pushed her chair back and stood up. "Thanks for the meal. I better get going. I don't want to impose."

Eve reached across the table and touched Mei's hand. "Stay. Please?"

"Why?" Mei paused. Her dark brows scrunched up in a frown. "You hardly know me." Then her eyes narrowed with suspicion and she glared at Eve. "You want sex? That's it, isn't it?"

Eve shrugged. "Sex is always an option, but only if you're interested. You're a link, Mei. Someone who knew me when I was a child. I have so few memories of friends from my childhood. In a way, you're the closest thing to family I've had since I left my last foster home. Stay, please?"

Mei cocked her head to one side. Obviously she still wasn't buying it. "Do you live here? In this motel?"

Eve shook her head. "No. I came back here on business, but I had car trouble. My friend is on his way to fix the truck. I expect him in a couple days."

"Boyfriend?" Mei pulled the chair out and sat.

"Could be. Some day."

"What happens when the truck's fixed?" Mei twisted a strand of her long, dark hair. Her constant motion told Eve a lot more than mere words. Her eyes, hands, smile . . . all spoke volumes of Mei's nervous energy and lack of trust. "Where will you go then? Where do you live?"

"Nowhere, right now." Eve sighed. "Montana, maybe. I've got friends there. Friends who want me to live with them, but I wasn't ready. Like the boyfriend. I think he loves me. It scares the crap out of me, that kind of relationship. I needed time to figure out what I want to do with my life. What I really need."

"Yeah. I wish I knew what I wanted." Mei laughed. "Other than a bath and a clean change of clothes."

Perfect! Eve stood up. "That I can do. We're about the same size. You can borrow some of my things for now. Get a shower, some clean clothes. Later we can get a cab and go shopping."

Mei blinked, but for the first time since entering the room, she sat perfectly still. Eve realized she was fighting tears.

"You'd do that for me? Buy me clothes?"

"Of course. You were my friend years ago, Mei. I'd like to think we can be friends again."

Mei nodded. Then she grabbed her purse. She didn't hesitate when Eve pointed her toward the shower. Nor did she seem to realize her thoughts were growing clearer by the minute as Eve consistently probed her mind. She had to be Chanku. Could Mei be the reason Eve had been drawn back to Florida? It was too perfect to be purely co-incidental.

Anton was going to love it! His ongoing argument with Stefan over fate versus coincidence was gaining credence by the day. Eve almost picked up the phone to call Anton. Almost. She hesitated, fingers spread in the act of grabbing her cell phone off the nightstand.

How easy it had become, to think of Anton, of Keisha, Stefan, and Xandi when she had something to share. Already she thought of them as family. Why hadn't her thoughts rushed to Adam? Or even to Oliver?

Because they scare the crap out of you. She wasn't ready for the powerful connection she felt with both men, but especially with Adam. Not yet. It was easier not to think of them. Knowing what little she did of the two men, she still expected at least one, if not both, of them to show up within a day or two.

Eve curled her fingers into the palm of her hand and listened to the sound of the shower. Mei was in there now, her slim body naked beneath the spray, her long black hair flowing with the rivulets of water as it sluiced over her shoulders, trailed between her breasts.

A sense of well-being poured into Eve, and she knew she was catching Mei's thoughts and feelings. She sat back in her chair and closed her eyes. She would think of Mei, of possibilities. Adam was on his way. Eve knew it the way she knew the sun would rise each morning. He was coming and he wasn't alone. She shivered with a strong sense of premonition. There was power in this room, in the woman blissfully enjoying the shower. Power in the throbbing arousal that surged through Eve's body at the mere thought of Adam, of Oliver . . . and Mei.

She wrapped her arms around her waist and bowed down until her head was between her knees. Desire shimmered, hot and sultry, pulsing in her veins, engorging her sex. Desire fueled by images of herself, of Adam and Oliver and Mei, a tangle of arms and legs, slick with the lush dampness of sweat and saliva and all the intimate fluids that bodies produced in the heat of passion.

She'd gone three weeks without sex. Three weeks of easing her own needs but never satisfying them. Three weeks with the powerful surge of arousal that accompanied each shift, growing and spreading with the same rush and power as the blood in her veins or the oxygen in her lungs. Arousal so much a part of her very existence she'd become one living, breathing, pulsing creature of lust.

She'd risked everything to bring two strange men to her room, just for sex. Thank goodness she'd survived that idiotic decision. The risk with Mei was different. With Mei, she could lose another bit of herself. Strangely, though, the need for independence that had driven her away from Adam and Montana somehow faded, now that she'd found Mei.

Even Adam wasn't as frightening anymore. She realized she missed him, wanted him for more than what he could do to ease her basic sexual needs.

That was definitely a step in the right direction.

Smiling, Eve stared at the closed bathroom door, imagining Mei. Picturing the younger woman's lean body slick from the shower, imagining Mei's hot mouth between her legs, licking and sucking, bringing Eve closer and closer to climax.

She leaned back in her chair and spread her legs wide, imagining and calling out silently, in the way of the Chanku. Calling to any mind willing and able to listen. Her breasts ached, her womb clenched and the need built. Eve closed her eyes against the growing arousal that had become as much a part of her identity as her name. She thought of Mei, and then she thought of Adam and Oliver and the things the four of them could do together, in that nice big king-size bed, back at the house in Montana.

But Mei was here, so most of all, she thought of Mei.

Mei closed her eyes as the hot water cascaded over her body. She'd not had a decent shower in weeks, bathing instead in the dirty sinks in public restrooms and quick showers at the occasional homeless shelter when she'd been lucky enough to find a bed. This was luxury unlike anything she'd experienced for far too long.

It felt wonderful. It felt beyond wonderful when she washed her hair with the expensive shampoo on the side of the tub and used the conditioner she'd never once been able to afford in her life. She'd grabbed a new razor out of a pack on the counter and, while she'd never had much body hair, went ahead and took the time to shave what was there.

Sleek and smooth and clean. It just didn't get much better, especially since there was still plenty of hot water and she didn't have to get out if she didn't want to. Suddenly Eve popped into her thoughts and just like that, Mei's nipples puckered up into tight, sensitive little beads and she felt a rush of heat between her legs.

What was it about Eve that turned her on so much? Mei had never been all that particular about her sexual partners, but she was most definitely heterosexual. At least she thought she was, until she thought of Eve. Eve was definitely beautiful. She was kind, and she smiled a lot. She had a fun sense of humor, but there was something in her eyes, something about the way Mei felt as if Eve were inside her, reading her thoughts, feeling her feelings.

Mei stood there for a moment longer with the water running over her shoulders, pondering the weirdness of it all. Slowly, the water cooled. Sighing, she turned the spigot off, wrapped her long mass of hair in the soft terry cloth towel and grabbed a second towel to dry herself. She glanced at the filthy clothes on the floor and kicked them into a pile.

She paused a moment, staring at the closed door. Was she ready to walk out into the room naked? Even with a towel around herself, Mei knew exactly where it would lead, but that was a good thing, for now, at least, as far as she was concerned. She felt drawn to Eve on so many levels, in so many different ways. Felt a connection to her that reminded Mei of the time they'd been together as children. Now though, there was a major difference. That same connection carried the weight and promise of two sensual women.

She'd trusted Eve then. She would trust her now. And just maybe, they'd still have time to shop.

Eve glanced up as Mei walked into the room. Mei's green eyes were wide, her skin glistened dark and damp against the white terry cloth towel. Mei looked around with studied innocence and shrugged. "I left my clothes in the bathroom. They're pretty dirty."

"No problem. I've got things you can wear." Eve slowly peeled herself out of the chair. Her heart pounded. Her sex throbbed and her nipples had puckered into such tight, needy little peaks that they ached. When she stood up, Mei stepped closer, the movement slow and subtle like a sinuous cat stalking its prey. Eve watched a single drop of water find its path from Mei's throat to the dark valley between her breasts. It slipped beneath the towel and she imagined its damp trail down the middle of Mei's belly to the soft thatch of dark curls beneath.

Eve realized she was staring and snapped her chin up. She caught herself in Mei's green eyes and sensed a pressure behind her own eyes, as if Mei searched her mind. Could she read thoughts? Did she have the Chanku power even now, before the nutrients had had time to work their magic?

Mei swallowed and the sound was loud between them. She blinked slowly and her pupils narrowed. They changed to vertical slits, then slowly returned to their natural round shape. The effect was oddly feline, reminding Eve of a Siamese cat she'd had at one of her many foster homes.

"I don't understand." Mei's whisper was a harsh counterpoint against the pounding of Eve's heart.

"What?" Eve asked. She shook her head. Her mind felt fuzzy and thick, as if everything moved in slow motion. "What is it you don't understand?"

Mei shook her head slowly, side to side. "I feel you in my head and my body responds to yours. There's a sense that we have to have sex, we have to touch and share, but I don't understand why. I'm not like this. Not usually."

Eve licked her lips. How could she explain without telling her secrets? Were explanations all that necessary? Now, when all she wanted was to feel, to touch and taste and share her needs and desires?

She didn't answer. Instead she reached out and cupped Mei's cheek in the palm of her hand. Drew the woman forward until the damp heat of Mei's body enveloped Eve. Mei smiled and shrugged, and her towel fell to the floor. She tilted her head and the one wrapping her hair slowly unwound and fell beside its mate.

Naked, she stared at Eve. Then, as if they'd done this many times before, Mei leaned close and kissed her full on the mouth. Her lips were firm, her tongue an insistent pressure against Eve's mouth. Groaning, her body throbbing with heat and lust, Eve wrapped her arms around Mei and pulled her slim, damp body close against her own.

She smelled of fresh soap and floral shampoo, of need and want and the subtle hint of forest. The mingled scents filled Eve's head, an aphrodisiac as powerful as Mei's sleek, wet body.

Eve opened her thoughts. Opened to whatever she could find in Mei's mind, and she was immediately swamped in the lush purity of Mei's arousal, in sensation and expectation and want. Weakened by the power of Mei's desire, Eve collapsed with her into the welcoming softness of the big bed.

They lay together, lost in the ripe sharing, the images passing from mind to mind without words. Heat spiraled through Eve's core, and she knew Mei felt the same intense wash of pleasure. Her clothing was nothing more than an inconvenience, so Eve slipped out of her shorts and panties. She held her arms up while Mei peeled the soft tank top over her head and tossed it aside.

Thoughts of Adam swept over her with a brief wash of longing. His taut, muscular chest and rippling abs, the long blond hair falling over his eyes as his body covered hers. But he was gone and Mei was here, all slim and soft. Their bodies met, breast to breast, belly to belly, mouths exploring, hands kneading taut buttocks. All senses and thoughts attuned, one to the other, they pressed close and clung. Bodies slick with sweat and shower, they explored, touching, tasting, plucking at turgid nipples, tracing fingers through damp clefts and warm openings.

There was something almost mystical about Mei's touch, the way her fingers brushed Eve's nipples with the barest of pressure, shaped the curve of her breast and followed the line of each rib. Eve copied the younger woman, following her lead, stroking along the smooth line of her hip, teasing the smooth mound between her thighs.

She felt Mei's response, the liquid rush of pleasure when Mei rolled her hips and helped drive Eve's fingers over her hooded clit. Eve rubbed small circles over that tiny bundle of nerves and felt the electric charge between her own legs, felt the rush of warm fluids, the pulsing in her labia as blood rushed to her sex.

Eve raised her hips in response and Mei slipped lower

on the bed to kneel between her legs. There was a feral look in her eyes, a needy, greedy sense of arousal that sent a shiver along Eve's spine. Something was different. At first Eve wasn't sure what, when it slammed into her, spiking her growing arousal even higher.

Mei was taking charge, usurping Eve's sense of control with nothing more than a glance. She caught Eve watching her and smiled, but her thoughts suddenly disappeared behind solid, protective walls. Eve shivered again, but her lips parted and her womb fluttered in response. She grasped the bedspread with both hands, anchoring herself as Mei shoved pillows beneath her hips, raising her.

Preparing her.

Three weeks of screaming need, three weeks without Adam, with a body growing more aroused after each shift, had left her primed on the edge of orgasm. Mei slipped her hands beneath the pillows and grasped Eve's buttocks in her long fingers. She lifted Eve's hips even higher, licked her lips and leaned close.

Her silky hair formed a black curtain, hiding Mei from Eve's view. She felt the brush of the long, damp strands across her belly and thighs and the muscles between her legs convulsed.

Warm breath touched her clit, a silky tongue parted her swollen labia and stroked her sex in one long, smooth sweep of heat.

Eve screamed, climaxing with Mei's first touch. She tried to squeeze her thighs together, but Mei's shoulders held them apart. That amazing tongue found her clit, circled it once, then twice. A second climax slammed through Eve's body. She tried to pull away, but Mei's fingers dug into her buttocks and held her in place.

Mei licked her now, long strokes from ass to clit, her tongue probing the damp entrance to Eve's sex, circling her clit, almost painful now as she forced yet another orgasm on Eve.

Whimpering, Eve gave up her struggle for control. Her thighs fell limply to either side, her fingers tightened around the bedcovers and she was carried away by sensation. Only then, with her surrender complete, did Mei allow Eve back into her thoughts.

They were filled with a jumble of twisted, tangled images. Confusion, arousal, curiosity. Obviously Mei didn't realize what she'd done. Didn't know the power of her own mind.

How, Eve wondered. How did this young woman wield power she didn't understand? Power obviously beyond what Eve herself could control. Body shuddering, legs trembling and jerking with each sweep of Mei's velvety tongue, Eve finally opened her eyes. She caught Mei sitting back on her heels, staring warily at her.

Eve reached out and touched the top of Mei's thigh. Mei jumped, blinked and turned her head slowly to look down at the spot where fingers met flesh.

"This is just too weird." Mei shook her head. Her body trembled, but Eve wasn't sure if it was from arousal or something else. "I felt you again, in my head. I knew what you wanted. Where to touch you, where to lick you, how hard. I felt as if you controlled everything I did. What's going on?"

Shocked, Eve scooted back and sat against the headboard. "I didn't feel that way at all. I felt as if you were in control, as if you'd taken control."

Eyes narrowing to dark slits, Mei covered her breasts with folded arms and glared at Eve. Her lips and chin glistened, still bathed in Eve's intimate moisture. "You were in my head. Admit it."

"As you were in mine." Eve patted the mattress next to her. "Come, sit here. I'll try and explain, at least as much as I'm able."

Moving warily, more like a frightened animal than a young woman, Mei scooted closer to Eve. At least she'd stopped trembling, and she used a corner of the sheet to wipe her mouth, scraping it defiantly across her face. "Okay. I'm waiting."

Eve nodded and took a deep breath. Anton had been very specific about not telling anyone about the Chanku, at least until she was certain the other person carried the same genes. With Mei, Eve was almost sure, but not quite.

She reached for Mei's hand, spread Mei's fingers out against her own, and admired their long, slender length and the perfectly shaped fingernails. Unusual, she thought, for a young woman who was homeless to have such perfectly groomed hands. Eve looked up and caught Mei's intense stare.

"I think," she said, "in a way, we are related. I can't explain all the details, at least not yet, but when my friend Adam arrives, I'll be able to tell you more. I'll know more. Adam and I can communicate telepathically. It's something in our genetic code. Obviously you and I have the same ability. I'm guessing you share the same genes, but I'm not certain. Have you ever been able to read minds before?"

Mei shook her head. Her eyes were wide and green, though her pupils narrowed once again to that intriguing vertical slit.

"The pill I gave you enhances that ability, but it's too soon for it to have had any effect on you. You must have a powerful mind if you can communicate and pick up thoughts without the nutrients in that capsule."

"You said it was just a vitamin."

There was no avoiding the accusation in Mei's voice. Eve dipped her chin, but she raised her head and looked directly at Mei when she answered. "I know. I couldn't say anything more until I knew for sure if it would affect you, but since you're already capable of at least a moderate form of telepathy, I'm going to assume you'll just keep getting stronger. I didn't want to lie to you, but I really needed to know. I sensed something in you from the beginning."

"Did you sense my need for you?" Mei surprised her when she leaned forward and kissed Eve. "Did you know my body was reacting to yours from the beginning?"

On safer ground, Eve grinned. "Oh yeah. The feeling was mutual. And ya know what? It's your turn, sweetie." She leaned over and caught one of Mei's nipples between her teeth, then sucked it into her mouth. Mei arched her back and moaned.

Eve's mind flooded with sensation and she felt the spike of need run directly from the nipple between her lips to the damp recesses between Mei's thighs. Mei didn't want subtlety, nor did she need slow and steady. She wanted to climax, needed an orgasm to soothe the roiling emotions and powerful arousal thrumming through her veins.

Sliding lower along Mei's sleek body, Eve went directly for her clit. Suckling the tiny organ between her lips as if it were a nipple, she tongued the underside at the same time her fingers were finding their way closer to Mei's damp heat. Suckling and licking, Eve lost herself in the unfamiliar flavors, the smooth yet surprisingly solid curve of Mei's clit, and the thick and swollen lips of her sex.

Mei groaned and her thoughts continued spilling over into Eve. She wanted penetration. She hovered, close now to coming, but she needed the sense of fullness only a man could give her.

Or a very large vibrator. Smiling to herself, blocking her thoughts as she suckled and licked, Eve reached for the drawer next to the bed. Her fingers locked on the smooth surface of her brand new vibrator. Shaped like a penis and made of some sort of gel-like substance over a rigid core, it felt almost lifelike in her grasp. She'd bought it because the large size, the broad crown, and thickly veined surface reminded her of Adam.

Holding this plastic imitation in her hand, Eve suddenly

realized how much she needed the real thing. Mei was the key. She'd found Mei, and her fear of Adam and the commitment he represented, seemed totally unimportant.

Mei whimpered and drew her back to the here and now. Eve rubbed the smooth, rounded tip of the dildo back and forth between Mei's legs, sliding across the sensitive nerves surrounding her anus, then slowly between her feminine folds to the base of her clit. Eve kept up her licking and sucking, well aware of Mei's frustration with Eve for not taking her over the edge.

Mei raised her hips, bucking against Eve's busy tongue and lips and she squirmed when the slick dildo slipped along the damp cleft between her cheeks, pausing to press just a little harder at her tightly puckered sphincter.

Eve pressed again and Mei moaned. Her body shuddered and her thoughts swirled incoherently. A sense of *want* and *need*, of delicious yearnings and anxious pleas for fulfillment drew Eve once again to the verge of coming.

Like Mei, she hung there, her own body awash in shared sensation, caught on the edge of her own climax, tuned to every touch of her tongue against Mei's heat, every small slide of the lifelike phallus over anxious nerves. Finally, hands trembling, Eve placed the thick head of the vibrator against the damp entrance to Mei's sex, clamped down on her clit with her lips and tongue and pushed the vibrator deep inside. At the same time, she flipped the base and turned it on.

Eve felt the tip press up against the mouth of Mei's womb, only it was Eve's womb that clenched against the vibrating phallus. Mei's thoughts swamped Eve's mind and the link was eternal, complete, the orgasm shared, one woman to the other. Mei arched her back and screamed. Eve's muscles went rigid as she climaxed as well. She held the fake cock deep inside Mei, and felt the shivering life in the damned thing as if it pulsed against her own cervix.

Only it wasn't made of plastic. Wasn't held in her own

hand at all. It was Adam pressing deep inside. Eve felt the roll of his hips as he thrust harder, heard his harsh, rasping breath as he struggled for control. Her mind swirled in convoluted eddies of fantasy and memory and shared sensation. Mei, Adam, and Oliver. The three of them mingling and becoming one.

Linked, all of them loving Eve. Loving Mei. A single entity, spilling out of Eve's thoughts, joining Mei's experience to Eve's, combining them all in a lush melding of pure sexual arousal and desire.

Gasping for air, Eve set up a slow and steady rhythm. She felt as if she fucked herself, as if each penetrating slide inside Mei stretched her own channel around the warm bulk of the vibrating phallus.

She moved it faster and found a rhythm to match the tight clenching pulse of Mei's orgasm. Images of Adam and Oliver faded away. Now Eve's mind raced with the sense of Mei's arousal, Mei's past, Mei's needs.

And over it all was a knowledge of something *other*. Something beyond Chanku. Something feral and cruel, powerful and alone.

Always alone.

Shaken by alien images and feelings, by unfamiliar sensations, and missing Adam and Oliver more than she ever would have imagined, Eve slowly pulled the vibrator out of Mei's channel. Mei whimpered, her clenching muscles grasping the phallus even as Eve pulled it free.

Breathing hard, Eve planted one more kiss on Mei's smooth mound, just above her clit, and then she backed away.

She wasn't sure. Couldn't tell why or what was different about this woman. Eve had very little experience of her own as Chanku, though she'd learned much from her links with both Keisha and Xandi. Still, what she felt now was totally alien, this feeling she had with the woman who sprawled boneless and sated in her bed. The woman who sighed with repletion, who gazed at her out of half-lidded eyes.

Mei was different. Chanku, yet not. Feral, intelligent, wild and free, yet trapped in her own world of images and half-memories.

Memories that confused and bedeviled Eve. Running her hand softly along Mei's trembling flank, she buried her worries behind a smile and thought longingly of Adam. He would know what was wrong. Adam always had answers. He fixed things, didn't he?

She lay down beside Mei and closed her eyes. She thought again of Adam and Oliver. They had belonged in her fantasy, but now she was surprised that for once their images came into her mind first, before the other members of the Montana pack. Still, the others were there as well. Stefan, so tall and handsome and full of fun, his mate Xandi, always practical but with a twinkle in her eye, her perfect baby boy snuggled in her arms.

Keisha, regal and beautiful, an African princess in bearing and action with her dark hair pulled back in braids and beads, her amber eyes aware of so much more than Eve had wanted to share. And then there was Keisha's mate, Anton. Just thinking of Anton sent a shiver along Eve's spine. He was all gorgeous male and pure mystery combined, powerful and aloof, yet an absolute pussycat where Keisha and their little girl, Lily Milina were involved. A Chanku shapeshifter, a wizard, a father, and a friend. He'd frightened her at first, but Eve knew Anton was someone she could always count on.

Just as she could count on Adam Wolf. And Oliver.

Why, when she thought of Oliver, did she always smile? Eve wasn't quite sure, but Anton's manservant-slash-friend was definitely special. Thinking of all the new men in her life, Eve rolled to her back and listened to Mei's breathing as it slowed, steadied, and took on the cadence of sleep.

Mei was a mystery. Obviously not purely human, yet not entirely Chanku, either. Adam would know what to do. Like Anton Cheval, Adam always seemed to have answers.

Eve really hoped he could fix the truck. She wasn't necessarily worried about Mei. Just curious, more than anything. Whatever mystery surrounded the young woman would eventually come to light, but damn, the truck was something else. She'd ripped a lot of stuff loose under the hood. Stuff that might be really important. She hoped Adam saw the humor in what she'd done. It wouldn't be nearly as great a plan if her actions made him angry.

She really shouldn't doubt his ability to repair her unskilled attempts at vandalism. Adam could do it. He could do anything. Hopefully, if he still wanted her, he'd recognize the reason for her actions.

Hopefully.

Feeling only moderately guilty for damaging Stefan's birthday gift, Eve closed her eyes and drifted into sleep.

Chapter 3

The sun hadn't yet crested the horizon and the day hung quietly in that strangely silent spot between the full darkness of night and the pale oyster-shell glow of coming dawn. Adam raised his muzzle from the warm cushion of Oliver's back.

Oliver sighed, but slept on, his wolven body curled tightly in the thick ferns where they'd spent the night. Adam blinked, gazing into the dark, seeing so much more through wolven eyes. He decided he really loved to travel this way, shifting and spending the night as a wolf, sleeping in the thick stands of forest they'd managed to find along the way. No need for camping gear or motel rooms— just a quiet, protected spot in the woods.

With luck they'd reach Tampa later today. Tampa, and Eve. A frisson of awareness, a sense of destiny raced across his spine when he thought of her. Damn, but he'd missed her, even though they'd hardly spent time together at all.

Eve. Her name filled his soul like a benediction. She'd sent for him, as surely as if she'd sent an engraved invitation. Keisha might think Eve only needed him to repair the truck, but Adam knew better. She'd merely needed an excuse, a ploy to salve her pride.

His body quickened with the image of the beautiful blond. Some day, soon, he hoped, she would be his. When she'd left Montana, Adam hadn't even tried to stop her, even when everything inside him begged her to stay. He'd known she had to leave. He'd expected it, though not quite so soon.

It was all about timing.

All about Eve.

Oliver stirred and stretched. Adam stood up and shook. His rumpled coat settled smoothly across his back. Oliver joined him, touching nose to nose in greeting.

They'd touched a lot more than merely noses last night, but before Adam had a chance to relive some of the details, he scented fresh game.

Rabbit. Brush near water. Circle.

Oliver nodded and immediately slunk off to the left under cover of a stand of thick willows. Adam moved quietly to the right, keeping the tall grass between himself and his prey. Three fat cottontails munched their way through a narrow band of grass growing alongside a small creek.

Adam's muscles bunched as he crouched within a few feet of the rabbits. His muscles quivered, but he held still to give Oliver time to get into position. He caught Oliver's mental signal. Heart racing, blood thundering in his veins and the power of the hunt lending him speed, Adam leapt just as Oliver burst through the bushes on the far side of the clearing.

Adam's jaws closed on the rabbit closest to him. Oliver snapped up another. The third rabbit bounded into the brush to safety as the first two died soundlessly, quickly in the viselike jaws of their captors. Within minutes, the only sign the rabbits ever existed were the small wisps of pale fur scattered over the closely cropped grass where they'd been feeding.

Oliver shifted first, knelt by the creek and washed his

hands and face. Adam did the same, bathing away the last vestiges of sleep and rabbit before he stood up and stuck a hand out for Oliver.

"Ready?"

Oliver nodded. "Thank you," he said. He wiped his hands against his bare thighs and laughed out loud. "Wow. This trip has been quite an adventure."

"You've had fresh rabbit before."

"I've never slept in the forest as a wolf before. Never bathed by a mountain creek after a night in the woods. Such freedom! I could grow used to this life." Oliver glanced over his shoulder at Adam and winked, but his heart felt full enough to burst. Adam really had no idea. Emotion washed over Oliver, deep and powerful emotion that left him shaken. His mood was thoughtful as he headed back to the small clearing where they'd left their clothing.

Never, if he lived a thousand years, could he repay Adam for the miracle he'd made happen. He'd forever changed Oliver's life. Because of Adam, he walked with a new sense of purpose, more pride and self-confidence than he'd ever known before.

He'd been reborn, physically changed from a mutilated freak to a whole man. For the first time in his life, Oliver could embrace all that was offered. His was a new life, one filled with power and strength and the potential for love. Physical love.

All because of Adam Wolf.

Only Adam had seen a way to fix his miserable existence. All the years Oliver had spent with Anton Cheval, working for the man he loved more than anyone else on this earth, Anton had been unable to help.

If Anton couldn't find a solution, Oliver had assumed no one could. It had always seemed impossible. How does one replace a missing set of testicles? He'd been castrated as a toddler and sold to a wealthy family as a playmate for their daughter. Oliver had no recollection of the surgery that cost him so much, but he'd never truly accepted his fate.

How could he accept that he would always live as half a man? He'd served Anton Cheval as well as he could. He'd taken the testosterone supplements Anton provided, but they'd done nothing to help him find his true heritage, that of a Chanku shapeshifter.

And then he met Adam Wolf. They'd connected from the very beginning, but Oliver hadn't had a clue what effect Adam would have on him. Not until Adam had linked, secretly at first so that even Oliver didn't realize what was happening. Until he'd given Oliver an erection. His very first.

Only Adam had known how to help him. First he'd shared his arousal in a powerful mental link, and suddenly Oliver was hard as a post. Later, Adam joined with him, linking once again, touching and sharing until Oliver finally knew what an orgasm felt like.

Even now, it still felt like a dream. Especially the night he'd spent with Eve. He hadn't shifted yet, still didn't have balls, but through Adam's link, Oliver had made love to Eve. She'd never known. Never guessed that the man who loved her was not fully a man.

Had not known, then, that she was the first woman he'd ever penetrated. That night was the first time he'd felt that sweet, hot clench of powerful feminine muscles around his perfectly erect cock. The first time he'd felt warm breasts cushioned against his chest, the gush of fluids covering his groin as Eve writhed and climaxed against him.

For that alone, Oliver knew he would always love the beautiful blond for showing him what true desire really was. He missed Eve. Not with the purely visceral need Adam felt, but with a longing, a sad and incomplete sense of what might be, what might have been.

Once she'd gone, though, Adam had taken his experiments with Oliver a step further. They'd linked and Adam guided Oliver through his first shift. It was amazing. Utterly, completely amazing, to follow Adam's neural pathways and suddenly find himself standing on all fours, his magnificent tail waving behind him, his teeth long and sharp, his eyes seeing clearly in the dark woods. He'd dreamed of such a thing. Wanted it as much, if not more, than he'd wanted balls. But then, shifting was all tied up in his sexuality, and it was something Oliver hadn't been able to do without the hormones produced by the male sex organs he lacked.

The organs he *had* lacked. Oliver shivered, remembering. Standing there as a wolf, living the fantasy he'd held for years, he'd become aware of an even more amazing difference. Yes, he was a wolf, but he was intact. There, between his legs, were testicles. Perfectly shaped, functioning, filling his body with a rush of natural hormones.

When it was time to shift back, he'd been terrified his balls wouldn't make the transition. For that alone he might have stayed a wolf forever, but Adam had promised him.

"I fix things, Oliver. That's what I do. I think maybe we've fixed you."

Goddess knew, he'd been broken. Oliver shivered, remembering the terror of that first shift from wolf back to human. He'd done it on his own, without Adam's help. He'd been almost afraid to look, standing there in the woods, naked and trembling, but his Chanku libido had kicked in even before the realization that his new set of balls had made the shift with him.

For the first time in his life, Oliver had a raging hardon! Even now, remembering, he was aroused. The others, Stefan and Anton, Keisha and Xandi, had all talked about how horny they were after a shift. He'd had no idea. The need to fuck, to find release, had raced through his blood and landed right in his cock.

Once again, Adam had fixed everything. He'd put his arms around Oliver and held him while he cried tears of relief. Then he'd fucked and sucked him until Oliver could hardly walk the next day.

Oliver sensed Adam's arousal as they entered the glade. He turned and felt the now familiar sweet ache of his own desire, the weight of his balls between his legs, the coil of heat resting at the base of his spine. His cock curved high and he reached down and encircled himself with his fingers. "Do we need to leave this early?"

Adam smiled and shook his head. "I truly did create a monster."

Oliver laughed. "It is a big one, isn't it?"

"Oh yeah. For a little guy you've got one hell of a dick between your legs. Got any plans for it?"

Oliver stroked his fingers along his length. He used to wonder what it would feel like to slide his foreskin back and have it actually stay behind the crown, held there by the sheer size of his erection. "If you have any rubbers, I imagine I could find something to do with this thing."

Adam licked his lips. "In the back pocket of my jeans. I was saving it for myself, but if you want it . . ."

The words trailed off, but Adam's growing arousal spilled out onto Oliver. He found the condom and ripped the packet open with shaking hands. They always used a condom for anal sex, for personal hygiene if nothing else, but Adam was the top. Always. Except for now. Oliver slipped the latex over his erect cock and almost climaxed from his own touch, from the thoughts whirling in his brain.

He'd never done this before. Never even considered it. Why now?

Why not?

Oliver's gaze snapped up to Adam's amber eyes. "You're in my head."

"It's a good place to be. You've got some amazing ideas

in there." Adam bridged the gap between them. The sky was growing lighter, birdsong welcomed the coming dawn, the forest was coming awake.

Oliver touched Adam's shoulder, trailed his fingers along his muscled chest. His arousal grew. So did Adam's. Oliver reached the thick nest of silky hair surrounding Adam's cock, trailed his fingers around the hard shaft, touched the wrinkled sac below. Their sensations sparked between them, feelings shared, needs open and begging to be filled.

Oliver dropped to his knees and licked the very tip of Adam's penis. The salty drop of ejaculate bathed his senses. The grass was soft beneath his knees, the air cool against his heated skin. Oliver sucked Adam deeper. He speared the tiny eye at the head of his glans with his tongue, cupped Adam's balls in his hands and rolled the precious globes between his fingers.

Then he released Adam and pulled him to the ground. Adam moved quickly, but with a question in his eyes. Did he kneel for Oliver? Should he lie on his back? Laughing at his own awkwardness, Oliver positioned Adam on his hands and knees and knelt between his calves. He ran his hands over Adam's taut buttocks and followed the crease of his ass to the perfect dip along his spine.

Then he grabbed Adam's cock in both hands and stroked him, tugging none too gently from root to tip. His own cock rode the sweaty crease between Adam's cheeks, but he didn't try to penetrate.

Adam groaned. Oliver felt his balls tighten against his body, just as Adam's did. Pre-cum filled his palm and he used it to lubricate Adam's tight ring of muscle. He ran his fingertip over the sensitive tissues, pressing harder with each pass.

Adam groaned and widened his stance, giving Oliver better access. He was so much larger than Oliver, his back broader, his legs longer, but his ass was perfectly positioned for penetration.

Oliver's arousal grew, but he continued his slow pressure against Adam's butt, spreading him wider, softening his sphincter muscle, relaxing it. Finally he was able to slip one finger inside, then a second, but his hands were smaller and he knew he needed more.

Adam's breath huffed in short, sharp puffs. Oliver felt him shiver. He swept his palm over Adam's cock and it twitched at the contact, spilling more thick, white fluid.

Do that again and I'm gonna blow all over your hand.

Laughing, Oliver ran his fingers once again along Adam's length, testing him further. Adam groaned, but his pleasure filled Oliver's thoughts.

Oliver covered the tip of his cock with Adam's fluid, then pressed hard. The sense of pressure was amazing as he slowly pushed forward. Adam adjusted his legs and lowered his head, thrusting his buttocks against Oliver's cock.

There was a sense of muscle giving, relaxing, then the tight ring slipped over the head of his cock and locked around the most sensitive part of his shaft. Oliver groaned and held still, fighting for control. Amazing. The sensation of being locked to Adam was purely amazing. Shivering with the need to come, to give over to desire, Oliver fought for control. It took him precious seconds to find it before he could push forward.

This was amazing. Totally new, totally unbelievable. He had no idea, even from the links he'd had with Adam, what it actually felt like to shove his cock deep inside another man, to experience the heat, the clench of internal muscles, the press of a tautly muscled ass against his groin.

He groaned and slowly withdrew. Adam's thoughts filled his head, the convoluted yet lush thoughts of a man on the edge. Oliver pressed deep again, then eased out.

Harder this time, faster, his hips swaying with a rhythm he found deep inside himself.

The pressure grew, the pleasure expanded. He reached around Adam's waist and clasped his cock in both hands, squeezing and stretching the full length of it in time with his own powerful thrusts.

Suddenly Adam threw his head back and yelled, his shout as incoherent as his thoughts during climax. Thick streams of ejaculate splattered against the grass and his cock jumped in Oliver's grasp.

Oliver felt the coil of his own climax, felt the sharp thrust of heat and power, the amazing sense of his balls squeezing hard and tight as he orgasmed deep inside the man who made him whole.

Body jerking, muscles tight, Oliver grasped Adam's hips and buried himself as deep as he could. It seemed to last forever, this mind-blowing, life-shattering orgasm, his first ever while buried in the clenching, spasming body of the man he loved. Gasping, lungs dragging in huge draughts of air, Oliver leaned forward and rested his cheek against Adam's back.

His hips still pumped, a feeble last blast of the waning spasms of what had to be the most wonderful climax any man had ever felt. He laughed, and even that sounded weak. "Holy shit."

Adam turned his head and grinned. "That all you can say?"

Oliver nodded, still numb.

Adam laughed out loud. "Works for me. Damn it all, Ollie. I didn't know you had it in you."

Oliver grabbed the base of his cock and held onto the condom as he withdrew from Adam's body and then rolled limply to the ground to lay beside him. "Actually, my friend," he said, "I had it in you."

"That you did, Oliver. That you did."

* * *

Mei handed her bags to Eve and climbed into the back-seat of the cab to sit beside her. "Sheesh. Ya think we bought enough stuff?" Laughing, she moved bags and shoe boxes out of the way, fastened her seat belt and leaned back in the seat.

Eve punched her lightly on the arm. "C'mon, now. Do you know any woman who ever has enough clothes? Or shoes?"

"Yeah, but hiking boots? In Florida? Where am I going to need those?"

Eve turned away and shrugged.

"What's up, Eve? What's going on?"

"I was . . . I'm hoping you'll come to Montana with me."

Montana? Mei hadn't allowed herself to think beyond the here and now for so long, it took a moment for Eve's comment to register. "I don't know. I . . ."

Eve held up one hand. "No. Don't give me an answer now. There's no rush. Adam should be here soon. Wait until you meet him. He can tell you more about it, about our friends. I never realized how much I would miss them, but now I've found you, I don't want to let you go, either."

Mei nodded, speechless, and stared straight ahead. She couldn't think about the bags and boxes piled around her, of Eve's quiet declaration. She couldn't think of leaving all that was familiar and moving to a state that might as well be a foreign country for all she knew about it. It was all so much. Too much, too soon. She'd never had so many beautiful things in her life, never had anyone spend money on her the way Eve had today.

Never had anyone care about her before.

They'd had a late lunch in a fancy restaurant with real china on the table and crystal glasses for drinks. She'd worn one of her new outfits right out of the store and felt perfectly dressed in a pale blue cotton skirt and a gauzy yellow top. The food was amazing. She'd had salmon and quiche and things she'd never heard of before, all perfectly prepared and served by an immaculately dressed waiter.

She might have been too nervous to eat, but Eve put her at ease, asking about her life, her goals, her dreams. It wasn't easy, admitting her goals of college and a family of her own were long forgotten and her dreams so strange she couldn't discuss them.

Dreams of running through thick forests and climbing steep cliffs and mountains, hearing the cry of night creatures, tasting fresh blood, thick and intoxicating on her tongue. She'd long ago given up trying to find an explanation for the strange places her mind took her at night. In some perverted way she actually looked forward to her dreams, to the escape they gave her from such a desolate reality.

Mei felt Eve's fingers wrap around her hand. She squeezed a silent reply as the cab took them back to the motel. Eve paid the cabby while Mei grabbed up all the packages. "I've got everything," she said. "Eve, I . . ." She stopped. Stared.

The hood on the black pickup was raised. There was a man, his broad back glistening with sweat as he fiddled with something on the engine. His perfect ass was covered in worn jeans that fit him like a second skin and from this angle, at least, he was gorgeous. Standing next to him, though, was the most beautiful man Mei had ever seen.

About her height and slightly built, with smooth, dark skin and a perfectly proportioned body, he stared intently into the bowels of the truck. He wore an immaculate white sleeveless tank top and khaki shorts with sandals. His hair was cropped close, his face a blend of many races. A very pleasing blend. As Mei stared at him, she could have sworn she felt a connection, an unseen link that reminded her of the sensation she'd felt the first time she and Eve were together.

The packages slipped out of her fingers and fell to the sidewalk with a rustle of plastic and the solid plop of boxes hitting asphalt. Spellbound, she let them go.

"Adam! You're here. I didn't expect you so soon!" Eve raced past Mei, as the man working on the truck turned around and stood up. He had a smear of grease across his left cheek, but it didn't take away from the perfection of his face.

Damn. Mei shook herself free of whatever spell seemed to hold her, suddenly aware the one she'd been watching had turned and now studied her. She glanced away, at the other one. The one Eve ran to. Both men were gorgeous. Totally different from one another and absolutely beautiful.

"Ah, so I was right. You were expecting me! I wondered about that phone call to Keisha." He held his arms out and Eve practically leapt into his embrace.

She was crying and laughing all at the same time, obviously thrilled to see this guy. Mei stood there, grinning stupidly with all the good feelings pouring out of the two of them.

"I'm Oliver. And you are . . . ?"

She jerked her head around and realized the other man had crossed the short distance between them. He held his hand out, but he was obviously sizing her up. She wondered if he liked what he saw. He certainly got her nod of approval.

"Mei. Mei Chen. I knew Eve years ago. When we were kids." She took his hand and saw his eyes widen almost imperceptibly.

Did he feel the same jolt she did, the same amazing current that seemed to arc between them when they touched? Mei held on to his hand, well aware his grip hadn't relaxed, either.

"Wow," he said. Softly, almost reverently. He glanced

down at their hands, at their fingers still entwined. Then he raised his head and smiled at Mei. "And wow, again. Like I said, who are you?"

Mei smiled and shrugged and slipped her hand free of his grasp. Little tingles of current continued to race along her arm, but she chose to ignore them for now. She nodded in the direction of Eve and her friend. They still hugged, Eve still cried, even Adam's face looked suspiciously damp. "I guess they missed each other, eh?"

"I guess so. Here, let me help you with these." Oliver picked up the packages Mei had dropped. She pulled the extra room key from her purse and opened the door. Oliver set the packages on the bed.

"Should we, like, disappear for a while and give them time together?" Mei glanced at Eve and her man. Their arms were still wrapped around one another and they appeared to be having a fairly intense conversation.

"Not a bad idea. We can take the Jeep." Oliver grabbed Mei's hand and led her back outside. "Hey guys. Mei, this is Adam. Adam, Mei Chen. I've missed you, Eve." He leaned close and kissed Eve on the lips. It was obvious she kissed him back. With feeling. Before Mei could figure out the dynamics among these three, and well before Adam could shake her hand, Oliver was dragging her away. "Mei and I are going to take a ride. She's taking me on a tour of Tampa. Figured you two could use some quiet time . . ."

"Oh, that's not necessary," Eve said.

"Yes, it is. Thanks, Ollie." Adam grinned and tossed the set of keys. Oliver snagged them out of the air.

They were in the car and on the road before Mei had her seat belt fastened.

Adam shrugged into his shirt as he watched the Jeep disappear down the highway. When he turned to Eve, there was a speculative look in his eyes. "She's Chanku, isn't she? How did you find her?"

"I'm not sure. I found her this morning. There's something about her . . ."

"I know. I sense it. Does she know?"

Eve shook her head. "No. I've told her the pills help with telepathy. I had to say something. She knew I was reading her mind. Her thoughts are so . . ." Eve waved her hands helplessly. "I'm pretty new at this myself. I'm not sure what to look for."

Adam took her hand and tugged her toward the open door to the room. "We'll worry about Mei later. Right now, you're the only one I want to think about."

"Oh, Adam." Eve wrapped her hands around his upper arm and leaned close as they walked to the room. "I feel like such an idiot for leaving the way I did. I just . . . I . . ."

"It's okay. Now. You had your reasons and they were important ones." He leaned down and kissed her, then closed the door behind them. "It was pretty intense. When you shifted ahead of me, I was so afraid I'd lose you, and then you were gone."

"I couldn't stay. Something seemed to draw me back here."

"Mei?"

"I don't know. I think so. I'm not sure. At first I thought it was just me, needing to understand myself, my independence. Now that I've met Mei . . . I imagine Anton will have a field day with whatever is going on."

Adam laughed. "Yeah, well, Stefan won't like it. One more instance where his coincidence argument goes down the drain." He brushed her hair back from her face and slowly, thoroughly, kissed her once again.

Eve drew his breath into her lungs, his scent, the hard feel of his body against hers. She'd been so stupid, leaving this amazing man, but she'd had no choice. Something stronger than desire had drawn her back to Florida. "How was it?" She pulled away from his lips. "The first time you shifted. Was it absolutely amazing?"

"It still is. Every time. The hardest part has been shifting back, being human and so damned horny I ache. And you're not there."

Eve felt her smile spread, felt the warmth of his soft words like a caress across her heart. "I'm here now. So are you. Both of us here and very needy. Make love to me, Adam. I've missed you so much."

He took a huge breath and his chest rose and fell with it. She felt his confusion, his desire, but his thoughts were blocked, hidden from her searching mind. He suddenly turned and walked away from her, toward the small bathroom. Eve followed and watched while Adam carefully washed the grease from his big, battered hands and used the damp towel to take the smudge off his cheek. He led her back out into the room and stood with her beside the bed.

It was freshly made. Eve thought of the rumpled and sweaty sheets she and Mei had left this morning, but housekeeping had obviously come while they were gone. She wasn't sure how Adam might feel about her morning with Mei. There was so little she really knew about him. What they'd had was intense, but still very new. Swallowing back a million questions, Eve carefully put her own shields in place and blocked her thoughts.

Adam slowly raised his hands to cup the sides of her face in his callused palms and all thoughts of Mei fled.

Gentle yet so very strong, he held her immobile while his lips touched hers with a sense of reverence she'd never experienced. His mouth was soft and searching and he kissed her thoroughly, licking and nipping at her mouth and then carefully tracing the seam between her lips with the tip of his tongue.

She parted for him, sighing with a sense of expectation. The arousal he built inside made her ache for more. His muscular thigh slipped forward between her legs and he pressed against her pubes, a gentle pressure that merely hinted at his strength.

Moaning, Eve tilted her hips and rode his thigh. Her short skirt slipped higher up her legs and her sex throbbed with each scrape of worn denim over damp panties and needy clit. She wrapped her arms around his waist and sucked his tongue inside her mouth.

Adam's body trembled, yet he still moved slowly, carefully, as if she were made of crystal. She wanted more. Wanted the long, lean naked strength of him pressed against her, wanted the thick length of his cock buried deep inside her sex, but he kept the pace slow, almost languorous as he carefully made love to her mouth.

She felt the slide of his palm against her throat, over her shoulder, on her breast. His hands were scarred from years of working on cars and other mechanical things, and the rough calluses and ridged flesh added another layer of sensation to her already sensitized skin.

Her nipple tightened immediately and he rubbed his hand over the hard nub. She wanted the feel of his hand on her skin, not through layers of fabric, through bra and cotton blouse. As if reading her mind, Adam flipped the top button free, then the next. He kissed her and the pressure between her legs grew.

His left hand pressed the back of her head, holding her still while he plundered her mouth. She remembered him as a careful, thorough lover, but this was taking *careful* to new heights. Eve tilted her hips forward, bringing more pressure against her clit. Adam laughed and pulled his mouth away. "Slow down, sweetie. I've waited too long to rush this."

Eve laughed and rested her head against his chest. Her breath huffed out of her lungs and she rolled her forehead against him. "How about we rush this first time and take the next one slower?" She raised her head and laughed again at the expression on his face.

"You're telling me you want it hard and fast?"

"Oh . . . yeah. Definitely. The harder the better. I am so

ready." She walked her fingers down his chest, paused a moment over his heart and felt it thundering against her palm. She reached his waistband with both hands, tugged his shirt free and slipped her hands inside against the warmth of his belly. "Why'd you put this back on? I want skin. Yours against mine. You inside me. Now."

"Oh, yeah. Right now." He kicked his shoes off, slipped out of his jeans and ripped off his shirt. Buttons skittered across the floor. Eve watched, slowly unbuttoning her blouse and sliding her skirt down her legs. When Adam turned to her, his thick erection curving up and out of its nest of dark hair made her mouth go dry.

She reached for his thoughts and found only need and want and a powerful longing—every bit as powerful as her own. Overlying everything was an edge of fear. She wasn't certain why or what, but it unnerved her, to know this powerful, intelligent man feared something about her . . . or for her.

Eve unhooked her bra and dropped it on the floor. She slipped her bikini panties down over her legs. Naked, she watched Adam watch her while the tension between them grew. He was beautiful, even more perfect than she remembered. His tall, rangy body and rippling muscles were formed of hard work and physical effort, not hours with a trainer in a sterile gym.

His hair was longer now, some falling across his forehead, the rest swept back behind his ears, sun-bleached an even lighter shade of blond than she recalled.

His chest glistened and he smelled of clean, warm man and something more, something feral and free. His Chanku spirit was strong and the needs of the wolf paced restlessly just below the surface of his humanity.

That wildness drew Eve closer, opened her mind and her heart as she sensed the spirit of one like herself. *I need you. Now, more than I've ever needed anyone or anything in my life.*

I know. I've been praying you would want me, that you'd finally realize we'll be good for each other.

Love me, Adam. She held her hands out to him and at the same time, opened her thoughts even more, baring her soul as completely as she bared her body. He lifted her in powerful arms and stretched her out on the bed. She felt tiny and feminine, an unusual sensation for a woman who stood almost five eleven. When Adam came down beside her, his eyes glittered with arousal and his muscles were taut and trembling.

His mind opened. His thoughts shimmered clearly into her mind. "Oh, Adam." She was the source of his fear. That she might not want him, might choose to continue her journey alone. "No," she whispered, touching his face lightly with her fingertips. "Leaving when I did was something I had to do. I don't need to leave you again. I think Mei drew me back here, as much as my desire to feel totally independent for once in my life. I've learned something important these last few weeks. Independence means nothing without you to share it."

He didn't answer. He simply rolled over and covered her body with his. His cock slipped between her legs and he found her wet and swollen sex. With one powerful thrust, Adam entered her. She arched her hips with the smooth glide of his thickened shaft between her folds. Groaned with pleasure when he nudged against the mouth of her womb with the thick flare of his glans.

It was the first time he'd loved her without a condom, the first time she'd felt him bare inside her. Now they'd both shifted, there was no need to fear disease, no need to worry about an unexpected, unwanted pregnancy. Free to love, to experience everything in its rawest, most powerful form.

It was electrifying, exciting, unbelievably arousing. Eve arched her hips. She drew him deep inside and he seemed to swell even larger, fill her more completely.

I want to do this when we shift, when we're wolves. I want to lock your body to mine, lock your thoughts and your needs deep inside me. But I'm still afraid to say I love you, Eve. I'm afraid you'll leave me again.

I'm through running. I'll say it for us both. I love you, Adam. I want you. Always.

Adam raised his head, his body stilled. "You're certain?"

Eve touched the side of his face. "I'm certain. I don't think either of us ever had a choice. It was destiny that we meet, destiny that we fall in love."

Laughing, Adam kissed her hard and fast. "Stefan is going to hate this."

"Yeah, but Anton will love it. He's always arguing against coincidence. Now forget them and make love to me."

Adam nuzzled the tender skin along the line of her jaw. "I love it when you give me orders. My very own alpha bitch." He slipped out of her hungry folds and scooted down between her legs. Eve gasped when he dipped his head and nibbled at her clit. She tangled the bedding in her fists and closed her eyes to the persuasive pleasure of his tongue.

She was lost in sensation, lost in the length and strength of his tongue as he swept her folds and valleys, licked the crevice between her cheeks and swirled deep inside her pussy.

Impossibly deep.

Caught on the edge of orgasm, Eve opened her eyes and gasped. The beautiful wolf between her legs raised his head and panted. He wrapped his long tongue halfway around his muzzle, licking tiny drops of her fluids from his stiff whiskers. Then he dipped his head to feast once more between her thighs, lapping her cream and circling around her sensitive clit.

It was too much, too different, too soon. Not what Eve

expected, not anything she'd ever imagined. She tried to close her legs but he held her down with thick paws and powerful forelegs. His mood was playful, flirtatious, and she felt no threat from him. When she caught the laughter in Adam's thoughts, Eve flopped back down on the bed and spread her legs even wider.

What had seemed ugly and bestial suddenly morphed into the most powerful sex she'd ever experienced. His long, mobile tongue swept deep, twisting inside her to touch every sensitive nerve, every rippling bit of flesh. Eve shuddered as her body spiraled into one orgasm and then another. She cried out, a high, keening wail that seemed to come from some unknown part of her soul.

No more. She couldn't take anymore, but she clenched the sheets in her fists and arched into him just the same. Then the shape of his tongue seemed to change. Softer now, lapping gently between her legs, Adam brought her down slowly, and she knew he'd shifted once again. He crawled back up her body, and this time when he thrust his swollen cock inside her sex, Eve tumbled once again, gracelessly over the edge of orgasm.

Pumping hard and fast, Adam rose up on his knees and pulled Eve's legs over his shoulders. He filled her even more in this position, thrusting furiously with a sleek roll of his hips and a driving tilt to his cock. Again, unbelievably, Eve's pleasure rose, spiraling higher, dragging her close to yet another climax.

She shared her arousal, her approaching orgasm. Adam's fingers tightened against her buttocks, he threw his head back and shouted, filling her for the first time tonight, finding his own release within the pulsing, clenching muscles of her sex.

When he fell forward, bracing himself on his forearms, there were tears in his eyes and a soft smile on his lips. He kissed her gently, sweetly, his mouth against hers promising more than Eve ever imagined possible.

"I love you, Adam. I'm not sure why or how it happened so fast, but the doubt is gone. The fear is gone. I want you."

He nodded and kissed her gently once again. *Tonight. We run as wolves tonight.*

Chapter 4

Mei fastened her seat belt, fingers fumbling with the latch as they sped away from the motel. The damned thing finally clicked into place. She glanced at the man driving and caught him looking at her. Blushing, Mei turned away and stared straight ahead. Her heart pounded and her hands felt sweaty. She wished she understood what was happening to her, why he affected her so.

Who the hell he really was. "Where are we going?"

She glanced up and caught his smile. Brilliant white teeth set against dark chocolate skin. Perfect lips. High cheekbones. Gorgeous amber eyes.

"Wherever you like," he said. His gaze lingered on her a moment before he turned his attention back to the road ahead. "I don't know Tampa very well. I've not been here for years."

His soft voice sent waves of shivers across her arms. Mei loved the sound of it, the perfect enunciation, the slightly clipped British accent. He sounded well-educated. Smart. She rubbed at the gooseflesh on her upper arms.

"Are you chilled?"

"No." She shook her head. "I'm fine." She forced herself to relax. She didn't know him at all. Normally she'd never go off in a car with a strange man, but Oliver was Eve's friend, and Eve was okay. Better than okay. Mei sensed Eve might be the one to finally help her get somewhere with her life.

Get her out of the pit she'd been sinking into, deeper and deeper each day.

"I prefer the outdoors." Oliver flashed her another of those gorgeous smiles. "Can you think of someplace where we might go for a hike or walk?"

She thought a moment. Even though she'd lived in the Tampa area all her life, she really hadn't had the chance to explore very much of it. Mere survival took most of her time and energy, but there'd been one place she loved. One spot that called to her when the urge for solitude and nature coincided with enough money for transportation. "There's a park, not too far from here. It's got easy hiking trails." She glanced down at her sandals. She wasn't dressed for rough trails. "It's pretty."

"Sounds perfect. I doubt Adam and Eve will want us back any time soon."

Mei blushed. She couldn't help but think of what she and Eve had done this morning. That, of course, made her think of doing the same thing with Oliver. She'd never felt such a powerful attraction to a man, especially one like him. Usually she liked big, tall guys with lots of muscle. Oliver wasn't much taller than she was and his frame was fairly slight, though he certainly had the muscles.

His sleeveless T-shirt didn't cover much. It stretched across his torso, accenting what little it hid. What might have looked ridiculous on another man merely emphasized the spare beauty of his broad chest and smoothly muscled arms.

Mei sighed. She'd better pay attention or he'd think she was an idiot. "You're probably right. Eve told me about Adam. She's not sure, but she thinks she's in love with him."

Oliver laughed. "I imagine she'll be sure by the time we get back. Adam can be very persuasive."

"Have you known him long?"

Oliver shook his head. "Not really, though I feel as if I know him very well. He's had a huge effect on my life."

"Turn here." Mei pointed to an exit that would take them to the park. "In what way? What did he do?"

Oliver glanced over his shoulder as he merged onto a busy highway. "It's a long story," he said. "I'll tell you one day." He smiled at Mei. "I'd rather hear about you. How did you know Eve and how'd you get back together?"

"We were foster kids together. I was a lot younger and Eve looked out for me. We ran into each other just this morning." She didn't think he needed to know Eve had saved her butt when she got caught shoplifting. Not a good way to impress the man.

"Really? Eve's never said much about her childhood. I had the feeling it wasn't real happy."

"It rarely is when you're a foster child."

Oliver nodded and turned his attention to the heavy traffic. Mei wished she could tell what he was thinking. She'd certainly been able to pick up Eve's thoughts. She leaned back against the seat and concentrated on the man beside her. Opened her mind and relaxed whatever barriers Eve had tried to explain existed. This was such a new concept, the idea that she might actually be able to hear another's thoughts.

She didn't actually pick up words, but a warmth spread through her center, an obvious sense of arousal that Mei had been only slightly aware of earlier. Was she feeling Oliver's or her own?

She wasn't sure, but her breasts tingled and she suddenly felt her clit, something she wasn't generally all that aware of. Right now it throbbed in time with her heartbeat, a constant, rhythmic reminder of its existence. Mei forced herself not to squirm in her seat.

She chanced a surreptitious glance at Oliver's crotch. The khaki shorts were comfortably baggy, but he did appear aroused. Something filled the front of his pants. Imagining what his package looked like made her even warmer than she already was.

Mei smiled, wondering what it would be like to make love with a man so close in size to herself. She'd not had all that many lovers, but they'd all been large men. Powerful men. Scary, sometimes.

Oliver, for his slight size, exuded more power than the largest man she'd known, but he didn't frighten her. Just the opposite. She felt safe with him. There was a quiet dignity about him, a sense of self-awareness and confidence that was terribly exciting. She wondered what kind of lover he'd be, and with that thought came the assurance he would, indeed, become her lover.

She turned her head and caught him smiling at her. A knowing smile, one filled with promise. Mei's mind suddenly filled with images. Definitely Oliver's images, but she was ready for his thoughts and accepted what he shared. She saw the two of them in bed, like caramel and chocolate, her long, black hair wrapped in one of Oliver's hands as he controlled her for a long, drugging kiss.

She licked her lips and let the images take her. His tongue filled her mouth, his swollen cock pressed perfectly between her legs and she was shocked by the size of him, the heat and strength and heavy length. Even more shocking was her need, the feeling she had to have him inside her. Needed to feel him thrusting hard against her womb . . . needed to taste him. She licked her lips, imagining. There was a long, slow ripple of muscles deep inside that had Mei squeezing her thighs together. She couldn't even look at Oliver. Wasn't sure what she would say if he spoke to her.

The car slowed and Oliver took an exit onto a side street.

Mei blinked. "This isn't . . ."

"I know." His voice sounded tight, almost as if he were

angry. He pulled in front of a small, older but immaculate looking motel and stopped the Jeep, but he didn't look at her. He stared straight ahead. "You're in my head, Mei. Your thoughts are killing me." He laughed, a short, harsh burst of sound. "I know you don't know me, but your thoughts don't seem like those of a stranger. Do you really want me as badly as I want you?"

He didn't question her ability to hear his thoughts. He knew what she felt, what she wanted. Mei smiled with a surge of unusual self-confidence. At least there was no doubt they were on the same page. His profile made her want to touch him, to trace the perfect line of his nose and run her fingertip over his beautifully curved upper lip. His fingers beat a tattoo on the steering wheel. She watched his throat contract when he swallowed and sensed this wasn't something Oliver took lightly.

He took a deep breath. Let it out. "The vacancy sign's lit," he said, "but it's entirely up to you."

This morning, she'd followed her instincts with Eve and it had been wonderful. Her need for Oliver felt even stronger this afternoon. "I didn't bring my purse," she said, and then she wondered why she would even say such a stupid thing.

"I've got protection." For the first time since he'd stopped the car, Oliver turned and looked at her, and the expression on his face was priceless. Empowering. "Protection and a credit card. What else do I need besides the most beautiful woman I've ever seen in my life? You're amazing. Your thoughts are amazing."

"Yes."

"What?"

"Yes. I'll go with you. But Oliver . . ." She touched him then. Wrapped her fingers around his wrist, and the steady tapping of his fingers against the steering wheel stilled. "I don't do this. I never do this. I made love with Eve this morning. I need to tell you before we go inside. I have to know that doesn't make a difference in how you feel about me."

Oliver leaned his head back and laughed out loud. "Eve was the first woman I ever had sex with. See? We've got her in common."

Before Mei had a chance to work through his comment, Oliver was out of the car and opening her door. She went with him into the motel office, waited while he paid for the room, and followed him to the end of the long row of identical doors to the room they'd gotten on the end.

Oliver opened the door and held it for her. Mei stepped inside. The room was small but clean. Shades kept it dark and cool and the air conditioner hummed quietly from one wall. She wrapped her arms around her waist, shivering.

Nerves or the cool air? The door clicked shut behind her. Oliver flipped on a light. She couldn't believe she was doing this. She'd never, not once in her life, gone to a motel room with a strange man. She'd had sex in some odd places and some pretty cheesy motels, but never until she knew the man. A girl had to have standards.

Hers had just flown right out the window.

Oliver stepped up behind her. His hands rested on her shoulders and he put his face against her neck and kissed the sensitive skin just behind her ear. Mei went rigid.

"We'll only go as far as you like. If you just want to talk, that's all we'll do. If you want me to make you come without penetration, I'll do that for you." He kissed her again. "If you're a complete deviant and want to do anything, no matter how weird, I'm all for that, too." He nipped her earlobe. "I thought I should throw that one in . . . just in case."

The nervous tension fled. Mei took a deep breath. "This has been a most amazing day. Meeting Eve, realizing I could hear her thoughts in my head and learning she heard mine, too. Making love with her and having the most powerful orgasm I can recall. Shopping in stores I've never had the nerve even to go into before."

She turned around, knowing she had to explain a bit of herself to Oliver. Wanted to know that he at least knew why she'd so quickly agreed to have sex with him, a man she didn't even know. "We talked at lunch and Eve told me about you and Adam. She didn't mention making love with you, but I sort of got the idea you had. She said she thought you and Adam might be lovers as well. You know what's really weird? When she talked about you and Adam having sex I got so turned on I creamed my panties, right there in the restaurant. I've never thought much about two guys together before, but something about it, about the way she described the two of you, made it sound like the sexiest thing imaginable."

"We are lovers. The three of us have made love together. I've never been alone with Eve. At least not yet."

"Ah, but it is a possibility, right?"

Oliver smiled and leaned his forehead against hers. "Definitely. Can you tell what I'm thinking right now?"

Mei concentrated, but there was nothing. No images, not even a stray thought. She shook her head.

"I'm imagining all four of us together, our bodies twisted in a hot and sweaty tangle and we're sucking and licking and touching every erogenous zone possible. I've got my head between your legs. You taste utterly delicious, by the way, and while I'm licking and sucking you, Adam's working his cock deep in my ass and Eve has my cock in her mouth and her fingers on my balls."

Mei drew in a harsh breath as her level of arousal deepened. Oliver's nostrils flared. Her panties were soaked and she was almost certain he smelled her arousal. She should have been embarrassed. Instead she was more turned on than she'd been just minutes before.

Oliver cupped her face in his palms and kissed her.

Slowly, methodically, he made love to her mouth. Mei rolled her hips in a futile attempt to make contact with his, but Oliver kept enough distance between their bodies so only their mouths connected.

She moaned, parting her lips wider, sucking his tongue inside, tangling the moist flesh in a sensual dance. She reached for Oliver's waist and planted her hands on his hips to steady herself. He walked her slowly backward. The backs of Mei's legs connected with the side of the bed. Oliver leaned her back until she lay on the mattress with her knees bent over the edge.

He leaned over her. Her skirt rode up when he planted his hips between her thighs. The hard ridge of his cock pressed against her wet panties like a burning brand. He kept right on kissing her but she arched her hips, reaching for more contact with that solid bulge of fiery muscle against her clit.

Oliver pulled back and drew in a couple of huge breaths. "Take off your blouse," he said. Mei didn't hesitate. She slipped the buttons free and pulled it over her head. He gazed at her breasts as if he wanted to devour them. Then he took a slow, deep breath and knelt between her legs. He reached for the elastic band on her skirt. When he pulled it down, her panties slipped off her legs as well. Even without a single touch, her muscles had taken up a rhythmic clench and release and she moaned softly. "Oliver?" Her voice sounded soft and raspy, totally unfamiliar.

"Mei?"

She raised her head and realized Oliver's mouth was barely an inch from her swollen sex. Her first thought was how glad she was that she'd shaved herself bare this morning, but all conscious thought fled when he leaned forward and licked her. A single long, slow glide of his tongue from her perineum to her clit. He merely teased that tiny bundle of nerves before repeating the same, slow sweep of his tongue. This time he paused between her folds and sucked first one of her lips, then the other into his mouth. She felt him nibble lightly and cried out when his fingers slipped inside her wet heat. She cried again when he pulled them free. He sucked her clit next and she felt his thumb enter her pussy.

She tightened her muscles around his thumb and clutched the bedspread to keep from grabbing Oliver's short-cropped hair. His tongue circled her clit, his thumb pumped slowly in and out of her pussy, and his fingers trailed down the damp crease of her ass and pressed against her anus.

One finger circled the tight ring of muscle and her body seemed to leap into another level of arousal. Her breath came in short, sharp huffs as she fought to hold her climax at bay. This felt too good, too intense to go over the top right now. She wanted it to last, wanted the sensations to grow and develop even more.

Her mind whirled with a kaleidoscope of sensation. Oliver's warm, wet mouth suckling her clit. His thumb buried deep inside her sex. His middle finger pressing steadily against her sphincter.

Suddenly he was through, slipping into her body, stimulating an entirely new set of nerves. She jerked against the pressure, the amazing sense of so many nerves firing at once. Her mind seemed to blank, to overload on sensation and suddenly he was there, his thoughts so clear and bright he might have spoken aloud. She felt the pressure of her sphincter holding tightly against his finger, but it was her finger she squeezed. It was her own thumb sliding in and out of the slick, hot surface, rubbing against her inner walls, thumb and finger connecting through the thin membrane, reaching deeper on each slow thrust. Most amazing was the taste, her own taste, ripe upon her tongue, rich and salty and, in Oliver's eyes, totally addictive.

She might have come. Should have, but the images were

so intense, the sensation of sharing her own body through another's eyes so fascinating that she held her orgasm in check, sliding easily into Oliver's experience in order to control her own.

He could do this for hours. She realized he'd never grow tired of touching and tasting and learning her body, but she wanted more. She craved the fullness of a thick cock stretching her folds, wanted the hard thrust of hips against hers, the scrape of his pubic hair against her freshly shorn mound.

She told him this, speaking from her heart, silently in Oliver's mind. He raised his head in surprise. His lips and chin glistened with her fluids and he swept his tongue across the dampness.

"You are amazing," he said. "Do you know that? Absolutely amazing."

He withdrew his fingers from her body and slipped his shirt over his head. He tossed it on a nearby chair. He pulled a condom out of his pocket, then unsnapped his pants and dropped them to the floor. His underwear followed and he kicked them aside, along with his sandals. Mei stared, wide-eyed at the absolute perfection of his body.

His chest was smooth and glistened with sweat and his abs rippled with each breath he took. He had a perfectly shaped ass, so round and yet well-muscled that Mei wanted to bury her face in the sleek globes. His legs had the kind of long, lean muscles that swimmers and runners develop and he was perfectly sleek and smooth, with very little body hair.

But it wasn't his abs or his legs or even his perfect chest that caught her gaze and held it. No, she wouldn't even try and deny the fascination she suddenly developed for his amazing cock.

Oliver might be slight of build compared to the other

men she'd dated, but he more than made up for it with the amazing package between his legs. His cock was huge. Thick and long with veins running down the dark length, it jutted out of a silky nest of black curls at his groin, aiming directly at her crotch. He was uncut and his foreskin had rolled back behind the bulbous head, leaving him wet and glistening with a pearly drop of white on the very tip.

She knew he must be highly aroused, not only because he was obviously hard as a post, but she saw that his testicles were drawn up tight between his legs, barely visible beneath the thick girth of his penis. Without even considering the act, Mei leaned forward and kissed the very tip, licking the single drop of cream from the end.

Ohshitohshitohshitohshit . . . .

Blinking, Mei raised up and stared at Oliver. His head was tilted back, his eyes were closed and his lips moved in a silent litany. The condom was clutched in his right hand and his struggle for control couldn't be plainer. Smiling broadly, she pried his fingers loose, took the condom and ripped the packet open. Oliver never moved, though he groaned when she cradled his cock in her palm and stroked slowly back and forth a couple of times.

He was too large for her fingers to wrap all the way around, and she wondered if he'd be able to get all of that big thing inside her. He seemed to grow even larger as she stroked him. She slipped the condom over his glans and slowly rolled it down his shaft. Then she leaned back on the bed and guided Oliver toward her sex. He was shivering when his cock finally touched her, but he didn't press forward.

He must be right on the edge. Mei was close as well, but she didn't want him to lose it before she climaxed. It happened so often with men, but she hoped Oliver was different. She grabbed his cock at the base, squeezing tightly as she swept it along her slit. She used him to drag her fluids from her clit to her ass. The slick head of his cock left a trail of heat as she used him to gently masturbate herself. It took all her strength not to aim him inside, but she wanted to tease him, not take him over the edge. In a matter of seconds, though, Mei was the one ready to climax.

She didn't want to go alone. She glanced up and caught Oliver watching her. His eyes glittered. His jaw was set, his mouth a firm, tight line. Mei nodded and spread her legs farther apart. Oliver tilted his hips just enough. She pressed his latex covered glans against her wet and ready center. Oliver pressed forward slowly. Her nether lips parted and the head of his cock disappeared inside. He stopped, just barely inside her, and her muscles clamped down and held his cock in place. Mei wriggled her hips a bit to help him fit. He was huge inside her, stretching her vaginal walls with each small forward motion.

Her body adjusted, slowly drawing him in. She bent her knees and grasped her ankles, opening herself completely. Oliver leaned over her with his hands on either side of her body, his feet still planted firmly on the floor. He withdrew just a fraction, thrust a bit harder, then pulled almost all the way out. A thick, wet, sucking sound followed him when he retreated. Mei's moan drowned out everything else when he thrust back inside.

He was so large she felt stretched to the point of pain, but he moved slowly and carefully. The burning stopped as her body adjusted to fit his. Oliver picked up his pace. He was smiling now, obviously more in control and his actions were smooth and self-assured. He reached for her breasts and pinched her nipples. She felt the jolt all the way to her clit.

He did something with his hips, a little twist that put the base of his cock right against her clit on every downward stroke. Then he slipped his hand between their bodies and rubbed the slick little nub, barely touching it enough to register contact. His thrusting took on a rhythm, a perfect counterpoint to the beat of her heart, the rush of blood in her veins.

Mei felt herself spinning higher, faster, out of control. Their bodies had melded perfectly, so completely in sync that she knew he breathed for her, his heart beat for her.

Oliver covered her now, his slick body tense, his muscles shimmering with sweat, his balls slapping against her on every downward stroke. He held her hands over her head, rubbed his chest across hers, kissed her open-mouthed. His tongue fucked her mouth as his cock filled her sex.

Consumed by him, overwhelmed by sensations, by the mental barrage of passion and lust, by the pure physical power of his body filling hers, Mei finally turned herself free. She felt it spiral up out of her gut, a shock of power unlike anything she'd known before. Heat and light and emotion—so much emotion she knew she would cry from the pure beauty of passion.

This morning with Eve had been merely a hint of the orgasm Oliver was wringing from her body. She felt him tense, knew his climax was coming, felt her own sweeping through her body with the power of a nuclear explosion. Her hips arched up to meet him, her mouth opened in a silent rictus, a scream that would have torn from her throat if Oliver hadn't pressed his mouth to hers, hadn't melded with her and sucked the sound into his own body.

Crying now, tears cascading down her cheeks, her body shivering and shaking in the aftermath of the most powerful orgasm she'd ever experienced, Mei slowly brought her arms up and wrapped them around Oliver's neck, held him close against her body and wept even harder.

There were no words. No way to explain what had happened here. She felt him deep in her soul, in her heart, a wild, feral creature such as herself. Wild but not the same. No matter. She would not let him go. Her way had always been alone, but for the first time, she'd found a man who could please her. One who took her beyond her miserable life and showed her the purity of love.

Oliver knew he should hold his weight off Mei, but he was absolutely boneless, his muscles refusing to respond, his mind unwilling to work. His heart pounded so that he heard the blood rushing in his veins and he still felt the slow, steady pulse of his cock. The condom must be filled to bursting by now. Thank goodness he'd worn one.

Only a Chanku female could prevent conception. Mei might be able to link with his mind, but he couldn't say for sure that she was Chanku. There was something totally different about her. Something every bit as wild as the other shapeshifters, but as alien as Eve was familiar.

He lay atop her chest, listening to her heart pound every bit as fast as his own. Her blood raced as well, her lungs straining against his weight as much as against the need for more air than they were designed to deliver. Oliver lifted himself away from Mei to give her more breathing room.

She latched her hands around the small of his back and held him close. "No. Don't pull out. You feel so good inside me."

He had to agree. Her pussy clenched and rippled over his cock, dragging every last drop out of him. He was still erect, though he'd come harder than he ever had in his life. Of course, this was a first. Mei was a first. The very first time he'd made love to one woman, all by himself.

It felt wonderful. Life affirming.

Life changing. He rested his forehead against hers. "Mei, that was amazing."

She ran a finger along his cheek, touched his lips, traced the seam of his mouth. "I agree. I've never done that. Never come like that. Wow . . ."

WOLF TALES VI / 71

"Wow is right. I need to pull out. I don't want to lose the condom."

She giggled. "Okay. I'm not ready for babies, thank you very much. We hardly know each other." Her giggles turned to full-out laughter.

"I want to know you better. I want to know everything about you." He grabbed the condom at the base of his cock and withdrew. He was finally beginning to soften. The squishy, wet sounds of slick muscle separating from clasping flesh made him instantly hard. Again. He hoped he had enough condoms.

Mei stroked his flank as he stripped the condom off his cock. "I need to toss this," he said, heading for the bathroom. He felt Mei watching him. His skin grew hot. His nipples tightened and he felt a connection to his cock. Hell, his nipples never had been a huge erogenous zone for him, but right now he felt as if Mei were to touch one, he'd come all over himself.

He'd been an intact male now for less than a month. He'd enjoyed sex once with Eve, many times with Adam, and a couple times with Stefan, Anton and their mates. He was forty-two years old and this lovely young woman, probably young enough to be his daughter had he been able to reproduce so many years ago, had made him feel like a god.

He tossed the condom in the toilet and rinsed off quickly under the shower. Then he went back to Mei. She lay under the covers with one arm over her forehead. Her eyes were closed.

"Mei?"

She opened her eyes and raised her head. "Hmm?"

"How old are you?"

She smiled. "Older than I look. I'm twenty-seven."

Twenty-seven? Okay. He could handle that. "I'm almost forty-three."

She pulled the covers aside and invited him into the bed. "Good. An older man. I like that. A lot. I want you again. I hope you don't mind?"

There was a hesitancy in her voice, a question he liked. She was as unsure of this as he was. Smiling, Oliver crawled into bed beside Mei. He pulled her close and she snuggled against his side. She was almost as tall as he. Probably as strong. He knew she was brave, a survivor. If she was Chanku, she would definitely be an alpha bitch.

Hell, Keisha was an alpha bitch, and Anton didn't seem to mind a bit. Somehow he'd work things out. Assuming, of course, that Mei was Chanku. If she wasn't, Oliver didn't know if he'd be able to stand it. Let her go? Not now. Never.

He felt her hand trail along his hip, felt her fingers creeping ever closer to his groin. When she cupped his balls in her palm, the balls he'd had for barely three weeks, Oliver almost wept. To think he'd missed this his entire life!

He had a lot to make up for. Mei pushed the covers aside and scooted down the bed beside him. When she took him in her mouth, Oliver groaned. Then he threaded his fingers through her long, black, silken mane and thanked the Goddess for giving him this chance at love.

It wasn't the Montana forest, but a golf course just outside of Tampa was better than nothing. Since making love all afternoon, the desire to shift had built until there was no ignoring the need. They'd joked about it, both of them new at this whole shifting business as it were. Adam wondered if they got horny because they shifted, while Eve thought maybe they had to shift because of the sex.

No matter the cause and effect, Adam insisted there was no denying the fact their newly energized libidos were a direct result of finally becoming Chanku and embracing their amazing shapeshifting heritage. Now he took Eve's bundle of clothing and stashed it along with his in a tangle of fan palms just inside the gated golf course. He touched Eve's face with his fingertips. She smiled and shifted.

Nose to nose they sniffed one another. He'd seen her as a wolf, but Eve had taken off before he was able to shift. Other than today, when he'd been between her legs in his wolven form, she'd never seen him like this. Now she studied him in the pale swath of moonlight and her thoughts spilled into his mind.

You're beautiful! So much bigger than me. I still can't believe we're doing this. C'mon. She put her nose down to her paws, wagged her tail and yipped. *I want to run.* Then she spun around and took off with Adam close behind.

Running with the pack had taught him what to expect, how the air would be filled with new and powerful scents, how the ground would feel beneath his paws and the way everything that should have been lost in the night would suddenly burst into focus with his wolven sight.

But following Eve along this sandy trail, soaking up her amazing scent and knowing she wanted him and only him . . . Adam's step faltered with the rush of feelings, the almost painful depth of emotion he felt for this amazing woman.

She'd found a quiet glade and paused while she waited for him to catch up. Adam caught her there and they touched noses. There would be no hunting here tonight. There were rabbits and possums and other small game, but it was too risky to leave any trace of their passing. Florida's only native wolf, the red wolf, was mostly extinct in the wild. The danger of discovery was high, but the need to shift, to touch base with his lupine heritage was strong.

As much as he wanted Eve, as much as he needed to bond with her, there was too much danger so close to homes and the risk of discovery. Anton had warned him, of the fact that the mating bond was so powerful they'd be unaware of danger approaching. He'd explained the physical act of sex between two wolves when their bodies locked, how they were literally tied together by the huge knot that formed in the male's penis. The time needed to disengage without harming his mate could prevent escape, should they be discovered.

So tonight they ran. Experienced the rush of sensation, the fullness of life that only the wolf understood. Ran and connected on another level of intimacy, beyond human, beyond man and woman.

Within a few hours his pace was slowing. Eve was panting by the time they got back to the place where they'd stashed their clothing, and the hot and humid night seemed to close in around them. Dressing quietly, Adam couldn't begin to still the racing of his heart, the song in his soul.

They'd not bonded tonight as wolves, but they'd certainly found a new, stronger level of friendship and love than they'd known before. He wondered about Oliver and Mei. If they were back at the motel or not, and where everyone was going to sleep.

He wanted Eve. Wanted her beside him, beneath him, their bodies so close it was impossible to tell where one ended and the other began. An image filled his mind, of himself and Eve and Oliver. And Mei. Together. All of them together in one big bed.

He glanced at Eve and saw the shock in her eyes. Shock that slowly gave way to arousal. "I wonder what Mei and Oliver have been up to since you ran them out?"

Adam took her hand and they headed back to the truck. "I didn't run them out. Whatever gave you that idea?"

"I'll admit, there was no hesitation on Oliver's part when you tossed the keys to him." She wrapped her fingers around his arm and held it close against her as they walked. "He seems different since the last time I saw him. More self-confident, maybe. I don't recall him having such beautiful muscles before, either."

They reached the truck and Adam unlocked Eve's door and held it for her. She rolled down the window when he shut the door, and Adam leaned forward with his arms resting on the frame. "So, you're checking out Oliver now, eh?"

"Like you haven't?" Her smile lit up her entire face.

"I'm not sayin' anything." He leaned close and kissed her nose.

"You don't have to. I saw it in your head a little bit ago, remember? You're obviously quite familiar with Oliver's body. I imagine you've been getting more familiar with it." She winked. "I'm also wondering what he and Mei have been up to."

Adam shook his head. That could be a problem. Mei was gorgeous and Oliver was obviously interested. There'd been no ignoring the gleam in his eye or the bulge in his pants. If Mei wasn't Chanku, where would that leave Oliver? Hopefully, her ability to read thoughts went beyond mere telepathy. With any luck, she was just showing the first signs of her Chanku heritage.

"Has she had any of the nutrients yet?" Adam walked around the truck and climbed in behind the wheel.

"Just this morning. Once. She was already able to sense my thoughts. It appeared to grow stronger the more time we spent together."

"According to Anton, that's usually a good sign. Do you sense the wolf in her? Is she Chanku?"

Eve shook her head. "I don't know. I'm so new at this myself. I'm hoping you and Oliver will be able to help." She turned and placed her cool fingers over his wrist. "Which reminds me—is Oliver Chanku? Keisha told me he wasn't, but you mentioned shifting with him and sleeping in the woods on your trip out here. What's going on, Adam? What's so different about Oliver?"

"That's one Oliver will have to tell you himself." Adam leaned over and kissed Eve's temple, then guided the truck out on to the dark and empty road. It was well after three in the morning. He wondered about Oliver, and Mei, as well. She was an unexpected addition to this trip.

An unknown. Not unwelcome. Not by any stretch of the imagination. But certainly unexpected.

Chapter 5

Mei snuggled next to Oliver's warmth and wondered what had awakened her. They'd come back to Eve's empty motel room a couple hours ago. It was absolutely amazing to be sleeping in a comfortable bed after being homeless so long. Even more amazing to have the protective arms of a gorgeous man wrapped around her waist.

She heard it again. Voices, just outside the door. She recognized Eve's and relaxed. The bed was big. Oliver said they were all used to sharing. She should have been shocked, but for some reason, coming from Oliver after she'd already made love with Eve, it seemed perfectly normal to just slide over and make more room for Eve and her man.

Which in and of itself was totally weird. She'd been alone for so long. Maybe it was just human nature to occasionally need the contact of other warm bodies, but she'd never spent the night in bed with a man in her life. She'd had sex, but always managed to leave before dawn. Her need for solitude had outweighed her need for personal contact. Now she was going to be sleeping with two men and a woman? Go figure.

The door clicked open and a swath of light from the bright lamps in the parking lot cut a golden streak toward

the bed. Two people slipped into the room. "Oh. Adam."
Eve's whisper made Mei smile. "I didn't even think of
Oliver and Mei being here. I guess I just assumed Oliver
would have gotten another room."

"It's okay," Mei whispered, just as softly. "Oliver said
you wouldn't mind sharing."

"Adam's with me."

"I don't mind. It's a big bed. Oliver's out like a light."

"No, I'm not."

She felt him raise up on one elbow. "What time is it? I
wasn't sure when you were coming back."

Adam stepped into the room. "It's after three. Sorry we
woke you. I'm going to take a quick shower. You sure
there's room? Eve said there's a rollaway in the closet."

Mei laughed softly. "Tell you what. You guys figure it
out and wake me in the morning, okay?" She flopped back
down on the bed and snuggled close to Oliver. Before long,
she drifted off to sleep to the sounds of Adam and Eve
making love in the shower, and Oliver's soft, steady
breathing.

*Running hard and fast, big paws padding softly, barely
rustling the dry grass. The wind tickles across the tips of
sensitive ears and brushes past even more sensitive whiskers.
The air is fresh and the scent of rain fills questing nostrils.
Pause. Listen. Leap forward, following the night sounds.
Sounds that bring speed. The taste of blood is fresh. The
tongue remembers the way the rabbit twisted and leapt to
avoid the lethal snap of powerful jaws. It is good here, in
the woods. It's always good to run with the freedom of
four strong legs and long, sharp teeth.*

*Tonight, though, something feels different. Head lifts.
Air is scoured for scent. New scents, not crossed before,
sounds of others nearby. Unusual. The way is alone. Solitude is life. Pausing, head raised. No! What's happening?*

The world changes, shifts. No! There is no air. Suffocating! Trapped. No way to move, no idea where or who, no . . .

Mei blinked, held herself perfectly still and forced her racing heart to calm. It wasn't all just a figment of her dreaming mind. She *was* trapped, sort of. Oliver's arm wrapped around her waist from behind. Adam's nose pressed between her breasts and one long leg stretched over her uppermost thigh. Eve was snuggled against Adam's back, but the hand she'd thrown over his slim waist rested on Mei's hip.

Mei felt like the runt in a basket of puppies, buried under so many warm bodies. Her heart still raced but she managed to extricate herself without waking anyone. Adam groaned, Oliver squirmed closer, and the three of them settled back into sleep.

Mei used the bathroom and washed her hands and face, moving like she was on autopilot. So much of the last hours of her life felt as if someone else had lived them, some other woman experienced them. She scrubbed her face dry with a clean towel and glanced at Oliver's wristwatch on the counter. It was barely six in the morning. The others had come in so late, Mei was sure they'd sleep for hours more, but she was wide awake. After a moment's hesitation, she stepped into the shower.

The sharp sting of warm water woke her even more. She washed her hair and decided to shave her legs again. Would Oliver touch her today as intimately as he had last night? He'd seemed fascinated by her smooth skin, especially at the juncture of her thighs. She frowned as she ran the razor carefully across her slippery mound. She wanted to be certain everything, everywhere, was sleek as silk, but she still wasn't all that sure what had happened yesterday.

Sex with Eve. Then with Oliver, both of them essentially strangers, yet more intimate than she'd ever been with anyone else. She felt as if her life was changed forever. As if both of them had become terribly important to her. As if her heart would break should either of them leave.

She never let other people into her life. Not ever. She had no friends, no family. Now, suddenly, she had Eve and Oliver. And, from the looks of things, Adam Wolf as well—a man she hadn't even been properly introduced to, yet he'd spent the night with his body next to hers, his warm breath tickling the curve of her breast. Feeling terribly insecure and confused, she twisted her wet hair in a towel and wrapped another one around her body. Then she went back into the room and cuddled up in the big chair near the window.

She needed time to think. Time separate from the others.

Separate from the three beautiful people who slept on in the big bed. Without her. Mei felt a quick stinging in her eyes and swiped the back of her hand across her face. She would not cry. There was no need for tears, but her emotions were all tangled up, just like those bodies on the bed.

She'd been alone for as long as she could remember. She'd never spent as much time with other people as she had in the past twenty-four hours. It hadn't even been that long, actually, since Eve had saved her butt from a fine or worse. She could have gone to jail, and that would have killed her.

Mei sighed and watched the three of them, still sleeping so soundly, so comfortably together. They were all curled so close together there was plenty of room for her if she wanted to crawl back in bed with them. Adam and Eve, both so blond and beautiful, Oliver dark and mysterious, but with such a wonderful way about him. She loved his voice, his gentleness, the way he'd made love to her as if she were the only one for him. He made her happy. Made her want to forget what a shitty life she really led.

But Montana . . . that was a huge step. Leaving the one

place she'd known her entire life and just going away to a new part of the country? Wow . . . that was a major move. Of course, it wasn't like she had anyone here who would miss her. The few friends she'd had over the years had all moved on and forgotten her, or they'd ended up dead from drugs or worse. She'd quickly forgotten all of them. Even Eve, until they'd found each other, and that had been just a bizarre accident of chance. There never had been any family.

She would never forget the way one of her foster mothers told Mei how she'd been abandoned in a park. She didn't even know which one, but a little kid had found a newborn wrapped in bloody newspapers, her umbilical cord still attached.

Attached to a placenta, but not to a mother. Whoever had birthed her there in the bushes had just left her wrapped in papers like so much garbage and walked away. She couldn't imagine that. Carrying a baby under your heart long enough for it to live, and then just shitting it out on the ground like so much waste.

That story had taught her something powerful, though. She was a survivor. She had no one to count on but herself, but she'd survive. Since she was a little girl, she'd depended on herself for everything, though she'd obviously not done a stellar job at it. If she had, Eve wouldn't have caught her shoplifting in a cheesy little mini-mart.

It really was embarrassing when she thought about it. She was better than that. She shouldn't have been caught. Unless, of course, it was meant to happen.

Mei shivered in the muggy warmth of another Florida morning. She tucked the towel under her butt, wrapped her arms around her legs and thought of the odds of Eve being the one to find her. Thought of the odds they'd share this weird telepathy thing.

She rubbed at her arms, scratching at the unusually itchy skin, and stared at the three in the bed. She wondered what they were thinking as they slept. Did they dream of rocky cliffs and dark forests, of long legs stretching out in front of thick paws and a sensitive nose? Were their nights filled with exciting hunts and the taste of fresh blood?

Mei's dreams were just plain weird, and she couldn't help but wonder if Eve or Oliver or even Adam ever had dreams like hers. Then an errant thought drifted lazily through her mind and Mei smiled. She could open herself to the unexplainable. Maybe while they slept their thoughts would come to her, just as Eve's had yesterday. Settling herself more comfortably in the chair, Mei yawned, stretched, and turned her thoughts free.

Oliver's dreams felt as if they'd been filtered through a soft layer of contentment. Though he'd always dreamed of life as a wolf, it had only been the past few weeks where those same dreams were actually based on reality.

He'd not run last night, not even thought of shifting for the first time since becoming Chanku. No, his time with Mei had been absolutely amazing and his body still hummed with the sense of completion she'd given him. He thought of her now, caught up as he was in his dreams. He was the wolf. He was Chanku and she was near. He felt her as if she were already a part of him, as if the mating bond held them close, but now she strayed, just beyond his sight. He sensed her nearby and knew she paced restlessly, but she remained elusive, separate from him.

Oliver moved deeper into the dream state, aware on some level that it was indeed a dream, yet a part of his reality at the same time. He concentrated on his surroundings, on the thick carpet of grass beneath his feet, the myriad scents of wild things just out of sight. The woods were close and dark around him, the sounds of the night a gentle yet persistent symphony.

Confused, he sat back on his wolven haunches and searched for Mei. The cool air ruffled the thick fur on his back. It felt delicious after the stifling heat of the day and he wanted Mei close. Wanted the heady scent of her arousal, the proof she loved him as much as he loved her. He raised his nose and searched once more for her unique scent.

It was there, tantalizingly close, amazingly addictive. He sniffed again. Her familiar scent seemed different tonight. He drew her into his lungs, tasted her on his tongue and searched for her in the darkness. He heard the soft pad of paws on thick grass, turned his head in the direction of the subtle sound of movement through the forest. Her scent came to him, stronger now. It raised the hackles along his spine. He stood up, turned in her direction, and growled.

Mei jerked, surprised to realize she'd fallen asleep in the big, overstuffed chair. She blinked, and looked into Oliver's eyes. He'd raised up on one elbow in bed and was watching her. Before she could speak, he put a finger to his lips for quiet and carefully crawled out from under Adam's arm where it rested across his waist.

Adam turned over and rolled closer to Eve, and the two slept on. Naked and gloriously aroused, Oliver walked past Mei, leaned down and kissed her lightly on the mouth, and went on into the bathroom. She heard the shower run, the toilet flush, the sound of him brushing his teeth. She thought about his kiss, the fact a simple peck on the lips could leave her body tingling and her heart racing. She thought of his cock and the perfectly beautiful morning erection he'd carried, and almost followed him into the bathroom.

Before she could act on impulse, he came out. He'd dressed already and was wearing a clean T-shirt and shorts. He leaned over her body and she smelled the sharp, lemony scent of his shaving lotion and the subtle fragrance of the soap and shampoo he'd used, but beneath it all was Oliver, and that was the scent that heated her blood.

"Get some clothes. We'll go find something for breakfast. Those two could sleep for hours and I'm hungry."

She nodded and grabbed for one of the bags she'd not even unpacked after shopping. As quietly as possible, she searched through it until she found new panties, a short cotton skirt and a halter top. Mei went into the bathroom and dressed quickly, combed out her still-damp hair, brushed her teeth and met Oliver outside the room.

She stepped out of the motel room and quietly closed the door behind her. Oliver watched as Mei raised her head and scanned the parking lot, looking for him. He waved his arm and she smiled. He stayed where he was, leaning against the hood of the Jeep, and watched her walk toward him. It wasn't quite ten in the morning, but heat already shimmered off the black pavement and it gave Mei an even more mysterious quality. Damn, she was gorgeous. Long caramel-colored legs stretched forever beneath a short white skirt. Her long black hair swung loose against her hips with each step she took. She moved with a feline grace and it touched him deeply, that she allowed him to love her.

She stopped in front of him and Oliver took her hands in his. "Good morning."

"Good morning to you, too." He leaned close and kissed the tip of her nose. He was afraid to kiss her mouth. Afraid he wouldn't be able to stop with just her lips. She grinned at him and backed away, still holding his hands.

"Coward." She grinned broadly when she said it, obviously flirting with him.

"No argument there. What sounds good to you?"

She blinked owlishly. Then she blushed and laughed out loud. "Oh. You mean food? Whatever."

"For now, anyway." Oliver opened the door and helped her into her seat. When he leaned over to fasten her seat belt, his left arm brushed across her breasts. No bra. His cock twitched to attention. He wondered if he'd ever get used to that. He clicked the latch into place and closed her door and his heart thudded loudly in his chest.

She was so perfect. So beautiful. But was she Chanku? The strange dream that had awakened him left more questions than answers. Something about Mei was unique. His human side didn't notice, but the wolf in him was aware that all was not as it appeared.

"There's a little coffee shop about three blocks over." Mei pointed east.

Oliver turned on the street she indicated and found the restaurant. They parked and went inside. Neither of them spoke, but the silence felt comfortable. Natural, even, as if they'd known each other for years, had shared a bed and meals and the daily details of life for much longer than a night and a day.

This late in the morning, the restaurant was practically empty. They found a quiet booth near the front window with a view of the street. The waitress handed each of them a menu and left them alone.

Oliver took Mei's hands in his. "It's hard to believe we started out yesterday as perfect strangers. Thank you for last night. It was . . ." He paused, his throat suddenly choked with emotion. "I need to tell you about myself, but I can't, Mei. Not yet. There are things . . ."

She nodded, but she didn't look all that happy. "It's okay. Eve said sort of the same thing, but she promised me it was nothing illegal. It's not, is it?"

Mei frowned and Oliver laughed. "No, I don't think it's illegal. It has to do with the telepathy. We're learning more about you every day. When we know enough . . ." He shrugged. "It's complicated."

Mei pulled her hands free and picked up her menu.

Oliver shrugged and did the same. The waitress brought coffee for both of them, took their orders and left. Mei sipped at hers and watched Oliver over the thick porcelain rim of her cup. Her green eyes were flecked with specks of gold, almost hidden behind sooty lashes, but he sensed her unease over his secrets.

He couldn't blame her a bit. He was a complete stranger to her, yet they'd made love for hours, explored one another's bodies as if they'd been lovers forever. "There is something I need to tell you." He set his cup down. "Yesterday, last night . . . it was more than just good sex with a beautiful woman. Better than good. Absolutely exquisite." He laughed softly, remembering. "Shit, Mei. It was damned near perfect. You are perfect. I want to know you, Mei. Everything about you. I need you to believe that what happened between us was very special."

"It was special for me, too." She looked away and he knew her feelings were still hurting. "There's nothing about me to tell. I was abandoned when I was born. They found me under some bushes in a park. I was wrapped in newspaper, still covered in blood and stuff." She flipped her fingers as if it was no big deal, but Oliver felt her pain as if it were his own.

"One of the paramedics named me Mei, after his sister, and the county gave me the last name of Chen because it's common in various Asian communities. I'm not even sure what my racial mix is. Chinese mostly, I think. Maybe some Vietnamese or Korean." She shook her head. "I'm really not sure."

The waitress brought their food. They'd both ordered scrambled eggs and fried potatoes and bacon. Oliver's mouth watered as the delicious aromas hit his nose. He'd not eaten much last night but he'd certainly burned a lot of calories.

Mei seemed just as hungry. The two of them ate in silence for a few minutes.

"I'm not sure, either."

Mei raised her head. "Sure of what?"

"What I am. Who." He took another bite.

"What happened?"

"I was born on Barbados but my family, for whatever reason, sold me to a man when I was barely more than a baby. I grew up, essentially, as the pet of a little girl in a very wealthy family. When she got too old to want a play-mate, they planned to sell me to one of the local factories as a worker, but I heard about it and ran away. I was a teenager, but I'd learned a lot living in that house. It took me a few years, but I got to the United States."

Mei stared at him, her meal obviously forgotten. "That's horrible. What happened next?"

"I found a job with the circus. I tended the animals and such. They weren't too careful then about papers and I was here illegally. Eventually I met an amazing man, a ma-gician. His name is Anton Cheval. I have worked for him for most of my life. He helped me get my citizenship and since I needed a name, I took his. My legal name is Oliver Cheval, though I rarely use my full name. I was just Oliver for so long, it's how I think of myself."

Mei leaned forward. "Cheval? That's the man in Mon-tana. Eve mentioned him. She said he was absolutely bril-liant. She told me the same thing, that he's a wizard. I didn't think there were real wizards."

Oliver nodded and took another bite of his breakfast. "Anton will make you believe. As will Stefan, his . . ." Oliver took a sip of coffee. He'd almost referred to Stefan as Anton's packmate. He'd have to watch himself, at least until he knew more about Mei. Damn, but he hated this part of the process of discovery. Never had it meant so much to him that he be right.

"Anyway, where this convoluted story is . . ."

"No!" Mei interrupted him. "It's a fascinating story. I want to know more." She watched him, her heart in those gorgeous green eyes and Oliver realized he had to tell her as much of the truth as he could.

He shivered. His past was not something he thought about often. He preferred to leave it where it belonged—over and done with, bad memories he never wanted to resurrect. But Mei deserved more than bits and pieces.

"This is very private, Mei. Eve doesn't even know, but I want to tell you as much about myself as I can. I don't want there to be secrets between us." He took a deep breath and felt the cold shiver that always ran down his spine when he thought of his childhood. "When I was sold, the first thing my master did was make sure, medically, that I would never develop into a man, a sexual male. He wanted to make sure I'd be a safe playmate for his daughter."

He couldn't tell her he'd been castrated. Mei had suckled his balls between those glorious lips of hers last night. Thinking about it made him grow hard again, but there was no way to explain how testicles once removed could somehow grow back.

"But you're . . ." She held both hands up. "You're fine. You're better than fine, if you want to know." She blushed again. That swift rise of color made him hard as a post.

He had to take a deep breath to admit the truth. It was still all so new to him, this knowledge of what it felt like to be a man. To make love to a woman. "Only since last month. When I said Eve was the first woman I had sex with, I wasn't kidding. You are the only woman I've been with by myself." He laughed. "Without Adam there beside me. He was there with Eve. What happened last night was . . ." He shook his head slowly. There were no words. *It was amazing, Mei. Perfect. I fell in love with you last night.*

Mei's eyes widened. She'd picked up his thoughts. "You did? Are you sure?"

Oliver frowned as he nodded. "I did, and yes, I am very sure." He reached across the table and took her hand.

"Please. Come back to Montana with us. With me. I can't stay here, but I can't leave you, either."

"I want to. I'm afraid. I don't know."

"I understand. Really." He sighed and went back to his breakfast. Then he remembered his pills, the nutrients that made him Chanku. Oliver reached into his pocket and drew out a small packet. He removed two of the large capsules and offered one to Mei. "Eve said you were taking these. Here."

She eyed the big pill for a moment, then plucked it out of his hand. "I'm still not sure about these."

"For what it's worth, neither was I." Oliver popped his into his mouth and took a swallow of coffee. "Believe me, it's worth it."

Mei swallowed hers with a sip of water. "This mental thing. Reading thoughts. Is it normal? I mean . . ." She grimaced. "Sometimes it happens, other times, not."

"Eventually it will always work. You're already pretty good." Oliver went back to his breakfast. So did Mei. The silence between them felt more comfortable again. Natural.

"How did it happen?" Mei stared at him, her face a mask of questions.

Oliver finished chewing the bite he'd taken. "The details aren't important, but it was Adam. He fixes things. Essentially, I was broken."

"And he fixed you?" Mei tilted her head. Her long sweep of dark hair fell to one side.

Oliver was so caught in the sensual slide of her hair he forgot to answer. "Yeah," he said, finally. "Adam made it possible for me to heal. I owe him for that."

Mei glanced down at her plate, then back at Oliver. "So do I," she said, and once again she blushed. "So do I."

Mei wished this didn't all feel so totally surrealistic. Only yesterday she'd been stealing food because she was weak from hunger, and now she had this absolutely gorgeous man telling her he loved her. Obviously, something was wrong.

Her body still thrummed with the amazing sex they'd shared yesterday. Truth be told, she wanted him now, but even though they were already in the Jeep and headed back to the motel, Adam and Eve were still there.

Probably sleeping . . . or maybe having sex. Mei flushed hot and then cold, imagining those two gorgeous bodies together. She knew what Eve was like, how she tasted, how she touched and the way her body shuddered in climax. The mere thought of Eve's mouth between her legs made Mei slide from chilled to boiling. She glanced up at Oliver and realized he was watching her, but her panties were wet from thinking about Eve and he had to know she was turned on.

That was the only drawback to this mind reading stuff. How did you keep anything a secret? Of course, if she wanted to know what Oliver was thinking, all she had to do was . . .

His thoughts slipped into her mind. Effortlessly. As clearly as if he spoke the words aloud. His eyes might be back on the road, but he was definitely thinking of Mei. She closed her eyes and leaned back against the seat and listened.

Maybe we can go to that park she talked about. Find a quiet place there, or I could just get us our own room . . . damn, she is so hot and just absolutely perfect and I can't believe how much I want her again, but she's not ready for all of us yet. Hell, even though she said she's had sex with Eve, she doesn't even know Adam so I can't very well expect Mei to want to fuck a strange man. That's asking way too much of any . . .

"No, it's not."

Oliver hit the brakes and barely missed the back of a big Cadillac Escalade stopped at a red light in front of them. His head whipped around. "What? What do you mean?"

Mei shrugged. "Well. I'm working on that mental stuff and I'm listening to your thoughts. You're afraid I won't want to have sex with Adam." She shrugged, absolutely loving the shocked expression on Oliver's face.

The car behind them honked. Oliver glanced up at the green light and pulled ahead, but he kept looking back at Mei. "You've already gotten that good? You can read me that clearly? I thought you could maybe catch a word or two . . ." His voice sort of squeaked on the last word. Mei thought it was adorable . . . and sexy as hell to know what he'd been thinking.

"You wondered if you should take me to that park I told you about, or if you should get another room at the motel. You also wondered how I'd feel about sex with Adam."

He was breathing sort of hard and fast and she loved the fact she'd shocked him.

"And?"

The word came out sounding kind of like the way a frog croaked.

"And I said I don't mind." She thought about that and realized she more than didn't mind. She was fascinated by the idea of sex with more than one person. Her always healthy libido had somehow gone into overdrive this past—she reached over and turned Oliver's wrist so she could see his watch, barely noon—this past thirty hours. Not even two full days and she'd had sex with Eve, sex with Oliver, and was contemplating adding another man. Mei leaned back in her seat again. Damn! Maybe sleeping in a real bed and eating good food had something to do with it, but for whatever reason, her life had definitely changed in a big way.

Oliver kept glancing in her direction, but he didn't say a word. She tried to read his thoughts again, but either he'd somehow managed to block them, or her great powers weren't so great after all.

Oliver parked beside the black pickup just as Eve stepped out of the motel room. She was wearing a cute summery dress and sandals and her hair was hanging shiny and clean to her shoulders. She waved when she saw them.

"Hi. Adam and I were just going for a very late breakfast. We'll be back in a couple hours. He wants to take the truck out and make sure it's running okay."

Adam stepped out behind her and walked over to Mei's side of the Jeep. He leaned in through the open window and kissed her right on the mouth. Shocked speechless, she kissed him back.

"Hi. We haven't been properly introduced. I'm Adam Wolf. Sure hope I didn't snore and keep you awake, sweetie. Thanks for sharing the bed."

Mei smiled and licked the taste of him off her mouth. What was it about these people that turned her into such a hussy? "It was my pleasure."

Adam's smile was pure male invitation. "Hold that thought. We'll be back later."

Eve laughed and lightly smacked his shoulder. "Adam. Watch your mouth. You'll scare the poor girl."

Adam straightened up, but his searing gaze never left Mei's face. "Oh, I don't think so. I wouldn't underestimate Ms. Chen if I were you. I think she's a lot tougher than she looks."

He stepped back and flipped a wave to Oliver. "Two hours buddy. Just as much time as you gave us. Thanks."

They got into the little black truck and drove off as Mei and Oliver climbed out of the Jeep. "What was that all about?"

Oliver took Mei's hand in his and led her toward the open motel room door. "It was about you and me and not having to drive forever to find that park of yours." He closed the door behind them and turned to Mei. She slipped into his embrace as if they'd always done this, always spent their days making love.

In the back of her mind, a voice whispered questions. Why was she so accepting of all these people? Why didn't their blatant sexuality scare the crap out of her . . . or at the very least make her wary of them?

The answer came to her in all its simplicity. Mei raised her lips to Oliver's without fear, without hesitation. For the first time in her life, she knew she'd found family.

Adam slid into the booth in the quiet little restaurant, directly across from Eve. He reached over the table and brushed her hair back from her eyes. She raised her head and smiled at him, but he still thought she looked troubled.

"What's up?"

"Mei. I'm worried we're rushing her. I just found her yesterday. She's already had sex with Oliver and I haven't given her a capsule today. What if . . . ?"

"Oliver gave her one with breakfast."

"He told you?"

Adam nodded. "Mindtalking when I was teasing Mei. She's had the second one. He's already noticed her rubbing her arms. Remember that irritating itch?"

Eve nodded and took the menu the waitress handed her and nodded again when the woman asked if she wanted coffee. It was almost lunchtime but her hours were all messed up. Breakfast sounded wonderful. "Good she took the pill. Did you find out anything else?"

Adam shook his head. "Not much. He thinks she's Chanku, but he said there's something different about her. He's known all of us, the members of the San Francisco pack as well as the ones in Maine and Montana. If Oliver thinks there's something different, we need to tread lightly."

"Have you talked to Anton?" Eve smiled at the waitress and took her cup of coffee. Adam sipped his as well.

"No, but that's a great idea. Drink your coffee. Order a really rare steak and eggs for me. I'll go out and give him a quick call."

He leaned over and kissed her, took another quick sip of his coffee and walked out to the parking lot. Anton would know. The man seemed to have an answer for everything. Leaning against the hood of Stefan's birthday truck, Adam punched in the number.

When he finished his conversation with the leader of the Montana pack and went back in to eat breakfast with Eve, Adam realized he felt even more confused than he had before he called.

Chapter 6

Eve's fingers wrapped snugly around Adam's and they walked along the flowered pathway through a lovely park. She imagined they looked like any young couple in love. No one passing would ever dream they were shapeshifters, able to become wolves in a time span barely longer than the beat of a heart.

Adam, with his tall, rangy build and sun-bleached hair would have looked equally perfect on the back of a horse or balanced on a surfboard, and Eve couldn't ignore the envious glances of other women who passed them.

If they only knew.

"What are you grinning about?" Adam pulled her into the shade of a mossy oak and looped his arms loosely around her hips.

"Thinking how much my life has changed. How no one we've passed would ever imagine how we spend our nights." She smiled up at him, inviting his kiss.

She hadn't known Adam all that long, but she'd never known him to turn down an invitation. His lips were warm and sweet when they covered hers. His tongue trailed along the seam of her mouth, but he didn't force entry. Instead he licked and teased before resting his forehead against hers.

"Do you think Mei will go through with it?" Adam took a deep breath and rolled his forehead over Eve's. "Anton said the only way we're going to find out more about her is during orgasm, when her thoughts will be totally open to us."

"I hate the subterfuge." Eve wrapped her arms around his waist, but her thoughts were on Mei. She knew so little about her, but already Eve felt a kinship with her newly rediscovered friend. "She's such a sweetheart and her life has been so tough. Can't we just wait? That's asking an awful lot of a woman you barely know, to share herself so intimately with three people at the same time."

"She seemed willing when I teased her about it. Besides, Anton wants us to head back in the morning, if we can. Tomorrow it will be her third day on the pills. She could shift at any time."

"Isn't that all you need? To see her shift? What more proof is there?"

"We can't hang around here forever and wait." Adam drew Eve against his chest and she went willingly into his embrace. "Some don't shift for a week or more."

"What's the rush?"

"Stefan's birthday—that truck parked under that tree is probably a big part of the celebration. Remember, that's his birthday gift you borrowed when you ran off."

There was no condemnation in his voice, but she felt it just the same. "Adam, I am so sorry." She felt terrible when she thought about it now. Damn, what a coward she'd been, to run away like a scared rabbit, just because she was terrified of the emotional intimacy, of losing her freedom. She'd caused everyone so much trouble.

"But you found Mei."

"You're in my head again, aren't you?" She looked up at him and grinned.

Adam nuzzled his cheek against Eve's. She wanted more, but now wasn't the time. "I love you," he said, brushing his lips softly over hers. "I want to be in more than your head. I want to run with you in the forest and make love to you when we're both Chanku. We've never done that. Never shared the most intimate mating two creatures can experience. I want to bond with you so that you'll always know what's in my heart. So you won't have any fears or doubts, ever again."

"Is there anyplace around here? A park or someplace private?"

Adam took her hand and started walking back toward the truck. "I want to go back to Montana, where we know we're safe from prying eyes, where we both feel comfortable in familiar woods. For tonight, though, let's plan a nice dinner out, some wine and time to get to know Mei better. We'll invite her to leave with us tomorrow, but hopefully she'll join us in bed tonight. We'll know better how to proceed once we can see who and what she is."

"It sounds so cold-blooded, to plan sex with an ulterior motive like that." Eve slipped her hand out of Adam's and wrapped her arms around herself. "For so many years, the men who fucked me did it for a reason. Never for me. It was all for them. I don't want to be like that with Mei. It's wrong. I don't know if I can go through with it."

Adam stopped and touched Eve's shoulder with his fingertips. She felt the warmth and strength in his hands, the power in his body and realized it was impossible to be upset with him for long. Odd, for her, anyway, to be so accepting so quickly. She asked herself, how well did she know this man? They'd only spent a couple days together. Very intense days, but not enough time to really know one another. Still, there was no doubt in her mind that Adam was hers, that she would bond with him. Whatever barrier in her heart had existed was no longer there. She wondered what it was about him that filled her with as much trust as love. "Convince me, Adam. Make me see this from your eyes."

"It's not like I want Mei to do anything she's not ready for, Eve. Oliver's already half in love with her, if not totally caught. I know you love her or you never would have taken her into your bed and you wouldn't be this worried about her now. I don't know her well enough to say I love her, but I find her extremely attractive and I know she's at least physically attracted to me. I'm only asking that you help me read her thoughts when she reaches orgasm. We can work together and get more clarity."

Eve shook her head, more certain now than ever. "Only if Mei approves. I won't sneak into her mind and look for things that even Mei doesn't know are there. We tell her our plans, or we don't do it." Eve put her hand on Adam's forearm and imagined the leg of the wolf, all sinewy power and coarse, dark fur. "Men have lied to me and used me all my life. I won't be part of that now. Not for any reason, with any woman . . . or man. If you truly care about me, you'll understand why this is so important."

"If we were bonded, I'd know." Adam slipped her fingers into the crook of his arm and started down the trail toward the car. "I'm not sure if this will work if she knows, but we'll do it your way. Do you want to tell her, or should I?"

Eve stopped in her tracks. "What? You're agreeing with me?" Laughing, she shook her head. "I don't believe it."

Adam's smile melted whatever was left of her heart. "Believe it. Get used to it." He tapped her forehead with his index finger. "You're a smart woman, Eve, and your instincts are excellent. You've just reminded me that honor and integrity are a lot more important than results."

She stood on her toes and kissed him soundly. "I know if there's a problem, you'll figure out a way to fix it."

"Yeah. Right." He glanced at his watch. "It's been almost three hours since we left those two. I imagine they've worked up an appetite by now. Let's see where they want to go for dinner."

* * *

Mei slipped into the shower behind Oliver. He glanced over his shoulder and smiled that sexy smile of his and her heart did a huge flip, right there in her chest. "Want me to scrub your back?" he asked. There was a promise of more in his voice.

"No. I thought you might need a little help yourself." She slipped around to the front of him and knelt down with the stinging spray beating hard on her back. Slowly, almost reverently, Mei took his cock in her hands. Such a perfect instrument of pleasure. Long and dark and thick, broad at the head with the foreskin rolled back behind the flare of the crown. She traced the thick veins along his length, cupped his wrinkled sac in her palm and felt herself cream at the mere sense of the weight she held. At the potential for pleasure.

They'd made love for hours. Her pussy should be rubbed raw, but instead she felt herself come to life once again, now, as she nestled his lovely balls in her right palm and stroked his solid, semierect penis in her left hand.

His size and weight increased as she held him. Oliver's physical response to her touch was amazingly sensual and she felt again the hot rush of fluid between her legs. What was it about this man? She should be sick of sex by now. She'd never been fucked in so many positions and so many times in a single day in her life.

Instead, each time she came, her body seemed to want more. Each climax left her hanging, as if there was more waiting, just beyond reach. Now, when she should have been lying in bed exhausted, she'd followed Oliver into the shower, knowing exactly what she wanted from him.

His cock in her mouth. His taste on her tongue. The strength of his thighs pressing solidly against her body and the knowledge she'd brought him, once again, to his peak. Steam rose around them both and she thought of the forest, barely tamed in this place. Thought of the heat when her body held Oliver's powerful shaft deep inside. She wanted to share that heat and warmth and sense of connection, so she stroked his dark length and put every bit of herself into her touch.

Gently stretching and rubbing his foreskin over the broad crown of his cock, using it to softly stimulate the sensitive glans, she wondered at the resilience of their bodies. He should be absolutely raw by now, considering the number of times they'd had sex.

Made love.

He really had loved her. Worshipped her body, treated her like an absolute treasure. It was new, this sense of being loved, of being important to another person. So many times, so many ways and with a depth of emotion that left her stunned. She'd marveled at the power of his loving, at her own body's ability to come back, time after time, for more.

She'd wondered, off and on, if Oliver used her to make up for all those years when he couldn't have sex. Was she nothing more than a vessel? Then he'd say or do something amazing, and her doubts would fly out the window. He did love her. He must, to make love to her over and over again, to always put her needs first. Not once had he climaxed without taking her over the edge, never had he done anything without Mei as his full partner, making love *with* her, not *to* her.

She slipped her mouth over the head of his cock and wrapped her fingers around his tight buttocks. Damn! He had a rock-hard butt and the muscles moved in powerful ripples beneath her hands. His cock swelled between her lips and she sucked him deeper. Steam rose hot and thick around them and Oliver leaned forward, bracing himself on the walls of the shower.

Mei slipped her fingers into the tight crease between his firm cheeks and traced him from ass to balls and back again. She paused to lightly tease his sensitive perineum, and felt his muscles tense. Her fingers were slick with soap and it wasn't long before she centered on the tight ring of puckered muscle at his ass. She pressed and released, pressed again, harder, and he moaned, dropping his head forward, shoving back against her finger.

The shower cascaded over Mei's head and shoulders, an endless stream of warmth. She felt the various trails of water touching the swell of her breasts, dripping from the tips of her sensitive nipples. More trailed the swell of her hip and raced over her clit. She felt it. Felt every drop like tiny fingers, touching her, arousing her body to a feverish pitch.

Her tongue played with Oliver's foreskin, stretched tightly now behind the flare of his glans, her finger maintained the same steady rhythm, pressing but not entering his anus. He groaned and she felt it wherever their bodies touched. She drew him deeper, tonguing the velvety surface of his cock, sucking her lips around the firm strength of his shaft. He grew longer, thicker. Her own hips were rocking now, moving to his rhythm, caught in the sound of water beating a steady tattoo against flesh and tile, in the short, sharp gasps of Oliver's breath, of her own heart pounding in her ears.

She relaxed all the muscles in her throat and did something she'd never attempted before. She swallowed him. Her throat muscles rippled, contracting around his cock. He went deeper, obviously controlling his thrust. She felt the muscles in his buttocks quiver, the thick penetration of his cock down her throat, and finally the soft pressure of his balls against her chin. Her finger pierced his sphincter, pressing deep, driving him farther down her throat when he would have pulled back.

She felt the tight ring of his muscle grasp her knuckle. Felt the slick heat inside his body and the clench of powerful muscles holding her tight. She pressed harder, burying her long middle finger to the knuckle and pressing forward, finding the small gland she'd heard of. It was there, just like a G-spot for guys, smooth and round, exactly the way she'd heard, and she softly massaged it as she suckled his cock.

Oliver's body tensed. Her mind filled with sensation as all he felt spilled out, unchecked, flowing into her, becoming a part of Mei. She *was* Oliver, her cock held in a wonderful vise of pleasure, the waves of sensation increasing tenfold with each press of her finger inside his body. It was totally different than stroking her clit. Oliver experienced a stabbing electrical jolt of pleasure each time she rubbed him, pleasure that seemed to coil around his spine and roll straight back to his balls.

She sensed his climax coming, knew hers wasn't far behind. The water seemed to ravage her clit, the gentle river of moisture equal to Oliver's tongue between her legs. She arched her hips forward, swallowed him deeper, tongue and lips adding to his arousal. One hand cupped his balls, her finger pressed deep inside his ass, all of it coming together in a maelstrom of pleasure.

His testicles tightened in her palm and his ass clenched down hard on her finger. She felt the veins in his cock swell, knew the moment when he tried to pull free and she held him in her mouth, not so far down her throat this time, but caught firmly between lips and tongue just the same.

He cried out, a long, low howl that was animalistic and ragged. She held him tightly and wondered if his knees would have buckled without her supporting grasp. She tasted him, not for the first time, but never had she felt such control, such a powerful sense of connection. Her own climax hit just as the first salty ejaculate filled her throat.

Sucking, swallowing, breathing in as much of the steam-filled air as she could through her nose, Mei felt as if her entire world shifted. She flew with Oliver, fell head over heels through shards of light and dark, her body a trembling mass of sensation. All the power, the pleasure, the heart-stopping rapture of his climax and hers, melded. They became one, a single roiling creature of passion.

It ended, finally, though her body still trembled, her pussy still pulsed, her lungs still strained for enough air. Oliver's erection lost some of its strength, though he filled her mouth, both with his size and the salty, bittersweet taste of his seed. Mei sat back on her heels as Oliver leaned over her. His chest heaved with each breath he took. His hands came down from the wall where he'd supported himself and he cupped the sides of her face.

She released him from her mouth, licking the length of his cock, rubbing her lips over the wrinkled sac below, and then she pressed her cheek against his groin. When she finally raised her head, there were tears on his cheeks and a look of profound shock on his face.

Silently, Oliver drew Mei to her feet and held her. The water was beginning to cool, the steam had disappeared. The world once again seemed to have righted itself on its axis. He leaned past her and shut off the water, grabbed a towel off the rack and dried her as he would a child, rubbing her hair, her shoulders and body, going down each leg.

Then he wrapped the towel around her and gave Mei a slight shove. "Get dressed. I'm going to want you again if I see you naked. I'm obsessed with you, do you know that? I will never have enough of you." He kissed her hard and fast and grabbed his own towel. He was still drying himself when Mei wandered, somewhat dazed, out into the other room.

Adam and Eve were waiting. They sat at the little round table and grinned at Mei as she closed the bathroom door behind her. "Good thing we took longer than three hours," Adam said. He laughed softly and he was holding Eve's hand. She smiled up at him and it was so obvious she loved him.

It was all there in her eyes, in the soft smile, the relaxed, well-loved look about her.

Mei thought they looked absolutely amazing together. Both so blond and perfect. Obviously so much in love. She wondered if they saw the same thing in her eyes that she saw in Eve's. She didn't answer Adam. She just walked straight to him, filled with confidence and the knowledge that life was good, leaned over, cupped his face in her palms and kissed him full on the mouth. She put everything she had into her kiss. Her tongue parted his lips, her hands grasped his shoulders and her towel fell loose in front so she knew he could see her breasts, her belly, her naked pubes.

Knew, as well, he must taste Oliver's essence on her tongue.

Before he could touch her, though, she backed away and grinned. "Thank you, Adam. You are amazing. I owe you. A lot."

He stared at her, a goofy smile on his face, a stunned look in his eyes. "What was that all about?" He glanced at Eve and she was grinning like crazy. "Not that I'm complaining, by the way."

Mei reached down and picked the towel up off the floor, wrapped and tightened it around herself. "Oliver told me you fixed some things that were broken. I just wanted to let you know you did one hell of a job and I appreciate it." She went over and stacked the pillows against the headboard and flopped down on the bed. Whatever Oliver had done to her must have stripped away the last of her reserves. Suddenly, she felt perfectly comfortable in this new reality she'd hesitated to accept. "What now?" she asked

"Now we figure out where we're going for dinner." Still grinning, Eve held up a map listing dining in and around Tampa. "I know a great steakhouse, and it's not that far from here."

Mei shook her head. "Would you believe I've never had steak in a restaurant before? That sounds great."

"Then it's time you did." Adam still looked a bit shaken, but he checked his watch. "Reservations for seven okay?"

"I can't believe this. It's gorgeous in here." Mei smiled at Oliver when he held her chair for her.

Adam watched the dynamics between the two of them, sensing the simmering sexual tension they barely held in check. Damn. He hoped like hell Mei was one of them. It would break Oliver's heart if she wasn't Chanku.

Adam seated Eve and took the menu the waiter handed to him. They had a quiet table in the back of the restaurant. It wasn't all that busy in the middle of the week and there were only a few other couples scattered about the dining room. Mei chattered on, excited as a child about the fancy restaurant and the simple yet beautiful black cotton dress Eve had bought for her the day before.

Adam glanced at Oliver, who sat back and listened. Then his thoughts sought Adam's. *I sense you and Eve have something planned. What's going on?*

Anton wants us home. Something's bothering him, but he didn't say what, exactly. Merely that he has concerns. I haven't mentioned that part of our conversation to Eve. He suggested we all make love to Mei tonight, get into her head, see if she is Chanku. We can't take her back to Montana if she's not.

Oliver nodded. His gaze was steady, his confidence in his own decision obviously unwavering. *I know. And if that's the case, I won't be going either.*

I figured as much. Adam acknowledged his friend's decision with a silent nod of his head, though he knew it would kill him to lose Oliver's companionship. *Eve said we have to tell her what we have planned. She didn't like the idea of our going into her thoughts and just taking the information without telling Mei what was up.*

Oliver turned and smiled at Eve. *Good. I agree.* He turned back to Mei and caught her rubbing at her forearms, one of the first signs of the body's need to shift. It was all going to work out. Whatever it was about Mei that had seemed different, almost alien to him, couldn't be that important. She was Chanku.

She had to be.

The waiter appeared to take their order. Adam and Oliver both wanted rare prime rib and Adam asked for a bottle of red wine. It was an expensive Cabernet Sauvignon, but tonight was a celebration of sorts, the first night he and Eve had ever gone out for a nice dinner.

It reminded him how short a time he'd known her. Eve asked for a filet mignon, also rare. Mei looked at Eve and Adam sensed her nervousness, her lack of confidence in this new situation.

"What should I get?"

"How do you like your meat?" Oliver smiled at her over his menu.

Mei shook her head. "I don't know. I like hamburgers that are still pink in the middle."

Adam interrupted. "Order the same as Eve. I guarantee you'll like it."

"What he said." Mei smiled at the waiter but she pointed at Adam. The waiter took her order, promised to bring their wine, and left. Mei turned and grinned at Adam. "Yesterday was the first time I ever ate in a fancy restaurant, when Eve and I had lunch. You guys must be trying to fatten me up for the kill."

Adam laughed. "Hardly that. We always chose a nice place when we have the opportunity, and we want you to enjoy yourself." *A lot,* he thought. *We want you to enjoy yourself as much as possible.*

The waiter left and Mei looked down at her hands, folded neatly in her lap. When she raised her eyes, she blinked back tears. "This past two days have been like a miracle. I've never had new clothes like these, never had friends like you guys." She took a deep breath and let it out before she placed her hand on Oliver's forearm. "Never had friends I cared about, or someone to love. It's been like a dream. A wonderful dream."

Eve reached across the table and took Mei's free hand. "I'm just glad I found you."

Mei giggled and the spell was broken. She looked at the bounty on the table and waved her hand, encompassing the tray of appetizers, the wine the waiter had just served, the crusty French bread with the tantalizing sourdough smell. Her mouth literally watered. "Me, too. Dumpster diving has nothing on this!"

Adam smiled as he reached across the table and took Mei's hand from Eve's grasp, but then he went all serious on her. The warmth and sincerity in his voice had her choking up again. She looked down at their clasped fingers.

"I've been homeless before, Mei." Adam squeezed her hand. "I know what it's like, how scary it can be. Most of all, how lonely."

Mei squeezed his hand right back before slipping her fingers free. She took a sip of her wine. Suddenly, that overwhelming need for solitude didn't seem as important. She was surrounded by friends, suffused with good feelings and the sense these people accepted her. Loved her. Nothing could go wrong. Absolutely nothing.

Or so she thought. Sitting beside Oliver in the backseat of the Jeep on the way home from the restaurant, Mei's naturally suspicious nature reappered. She wondered if this had all been some weird kind of setup, if these amazing people were some kind of cult. She'd heard about cults, how they sucked you in and convinced you they were right about everything until you didn't have a thought of your own. She wasn't like that. Wouldn't be like that. If nothing else, Mei had always gone her own way, made her own decisions. She'd lived this long without depending on anyone but herself. Maybe falling for Oliver was a huge mistake. Maybe he was trying to brainwash her.

Yeah, right. With the best sex you've ever had in your life.

But still . . . Dinner had been spectacular and her steak like ambrosia. She didn't realize the taste she'd been craving was rare meat, but she'd finished her steak and even eaten a couple of bites of Oliver's huge, blood-rare prime rib. She could have eaten more, but didn't want to embarrass herself.

They'd talked over dinner, mostly about Montana and the beautiful country where they lived, all of them with four other people on a huge estate. All of them living together. Making love with each other. Maybe it wasn't a cult. Maybe they just lived in a commune. She'd heard about those, too, but mostly that was something from the older generation, when there were hippies and people who believed in free love.

Before AIDS. Before diseases that could ruin your life. She had an IUD, one she'd gotten at the free clinic, so pregnancy wasn't that big a worry, but AIDS was. She'd lost friends to that one and no way was it going to get her. At least Oliver always remembered protection. She hadn't thought about it at all this morning in the shower. She glanced at Oliver sitting quietly beside her. Everyone was quiet now, on the way home, but the tension inside the Jeep was filled with promise, ripe with the sense of arousal, of barely restrained passion.

They were going to have sex when they got back to the motel. She just knew it. Felt it. She needed to ask Oliver if he was clean. If oral sex had been safe with him. She'd been totally out of control and that wasn't like her. Not at all. In fact it was just stupid. If anything, Mei Chen was not stupid, but damn, no matter how concerned she might be about everyone's motives, she couldn't get past the fact she liked them. Really and truly liked them.

She sneaked another glance at Oliver. He turned and smiled at her, but she sensed he was somewhere else. Probably in his damned Montana. She wasn't sure about going there. Going so far with people she hardly knew.

Adam drove into the parking lot and parked in front of their room. Eve turned and looked at Mei and she felt her friend's thoughts and knew she was the only one who heard them.

If anything happens, anything at all that makes you uncomfortable, tell me. I'll make it stop. Okay?

But what . . . ?

Oliver was already out of the car, holding his hand out to Mei. Still confused over Eve's warning—and it could only have been a warning—she quickly unfastened her seat belt and took Oliver's hand, got out and stood with him while Adam and Eve went ahead and opened the door to the room.

"What's going on? I can feel something, some kind of weird energy, but I don't know what it is."

Oliver squeezed her fingers. "Wait until we're inside. We need to talk. All of us."

She felt an apprehensive shiver race along her spine. This didn't sound all that good, but she followed Oliver into the room. Housekeeping had been by and the bed was neatly made. The bags of clothes had been stacked by the closet. A hint, maybe? Four of them in this room had certainly made a mess of things, but it was a nice motel and maybe the fact they paid top dollar let them get away with more. She didn't know. How could she? This was so far out of her experience.

Eve immediately slipped out of her dress. She didn't seem to mind a bit that both Adam and Oliver were in the room, but then Mei remembered Eve had made love to

Oliver in the past, so what was there to hide? Eve wrapped a pale green sarong around herself. It shimmered and outlined every curve and angle of her body. She looked even more lovely than she usually did. Mei felt an instant attraction to her and her mind filled with images of their lovemaking. Was it only yesterday?

Adam undid his tie and slipped out of his coat. Oliver hung his sports coat in the closet and unbuttoned his shirt. No one seemed to notice the fact they were all undressing together in the same room, so Mei slipped out of the new heels that were beginning to pinch her toes, and searched through her bags for the blue sarong Eve had bought for her.

Shyly she glanced around. No one was paying any attention to her, so she took her sarong into the bathroom. She slipped out of her dress in there, and wrapped herself carefully in the sheet of silk. The transformation was amazing.

With her long, black hair sweeping the curve of her butt and the bright blue fabric shimmering against her caramel-colored skin, she looked exotic, like some sort of island princess. She'd never seen herself like this, looking so mysterious. Never had thought of herself as pretty before.

Right now she looked beautiful. She stared at her image a moment longer, using it to build confidence. Then, feeling totally stoked with self-assurance, Mei walked back into the room. Eve and Adam were on the bed with the pillows behind them. Adam had on a pair of boxers. They were silky and loose, but they did nothing to hide the size of the package he carried between his thighs.

Mei felt a sudden rush of moisture between her legs, followed by an immediate sense of guilt. Oliver stepped out from behind the closet door. He'd wrapped a shorter sarong around his hips. The yellow fabric glistened and shimmered when he moved and looked gorgeous against his dark skin.

Again Mei felt a rush of arousal. What the hell was

going on with her? She couldn't be turned on by both men, could she? It wasn't right.

"Yes it is." Oliver stepped in front of her and put his hands on her shoulders. "You excite me. So does Eve. For that matter, so does Adam. It's the way we are. We're all lovers, Mei. Does that offend you?"

She started to back away, to tell him it was just sick, but the serous gleam in his eyes made her stop and think about what Oliver asked. If she really thought about it, did the fact the three of them made love seem wrong? She'd seen them together, watched the way they interacted. It was obvious what they had wasn't just about sex. It was more. So much more. They truly loved one another.

"The same way we want to love you." Oliver kissed her, then pulled her close in a warm hug. "The thing is, Mei, we need to know more about you. About who and what you are."

"You know who I am. Eve can vouch for me." She straightened up, out of his embrace. Who the hell did he think . . . ?

Oliver shook his head. "It's more than that. The telepathy thing? Very few people can do that. Only the ones who have a very special genetic background. We want you to be part of us, to come with us when we go back to Montana, but we can only take you if you're like we are."

"You'd leave me?" Mei felt her skin go hot and cold, all at the same time.

Oliver shook his head. "Adam and Eve would go back. I'm willing to give up my life with them to stay with you, but only if I absolutely have to. Exile from my own kind is not something I'd choose lightly. Not something I want to even think about. Thing is, I think you're like we are. Will you let us find out?"

She stared at Oliver, then glared at Adam and Eve. This was their fault. She knew it. "How? How will you find out?"

Oliver stroked her shoulder. She grew hot, just from the slight touch of his hand. Aroused even while anger simmered deep inside her. She wanted to step away from his touch, but already he was a drug. One she couldn't willingly ignore.

"We make love," he said. "All of us, together. You know how it is when the two of us climax?"

Oh, God! Did she ever! Just thinking about it made her palms sweat and a deep coil of heat swell deep in her belly. Mei nodded, almost speechless with the sudden rush of desire. How could he do this to her? "We hear each other's thoughts." She hoped he could hear her whisper, but she couldn't dredge up any more sound. Not for this. "It's like I'm you, and you're me. We're one person."

Oliver smiled. "Exactly. If we achieve a climax at the same time, all of us together, and if Adam, Eve, and I can focus our energy on you, on your thoughts when you're at your most unguarded, we'll be able to tell if you're just like us. It won't hurt, I promise." Oliver glanced over at Adam and Eve who waited quietly on the bed. "I have to be honest with you. We, me and Adam, thought about just doing it and not telling you. Eve wouldn't let us. She said it was up to you, that it's your mind and your decision."

Mei looked over at Eve and had to bite back the tears. She'd never, not since she and Eve were children, had anyone stand up for her before. It had been Eve all those years ago. Once again, Eve was protecting her. "You said that? You told them . . ." She nodded sharply at both Oliver and Adam, then took a deep breath. "You told them they couldn't do it without my permission?"

"I did." Eve practically glared at Oliver and Adam. "No man, or woman, has the right to our thoughts, or our bodies, without our permission. Not ever."

Adam nodded, agreeing. He took Eve's hand and held it against his heart, but his eyes were directly focused on Mei. "She's right. I'm glad Eve had the sense to remind me of the importance of honor and integrity. Sometimes we, not just Oliver and I, but men in general, focus too much on results. We forget the process is just as important, if not more so."

"What happens if I'm not like you?"

Adam answered first. "Then Oliver will stay with you, and Eve and I will return to Montana. He's already made his choice, Mei. He chooses you and exile from the rest of our kind. We don't want to go without you, and we really don't want to leave Oliver. He has more history with our group than either Eve or I do. The man loves you, Mei. Eve loves you. I want the chance to know you better, because right now I like you one hell of a lot, and I also find you extremely desirable. I know I could love you as well, given time to know you. But, we don't want to do anything you don't agree to."

Mei pulled out of Oliver's embrace. She stood back far enough that she could see all of them. See them, but not be touched by any of them, especially Oliver. She needed to make this decision on her own. Treat it with the importance the three in this room gave to it. It was a new feeling, knowing her decision actually counted.

These three offered her a choice that would change all their lives, for good or bad. Knowing her decision still might not alter the eventual outcome, should she not prove to be one of them, put even more pressure on her to think this through. Knowing three people would be probing the deepest recesses of her mind was even more frightening than the act of sex with all of them. *That* she actually wanted.

She studied each of them, considering her options. Did she trust them with knowledge even she wasn't aware of? Oliver, though slight of build, had a presence about him that defied description. Eve was just flat-out gorgeous, and she'd been so nice, and so kind. She'd stood up for Mei when they were kids, and she was doing it again, against her lover's wishes. That meant she was willing to take chances for a friend, and that told Mei she was brave. And sexy, too, when it came right down to it. Mei would never forget what they'd done yesterday morning.

The question was, did she want to do it again? Not just with Eve, but Oliver as well . . . and with Adam, a man she barely knew, added to the mix. Was she willing to turn herself over to them, knowing they planned to use the most intimate acts possible to see into parts of her mind where even Mei hadn't journeyed?

She tried to imagine sex with four people. Then she glanced at Oliver and remembered what he'd said yesterday, when they'd first gone into that motel room. Before they actually made love and he'd described his fantasy of the four of them together. The words were engraved on her brain and she drew them out now, remembering how passion had roughened his voice. How it made his accent more pronounced.

I'm imagining all four of us together, our bodies twisted in a hot and sweaty tangle and we're sucking and licking and touching every erogenous zone possible. I've got my head between your legs. You taste utterly delicious, by the way, and while I'm licking and sucking you, Adam's working his cock deep in my ass and Eve has my cock in her mouth and her fingers on my balls.

She'd gotten hot when he talked about it. Now, standing here in this room, faced with the chance to experience exactly what was in this scene, she felt her labia swell, felt her own moisture, thick and hot, breaking free and trickling down her inner thighs. Her breath caught in her lungs with the full realization she wanted to experience what he described.

Not only could she do this, she wanted it. Craved it. They were all going to get naked and have wild monkey sex, but with one feature not included in the original fantasy.

All three of them were going to be crawling around in

her head. Probing. Searching. Knowing her more intimately than she'd ever known herself.

Could she handle it? She, who prided herself on what little privacy she had and was proud of her lack of need for others? She took a deep breath. Admitted her needs. Almost laughed at her fears.

Well, things change, damn it! That they did. Mei nodded, slowly. "Okay. I think I can do this, but on one condition."

Oliver stepped close and put his arm around her waist. He kissed her cheek. "What's that?"

Mei laughed. She felt like flying, felt as if her world had expanded and opened up an entirely new future, one she would embrace with heart wide open and both arms stretched wide. "My condition is, I get the best damned orgasm any woman on earth has ever had. Bigger than what happened today, Oliver. Bigger than anything. If you're maybe going to kick me out of your lives tomorrow, you'd damned well better give me some great memories to take with me."

Chapter 7

Adam reached down beside the bed and pulled up a bottle of champagne he'd left in ice. "I think a celebration is in order. It's obvious Oliver has found a woman every bit as strong as he is, one who will stand beside him." He rolled off the bed, bottle in hand and took the crystal flute Eve handed to him.

Carefully, he filled the glass and held it out to Mei. She took it from him, hands trembling and eyes wide. Adam caught the wary look in her green eyes and tried to see what she was thinking.

Chaos swirled in her mind. So many images, so many thoughts it was impossible to discern which led where. The only thing he could be sure of was her difference. If she were truly Chanku, there was something about her unlike any he'd known. Different, and powerful.

Forcing himself not to frown while he pondered her myriad thoughts, Adam handed a second glass to Eve, the third to Oliver, then carefully poured one for himself. "To Mei Chen," he said, holding his glass high. The others stood, forming a perfect triangle with Mei at its center. Each lifted their glass, tapped the edge lightly. When the three tapped their flutes to Mei's, the air vibrated with an otherworldly ring, like the sound of a bell echoing from far away.

Adam sipped his champagne and soaked up the thoughts of those around him. Oliver, desperate to find out Mei was indeed Chanku. Eve, concerned for her friend, ready to fight even Adam if she thought he was treating Mei unfairly.

His own thoughts were more convoluted and hard to assess. He wanted her to be Chanku. Wanted it more than anything, for Oliver's sake if nothing else. He'd always been able to fix things, and he wanted to fix this situation. Failure wasn't an option, not ever again.

He would never forgive himself for his greatest failure. He'd not been able to fix the horrible mess that was his twin sister's life. No, it had taken someone else to find her, to correct a lifetime of injustice.

He thought of Manda now, a young woman he'd known intimately in his dreams for most of his adult life, yet hadn't known existed for real until just last month. She'd called out to him in a familiar and hopeless voice in nightmares of pain and loneliness, dreams that haunted him. He'd tried to comfort her, his imaginary friend, yet he'd never truly believed she was real. He'd not discovered his Chanku heritage, had no idea that shapeshifters existed, but that wasn't an excuse. He'd not believed her existence even remotely possible—a creature trapped in the middle, halfway between woman and wolf.

Thank the Goddess she'd managed to save herself with the help of his packmate, Baylor Quinn. Thankfully she held no animosity against Adam, no matter how little he'd done to help her, but Manda had been a lesson to him. *Believe, accept, and trust in love.* There was nothing more powerful. Manda loved him enough to forgive him. She'd said it was his love that kept her sane through years of agony and confusion, when she was held a virtual prisoner and treated like a lab specimen by scientists who neglected to see the woman inside.

Whatever happened tonight, Adam knew he had to make it possible for Mei to come with them to Montana.

He wasn't sure how he was going to manage, but he would. He had to, for Oliver's sake. Sipping his champagne, he made a solemn promise. No matter what the outcome, he'd not leave his friend behind.

Eve touched his arm. He felt the current from her fingertips all the way to his groin. He turned and saw the smile in her eyes, felt the love in her heart. *I'll not leave any of you, either. Stop worrying, Adam. It's going to be absolutely wonderful. I feel it.* She stood on her toes and kissed him. She tasted of champagne, but it wasn't enough to disguise the raw sensuality of her own personal flavors.

Adam finished off his champagne and set the glass aside. He wrapped one arm around Eve's waist and leaned past her to turn out the light beside the bed. A smaller one glowed in a corner of the room, bathing the area in a soft golden haze ripe with shadows. "I don't know about the rest of you, but if I don't make love to Eve right now, I think I'll explode."

He lifted her in his arms and her head fell forward and rested against his chest. Her lips teased the warm flesh just above his left nipple and he felt the jolt all the way to his balls. His cock swelled and stretched until it tented the front of his silk boxers. He turned toward Oliver and Mei. "Join us whenever you like," he said. "I'm not waiting any longer." Then he set Eve gently on the bed.

Oliver laughed. Mei remained silent, but everything— sound, even the presence of two other people standing silently at the foot of the bed—faded away until it was only the two of them. Adam and Eve, as it always should be. Adam stood beside the bed and stared at Eve for a long moment, savoring her presence, the fact she had finally said she loved him. He'd never doubted, had he?

Yes. He had to be honest with himself. The fear had been with him for the past three weeks. He admitted it, now, silently thanking the Goddess for giving him this woman, this perfect moment. Adam slowly untied the sarong and pulled it away from her body. Long and lean, she lay there, one leg slightly bent, her hands stretched up over her head. She arched her back, raising her flat belly and bringing Adam's focus to the small thatch of blond hair at the apex of her thighs. Moisture glistened in the soft curls. Her scent was rich, ripe with her arousal, an aphrodisiac all on its own. Groaning, he knelt beside the bed, leaned over and planted a warm kiss just below her navel.

Her muscles rippled beneath his lips. He kissed her again, nuzzling the silky hair. It was smoother now than the first time they'd made love, something Keisha, Anton Cheval's mate, had explained. It had to do with the shift. Keisha's thick, black hair fell in soft waves, totally unlike her hair before she became Chanku. Then she'd always worn it slicked back against her skull or in corn rows to contain it. Not any more. She'd said the same thing happened to any hair on the body. Even there, in that secret place between her legs.

His thoughts of Keisha passed through faster than a heartbeat as he used his tongue to part the blond wisps. Eve's clitoris peeked out, swelling away from its protective hood, glistening with her juices. Adam touched the slick bundle of nerves with the very tip of his tongue.

Eve moaned and arched closer to his mouth. He licked her this time, delving between her soft folds, teasing the inside of her labia with the sides of his tongue, then curling forward once more to lap at the base of her clit. She writhed beneath his mouth, following his tongue, pressing close against his mouth, and he forgot everything else.

There was only Eve, his Eve, lying here on the bed, her legs spread wide, her breasts upthrust, her juices flowing. Tempting, teasing him to ask for more.

There was something else he knew was important,

something he needed to do, but Eve's hand reached up, fingers splayed wide, and she threaded them through his hair, tugging him closer between her legs. Whatever urgency had caught him sifted away like so much dust upon the breeze.

Mei squeezed Oliver's hand so hard she was afraid she might hurt him, but she was rooted here, empty champagne flute dangling uselessly from her right hand, breath coming in short, shallow gasps.

Nothing could have prepared her for the pure eroticism of watching two people, people she already cared about, make love. It was obvious, as far as Adam and Eve were concerned, she and Oliver no longer existed. Standing just at the foot of the bed, close enough that her legs touched the comforter, she turned away, overcome by emotion. It was too much, from the combined beauty of Adam's powerfully lean body as he knelt on the floor and leaned forward, one arm covering Eve's thighs, his face buried between her legs, to the pure carnality of his tongue dipping between his woman's legs.

Mei's sex seemed to swell and thicken and she knew she was drenched, aroused already beyond belief. Oliver tugged her hand. As if she'd been drugged, Mei slowly turned to him and frowned. *What? What do you want?*

To join them, of course.

Mei shook her head. *Not yet. I want to watch. I had no idea how sexy it was, to be so close, to watch them. They're beautiful.*

Okay. We can watch, but I need to touch you. I have to feel you close to me. Eyes glittering and jaw set, Oliver untied his sarong and let it fall to the ground. He tugged Mei around in front of him. She swayed, drunk with desire, and leaned into his body when he drew her close, her back to his chest. Chuckling softly, Oliver took her champagne flute from her lifeless fingers and set it on the table beside them.

Mei's thighs bumped the foot of the bed and her toes curled when Eve's foot shifted and came to rest so close she could have reached out and touched her.

Oliver wrapped his arms around Mei's waist. His erect cock rode in the crease of her ass, a thick, burning brand between her cheeks. Slowly he raised the hem of her sarong, gathering it between his fingers. She felt the silk creeping up her legs, shimmering over her smooth skin. It slipped above her knees and she moaned. Oliver's erection slid between her cheeks, riding on silk and sweat. She spread her legs even as she clenched her buttocks around his thick length. She ran her hands along his arms, urging him on.

Adam crawled up on the bed and knelt between Eve's legs. His butt was right there in front of Mei, all taut muscle and dark cleft between. She clenched her fingers into tight fists to keep from reaching out and stroking his smooth flank. Her body trembled with the desire to touch him, to cup his sac in her palm and feel the weight and heat of him.

Oliver's cock grew longer and harder, the pressure against her more intense. She knew Oliver and Adam had been lovers, and she pictured them now together. Oliver's dark body covering Adam's fair one, thighs flexing and stretching with each thrust, his long, thick cock buried completely inside, their sacs coming together, balls touching on each thrust. One man dark. One light.

The visual, so clear in her mind, made her giddy, made her heart pound, her sex contract, and her legs tremble more as the image took hold. Her silk sarong reached the tops of her thighs and air moved over her drenched labia and smoothly shorn mound. Oliver grasped the fabric in one fist, clutching the flesh-warmed silk against her belly. His other hand was splayed across her belly and she felt him slide closer to that neediest part. One finger crept along the crease between thigh and groin, following an invisible line of sensation. He stroked her smooth mound, barely touched her greedy clit and circled the tight bud, then pulled away.

Mei clenched her muscles again and groaned. She heard Eve's soft moan of pleasure, a sensual echo to her own involuntary sound and a reminder she and Oliver were not alone in this room. Blinking like one coming out of a dream, Mei realized her focus on Oliver's fingers and cock had cut Adam and Eve entirely out of the picture. Oliver paused, barely touching her, his cock holding steady against her butt, trapped against her in the silken folds of her crumpled sarong, his chest pressed tightly against her back. She felt his heart beating and the rapid tempo telegraphed his arousal every bit as much as his hot thick shaft against her buttocks.

His finger traced closer to her, dipped inside her wet heat and stroked her thickened labia. Breathing in through her nostrils, taking short, sharp breaths and biting her lips to keep the sounds of her arousal inside, Mei felt like screaming her frustration. *Touch me. Damn it, Oliver, take me over. You're killing me!*

His finger brushed the side of her clit, slipped along the downside of the slick little bit of sensitized flesh and teased the wet and swollen entrance to her pussy. She rocked her hips against him. He pulled his touch away.

It wasn't enough, not nearly enough. She whimpered, a strangled sound. Not hers. It couldn't be hers, so needy and pathetic, and she clenched her teeth to hold everything else inside.

Adam rocked back on his heels. He lifted Eve, turned her as if she weighed nothing, grabbed the stack of pillows and shoved them under her belly. It raised her hips in the air and she buried her face against her folded arms. When she spread her legs, exposing her dark pink pussy, Mei felt her own sex shudder in response. Moisture not only glistened in Eve's folds, it ran in a shimmering stream down both sides of her inner thighs.

The same moisture that coated Adam's lips and chin. He turned his head and looked back at them, his eyes glazed with arousal, his lips and the lower part of his face shining. Mei felt as if he locked with her for a moment, unaware who he saw, who she was. He blinked, slowly, then turned back toward Eve.

Mei held perfectly still, body tense, heart pounding in her chest. She'd never played the voyeur, never realized how powerful such a visual feast could be. Oliver moved behind her and his cock seemed to grow even larger. She clasped her buttocks, holding him down even tighter between her cheeks. This time it was Oliver who choked out the strangled, needy cry.

Adam covered Eve. His legs were spread within the confines of hers and he leaned forward, his cock pressed somewhere between them, his hands tugging and twisting her nipples. Mei watched, transfixed. She felt every tug, every pinch, felt the pressure of Adam's cock, the slick heat as it rested against her warm pussy. It took her a moment to realize she'd caught Eve's thoughts, that she experienced Eve's sexual response to Adam.

Oliver rubbed gently at the side of her clit. Almost close enough. Not quite. She shifted her legs to bring the tip of his finger into contact. He moved away. The pressure built. She was a rubber band, stretching . . . stretching. Lord, she was ready to break but he wouldn't take her that last step over the line. Oliver's cock pressed harder against her, a thick brand of fire behind while his finger wove molten circles in front. Mei clasped his forearms until her fingers ached.

He held her there, on the edge of climax. He had to know how close she was. Each time he brought her to the edge, he stopped and her frustration grew. Her clit throbbed, begging for his touch. Her pussy wept and she pictured the glistening fluids coating her inner thighs as thick tears of yearning and need. Adam rocked back once more on his heels, grabbed his cock and thrust into Eve. Mei lurched with the thick slide as he filled Eve, felt Adam's heat as if he entered her, the sense of his massive size stretching her. Eve was in her head, and Mei was Eve and she was coming so close, so desperately close with each powerful thrust.

She felt his balls slap her mound and the hair on his legs roughed the backs of her thighs. But it was Oliver behind her and Adam's cock in her and everything was pulling and twisting until her thoughts flew in all directions. Mei closed her eyes and absorbed it all, tried to make sense of it, but she was overwhelmed in sensation and sense alone was impossible.

She didn't feel Oliver lift her, didn't know she'd moved from her spot at the end of the bed, but suddenly Mei was lying beside Eve and Oliver was kneeling between her legs. He spread her thighs with his hands and his tongue teased every bit as effectively as his finger. So close. Not close enough. She felt the bed dip and slitted her eyes open just as Adam moved away from Eve. His cock shimmered in the low light, wet with Eve's juices, and he turned his head and gazed directly at Mei. She felt the power in him, the absolute certainty that whatever happened tonight would be exactly right.

That she was exactly right.

He knelt behind Oliver, stroked his hand along Oliver's flank, reached around him and found his cock. Oliver's tongue speared Mei and he groaned against her labia. She felt the vibration race the length of her spine and settle in her womb. She glanced to her right at Eve, but Eve was sliding out of bed, reaching for something in her bag. She came up with a tube of lubricant, squeezed a huge dollop into her hand and crawled back on the bed.

Mei's heart raced. She'd visualized this scene after Oliver fantasized about it. Saw him licking her, but was even more excited by the idea of Adam's thick cock sliding deep inside Oliver. She raised up on her elbows as Eve carefully stroked Oliver's butt, her fingers disappearing between his dark cheeks.

Adam let go of Oliver's cock and spread his buttocks wide. Mei wished she could see when Eve rubbed the clear lube along his dark cleft, but she knew from Oliver's soft moans of pleasure against her clit that Eve knew exactly what to do, especially when she took Adam's cock in her hand, carefully slipped a condom over his shaft and guided him toward Oliver. Practically gasping for air, Mei watched, transfixed. Oliver continued licking and sucking between her legs as if they were the only two people in the room and she squirmed beneath his talented tongue.

How could he possibly continue, knowing what Adam was preparing him for? Eve held Adam's cock, rubbing back and forth from Oliver's balls to his ass. His tongue drove deeper, taking Mei closer to the edge and she threw her head back, giving herself over to Oliver's lips, his tongue . . . his wonderful, wonderful tongue.

Mei's reality shifted. Her mind suddenly filled with Oliver's arousal. Her balls ached as she fought the luscious sensation of Adam's cock pressing harder against her ass. She wanted to push back, to help him penetrate, but she was too caught up in the texture and taste between Mei's legs. With the thickness of her swollen labia each time he caught them between his teeth and lips, the softness at the base of her erect little clit where the tip of his tongue swirled.

Only, she was Mei, wasn't she?

No, Mei was a vessel for pleasure. She was Oliver and she was Adam, with the thick head of his cock pressing through the tight ring of muscle so slick and warm from the lube Eve had spread liberally about, sighing with the hot glove now surrounding his full length. She was Oliver, lost in the heady scents and flavors of the woman he loved. Adam again, slowly moving forward, thrusting deeper until his groin pressed against Oliver's buttocks and their balls touched, and the shock of intimate contact linked them both.

She'd lost track of Eve, but then she felt Eve's weight across her leg, Eve's hair brushing her inner thigh and Oliver's thoughts took over once again. Eve's fingers encircled his cock, pressing, releasing, pressing again. She lay beneath Oliver, her long hair draped over Mei's thighs and took the full length of his erection into her mouth. Her fingers caressed his balls, holding their weight, fondling the round orbs inside. She found Adam's too, touching, stroking, raking with her fingernails along the wrinkled skin.

Mei felt it all, embraced them all, and let her body fly. Tangled into a messy heap, the four of them made love gently, reverently, touching and thrusting, tasting and licking until their thoughts melded, one upon the other.

Mei no longer identified with the lovely Asian girl in the middle. She was Oliver, she was Eve, she was Adam. She was all of them, together, a single entity defined by more than passion, by the pure physical pleasure one body could give another. Her mind no longer catalogued, no longer cared who touched what or where. She felt Adam's slow and careful slide deep inside Oliver's rectum, and her darker nature welcomed this forbidden pleasure. She was Eve, wrapping her lips around Oliver's sac, tonguing each solid orb, then doing the same to Adam, comparing the difference between Adam and Oliver, the slightly tangy flavor of one, the saltier taste of the other.

The sensations built. The edge between body and mind, between sanity and the sweet release of orgasm grew more precarious. The pressure inside Mei screamed for release.

She raced toward some unknown yet cataclysmic eruption of fibers and tendons and muscle. Oliver suddenly tightened his lips around her clit and sucked, hard. Adam's hips slapped Oliver's buttocks, driving deep, shoving him into Mei. Eve took Oliver's cock deep into her mouth.

The night, already dark, went totally black. Mei's body arched as orgasm swept over her, catching all of them in its powerful wake. She opened her mouth to scream, but her cry went silent, caught in the sudden, crystalline brilliance of three minds filling hers, three separate entities searching, probing, discovering.

What they learned, she had no way to understand. Their discovery left her trembling, as much with the aftermath of orgasm as the knowledge that she was not what they hoped, not what they'd expected.

She was more. So very much more, and it scared the shit out of her.

They showered, the guys first because they were faster, then Eve and Mei together. "It doesn't make sense." Mei wrapped her long hair in a towel while Eve dried herself off. "I know I saw the same things you saw. We were all crawling around in my head together, right?"

Eve nodded. She'd been fairly somber since they'd broken apart, each of them shaken by the power of their joined climax and the depth of their discovery. She wrapped her arms around Mei and hugged her. "Let's wait to talk it over out there. I want the guys' take on all this."

Mei nodded. She grabbed a white T-shirt off the floor—Adam's, by the size of it—and slipped it over her head. The towel came off her hair and she felt clumsy and awkward when she rewound it. Her hands wouldn't stop shaking. She wondered if there was any champagne left.

At the same time, while her mind was spinning with a thousand questions, her body was practically humming. She'd never experienced sex like that in her life. Never had an orgasm so overwhelming. Adam must have taken her seriously when she said he'd better make it good.

With that thought in mind, it was easier to smile when she followed Eve into the bedroom. The guys had straightened the tangled sheets and remade the bed, and everything was pretty organized, considering the chaos they'd left the bed in. Adam sat in one of the chairs. Oliver stood by the window, staring out into the darkness. He'd opened the shades and the parking lot looked almost ghostly under the amber glow of the streetlights.

There was only one small light on in the room, casting all into shadows and darkness beyond the glow from the outside lights.

Mei crawled up on the bed next to Eve. When Eve's fingers wrapped around hers, she smiled. At least now she'd find out what was going on. Adam leaned forward with his elbows planted on the table and rested his chin on his palms. "I wish Anton were here. He'd have a better understanding of what we learned. I'm going to make a leap of faith, and assume that what we think we saw inside you is exactly what you are. It's just sort of hard to draw a definite conclusion."

Mei shrugged. "I have absolutely no idea what you're talking about. I saw strange animals and rugged mountains and snow-capped peaks . . . memories I don't even know about, other than in my dreams, occasionally. Were you looking into my dreams, my fantasy world? Where do all those images come from?"

"From your genetic past." Oliver pushed himself away from the window. "I know you dream, Mei. Tell us what you dream. Describe them as carefully as you can."

She looked from one to the other. "My dreams? You want to know what I dream about? You're kidding, right?"

Obviously, he wasn't. All three of them appeared deadly serious. When she tried to access their thoughts, she felt as

if she'd run into a solid wall. Wasn't this all about her telepathic abilities? Why would they shut her out now? Startled, feeling oddly cast adrift, Mei pulled back inside herself.
She looked down at her fingers, unable to face even Oliver
right now.

"Okay. So I have really weird dreams. Sometimes they're
like nightmares and other times they're not, but they all
seem connected. I dream a lot that I run at night. But I'm
on four legs, not two. Sometimes I can taste blood, like
maybe I've hunted and killed something."

She thought of that now, the coppery taste she imagined
in her mouth that should have disgusted her, but always
made her sleep more soundly. The solid feel of her front
paws hitting the ground, silently carrying her through dark
forests. The more she talked, the easier it became. She'd
had the same dreams, most of her life, at least since she
was twelve or so, but she'd never had anyone she could tell
them to.

Mei looked up from her hands and stared at her reflection in the window. It was nothing special. Merely the
image of a young woman. Asian, slim and athletic looking, she sat cross-legged in the middle of a bed, but she felt
as if this moment in time was pivotal and this recitation of
a lifetime of dreams carried substance. As if her entire future rested on what she said and felt about her dream
world.

She looked away from her reflection and chose Adam,
not Oliver as her focus. "I'm always alone, but that feels
as if it's the way I'm supposed to be. Alone, usually hunting. Sometimes it feels like a jungle. It's humid and damp,
the trees are covered in vines. Other times a forest. Mostly
on steep mountain cliffs where the air is icy cold." She
shrugged. "Nothing specific, and yet the images are very
clear to me some of the time. More the last couple nights
than ever before. I look down and see paws, but not all that
clearly. I don't remember ever being curious about myself.

Merely accepting of my dreams. I haven't ever really thought about what I was. Just that I wasn't human."

Adam nodded toward Oliver and smiled. Oliver looked as if he might burst out laughing. Eve reached over and grabbed Mei's hand once again. "We have something to show you. Oliver, will you close the blinds?"

Adam pushed himself out of the chair. "You're confirming what we saw. For some reason, you're different than we are. Your mental *signal*, for want of another description, seems unfamiliar in many ways, but it might just be due to your Asian heritage. We'll know in a couple more days when you finally shift."

"When I *what*?"

Oliver glanced at Adam. Adam merely shrugged and grinned. "When you shift," Oliver said, repeating Adam's words. "We're more than mere telepaths. Sweetheart, we couldn't say anything until we were certain. Until we knew you were one of us. We aren't actually human. We're something more. We, all of us, and I'm including you, are Chanku."

Chills raced down Mei's spine and she frowned, remembering. "I picked that word out of your head a couple times. What does it mean?" She scooted forward to the edge of the bed. Oliver stepped close and took both her hands in his. "Chanku are an ancient race, a separate species actually, that appeared at some time before recorded history on the Himalayan steppes. We don't know their origin, whether they evolved or were possibly planted here by some alien race, but they aren't like normal humans. They have the ability to shift their body structure. To become wolves."

Mei had to consciously tighten her jaws to shut her mouth. "You're shittin' me!"

Oliver glanced toward Adam. "Your turn."

Adam tapped his long fingers on the tabletop, as if taking a moment to gather his thoughts. "At some point," he said, "they left their homeland. Whatever the reason—climate change, a lack of good hunting—we'll never know. But they left without realizing they left behind the very nutrients that gave them the power to shift. As they spread out across the world, far from the necessary foods their bodies needed, they became almost like other humans. Their ancestors and their amazing abilities to walk as wolves became legend, at least until their unique abilities were rediscovered. We now know that there are many Chanku among us, almost normal humans living lives of quiet desperation, unaware of their unique abilities, yet always sensing something important is missing in their lives."

Oliver picked up the story. "Those pills Eve and I have given you? They contain the nutrients your body needs to fully develop a little gland near the base of your brain, next to the hypothalamus. It's the part of you that determines your genetic heritage. It makes you Chanku. Your mother must have carried the gene and you've always had it, but it's been inactive. It's passed on from mother to daughter. Sons can be Chanku, but they can't pass it on to their progeny."

Mei looked from one to the other. She still squeezed Eve's hand, holding on to her as if she were a lifeline. "Okay, I get the ancient heritage stuff. But what do you mean by shifting? You don't really turn into actual wolves. That's just an analogy, right?"

Oliver glanced at Adam. Adam shrugged. He pushed his chair back, slipped out of his underwear and stood there, a perfect male specimen. Mei's mouth went dry. It really was a toss up, which one of the men was more beautiful. She glanced at Oliver and he smiled. "Watch Adam."

"Like that's a hard thing to do?" She tried to laugh, but the sound caught in her throat. Adam stared at her and suddenly wavered. Before she could blink and clear her vision, he was gone.

No, not gone. Changed. "Oh. My. God." Mei slipped off the edge of the bed to her knees. She held her hand over her mouth, holding back a scream. Then she shuddered, took a deep breath and held out her hand. It shook, trembling uncontrollably, just like the rest of her body. A wolf stood where Adam had been. A beautiful dark wolf. Not entirely black. His coat was a deep russet, streaked with gold. Darker around the beautiful amber eyes and over his back, yet absolutely perfect. He sat totally still, watching her.

Mei continued holding out her hand, as if in supplication. The wolf moved forward, sniffed her hand and stood in front of her. Mei took another deep breath and let it out, drawing on whatever inner strength she had. *This is Adam. This is truly Adam.* She repeated the phrase in her head, over and over until she could run her fingers through his thick fur without fainting. Speechless, she could only touch him and wonder.

The Adam wolf licked her fingers, wrapping his long tongue around them, running it between her thumb and index finger. She felt a rich spike of desire from her hand to her pussy. Stunned. Mei looked over her shoulder at Oliver. Maybe he could give her more of an explanation. She glanced at him and burst into tears. He'd shifted as well. A huge black wolf sat behind her.

Beyond words, tears streaming down her cheeks, Mei glanced toward Eve. A pale wolf, more gray than brown, stretched out on the bed, staring at her. Pink tongue lolling, the wolf nodded her head in a most humanlike fashion. Then she shimmered and Eve lay sprawled across the bed, naked, in her place.

Mei walked past both wolves, pulled the bottle of champagne out of the ice bucket where it now sat in mostly water, popped the loose cork out with her thumb and held the chilled bottle to her mouth. She tilted her head back and drank, barely tasting the expensive vintage. She wished it was a bottle of brandy or whiskey instead.

When she turned around, Oliver was Oliver again and so was Adam and both men were pulling on their boxer shorts. Mei set the empty bottle back in the bucket, walked over to Oliver and slapped him, hard, across the face.

"How dare you?" Her anger simmered hot and dark. She rubbed at her arms, understanding now what the strange, itchy feeling was. Her body was preparing to shift. Preparing to change her into a wolf, just like the three of them.

"We couldn't say anything, Mei. Not until we knew for sure."

"And if it turned out I wasn't like you? I couldn't shift? Maybe I can't. We still don't know, do we? What then? What if I'm not what you think?"

"I've already told them. I plan to stay with you. I love you, Mei. Whether you're Chanku or not, I love you. I won't leave you."

"You'd be miserable without them." She swept her hand in a jerky wave that encompassed Adam and Eve. Both of them sat motionless, waiting. They probably thought she was crazy. Hell, she probably was crazy. Only a crazy woman would think she saw three people turn into wolves.

Adam finally spoke. "We plan to stay with you as well, Mei. We've shared too much to walk away from you, even if you weren't Chanku. That's not an issue now, though. We saw enough to feel confident you can shift. You'll be able to come with us. You're one of us."

She shook harder, her hands trembling now so that she had to clasp them together in front of herself to hold them steady. "How dare you scare me like that, get into my head and find out everything about me and not warn me this was what you were doing?"

"We had no choice." Eve looked about ready to cry. "We're sworn not to give away anything about ourselves to anyone who's not Chanku. Until we were sure . . ."

"I know you're angry, but maybe if you know more about us, you'll understand part of our problem." Adam moved across the room and sat next to Eve, but he faced Mei. "Oliver's been around shifters for years, but he only became Chanku about three weeks ago. That's when he made his first shift. Same for me, same for Eve. We don't know that much about ourselves, much less you. We're still learning."

Mei felt the air just sort of go out of her, taking the anger with it. They made perfect sense, so why was she being such a bitch. *Because I'm scared to death. Too much, too soon, too hard to explain.* She shook her head and glanced at Oliver. "I'm sorry. I never should have hit you. That was wrong and I apologize."

Oliver took her hands in his and brought them to his mouth. He kissed her fingertips and rubbed his lips against them. "You have a right to be upset. It's not every day someone turns into a wolf in front of you. Unfortunately, unless you see it, you're not going to believe it."

"That's for sure." Mei rubbed at her arms in what had become an unconscious habit over the past day. "When will it happen to me?"

"You'll have your third pill tomorrow. Some women change in three days, others take longer. Sometimes a week. That's why we want to head back to Montana as soon as possible. We want Anton close by when it happens."

"His mate, too." Eve scooted across the bed and hugged Mei from behind. "Keisha can explain a lot of things, like how we can keep from getting pregnant without using condoms or birth control."

"I've got an IUD."

Oliver burst into laughter.

"What's so funny?" Mei pulled out of his grasp and wrapped her arms around herself.

"Tala Quinn had an IUD the first time she shifted. Mik, one of her mates, said it fell out on the floor. Earrings, any piercings . . . none of that makes it through a shift. However, if you have injuries, they heal faster. We don't get any sexually transmitted diseases, or any other bugs that we know of, for that matter."

"You used a condom when we had sex."

"Because I could make you pregnant. You weren't Chanku yet, and not able to consciously stop the release of an egg. But Mei, we didn't have sex. We made love." Oliver slipped his arms around her. "I love you, Mei. When you can finally shift, you're going to realize what an amazing gift it is, to be Chanku. You will come with us, won't you? We have to go in the morning, unless you decide you're not going. Then we're all staying here, with you. I need to let Anton know."

Mei looked into Oliver's beautiful amber eyes and realized he spoke the truth. He would stay here in Florida with her. Give up his home, his friends, his life, to be with Mei. Adam and Eve had sworn to stay with her as well. She who had no one, suddenly had a family.

She reached out and touched Oliver's cheek, where the dull red of her palm print was still noticeable against his dark skin. "I'm sorry," she whispered. Her throat felt thick, her eyes filled with tears.

Oliver lowered his head. Resigned. Accepting. Mei smiled at him when she realized he'd misinterpreted her apology. Gently she placed her hand over the print that marked his cheek and raised his head. "I'm sorry I got angry, and even sorrier I struck you. I'll never, ever do that again. I promise. Here I was worried you guys were some kind of weird cult. Nothing like that . . . no, you just turn into wolves." She laughed, but it ended in more of a sob. "I guess I'd better start packing. It looks like we're leaving for Montana in the morning."

Chapter 8

Eve stared out the window and watched the miles slide by. Thank goodness they'd gotten an early start, because it was one hell of a long way back to Montana. It sure hadn't felt like this long of a trip when she'd made her mad dash east, but she'd been a little bit crazy then, chased back to Florida by whatever forces of fate wanted her in that little mini-mart in Tampa when Mei decided to steal the store blind.

She was still tossing that whole situation around in her mind, wondering how and why things happened when they did. Of course, she'd blamed it all on that desperate need to escape Adam and her stupid fears. What a fool she'd been. It scared her now, thinking how close she'd come to losing him. All because she was an idiot and didn't know her own mind.

Now she rode with him in the cherried out black Ford pick-up while Oliver and Mei followed. They kept a steady pace, winding up through Georgia and on into Tennessee, with only a few brief stops along the way, but she'd had plenty of time to think about all the dumb moves she'd made in her life. Leaving Adam was by far the worst.

By the time they reached Illinois, Eve felt as if her butt had melded to the seat and her eyes were practically crossed. And she'd pretty much run through the entire litany of all the reasons why Adam should never have come after her.

Thank goodness he had. He didn't even ask if she was ready to stop for the night. He had to have sensed her exhaustion. The fact she'd hardly said a word for the last three hours should have told him something. She was more than ready, though, by the time he turned the wheel and pulled into the parking lot of a nice looking motel just over the state line, turned off the engine and leaned his head back against the seat.

"Thank goodness." Eve leaned over and kissed him. "I was afraid you intended to drive all night."

He shook his head slowly. "I'm beat. It's not safe to drive when you're this tired, and I figured you were probably ready to stop, too." He looked up. "Here's Mei and Oliver." The Jeep pulled into the next spot beside the truck. "Let's get a couple rooms and something to eat. We can get an early start tomorrow."

"I don't remember it being so far when I drove out here." Eve laughed, but she felt foolish again, thinking of that crazy trip across the country when she was so intent on putting distance between herself and Adam.

Adam leaned over and kissed her cheek. "I hope you know I've been in your head for the past three hundred miles. Get over it. I love you and what's in the past stays there. You left, you found Mei, we're going home. End of story. Or maybe the beginning, at least for Oliver and Mei."

"What?" She snapped her head around and glared at him. "You've been snooping in my head?"

"Yep." He kissed her again and got out of the truck. Eve sat there with her mouth hanging open and watched him walk across the parking lot with Oliver. *Damn the man.* She sighed. He was absolutely infuriating, but she loved watching him walk.

Feeling like a complete idiot, again, Eve slowly unbuckled her seat belt, crawled stiffly out of the truck and stretched. She tried to touch her toes, but she was so sore and tight from sitting for almost twelve hours, she couldn't make it all the way down.

Damn, she wanted to run so badly! Wanted the wind in her face and the feel of fresh earth beneath her paws. Wanted Adam beside her . . . inside her. Now where the hell had that come from? She was so tired her thoughts no longer made sense. She heard Mei's door click shut, and gave up on the parking lot calisthenics. "Hey, sweetie, how're you feeling? Are you as beat as I am?"

Mei shook her head and rubbed at her arms. "I'm exhausted. I offered to drive but Oliver said he was okay. I know he's tired, though." She stretched her arms up over her head and grimaced when her spine made audible crackling noises. "Now that I know what those pills are supposed to do, I'm feeling really anxious. Oliver says it won't just happen without my control, but I kept thinking, what if I turn into a wolf while we're speeding down the highway? Wouldn't that freak out the people in cars around us!"

Eve laughed. "It's not quite that easy, especially the first time. Generally you want to be with someone else so you can link and follow their shift. It helps to imprint the right way to do it in your mind."

Mei nodded. "That makes sense. My arms are really feeling itchy and tight, but I haven't noticed any change in my vision or hearing. Oliver said that gets really acute before you shift."

Eve nodded. "I'd forgotten that. Yeah . . . all of a sudden the night isn't nearly as dark. I remember being able to identify different sounds I'd never even heard before. The difference between a mouse and a snake moving through the weeds, for instance. Before, I couldn't even hear them and now I can tell them apart."

"You girls ready?" Adam walked around between the cars and slipped his arm around Eve. "We've got a couple of connected rooms and there's a restaurant on the premises. No place to run, unfortunately. I was trying to make it a bit farther so we'd be near a forest or something, then I figured we probably wouldn't want to leave Mei behind. I'm beat. I'll probably just want to eat and sleep."

He raised his eyebrows in a suggestive leer and grinned at Eve. She shook her head, laughing. "Yeah, that'll be the day when you just want to go to sleep." She punched his shoulder, but she felt a coil of need just the same. Would it always be this way? She reached into the bed of the truck for her travel bag. "I'm just hoping the tub is big and the water's hot."

But really, she hoped for more. Eve wondered if she'd ever get enough of him. She certainly hoped not.

"Do you think we'll make it all the way home tonight? Mei's got to be getting close to her first shift. She had her fourth pill today. I want it to happen at home, not out here on the road." Eve realized that even though she'd only lived with the others in the pack in Montana for a short time, the beautiful big house in the deep forest was now the place she thought of when she wanted to go home.

"Not sure." Adam sounded distracted.

Eve looked away from the vast emptiness outside her window. "What's wrong?"

"Shit." He pulled over to the side of the road and glanced in the rearview mirror. Oliver pulled in right behind them. Steam billowed out from under the hood of the Jeep. Adam crawled out of the truck and walked back through a roiling cloud of white. He popped the hood.

Oliver walked around and stood beside him. "I've been watching the temperature gauge. It started climbing a few miles ago, then all of a sudden . . ." He waved both hands in the air.

Eve got out of the truck and went back to the passenger side of the Jeep. Mei looked like she was just waking up. "Want to get out and stretch? We might be here awhile."

Mei nodded and opened the door. Night had fallen and the air was cool for July. "I must have fallen asleep. What's wrong?"

Eve shrugged. "Whatever it is, Adam will fix it."

"It's nice to have that kind of confidence in a man." She glanced back in Oliver's direction. "It's new for me. To feel as if I can let someone else worry about things. Oliver's just . . ." She grinned. "He's so together."

"Wait until you see him in action. He runs Anton's entire household, essentially for the whole Montana pack. I imagine it's been chaos with him gone. That's probably why Anton's insisting we get back as soon as possible. Oliver keeps everything functioning the way it should."

"He may do households, but he said he's not good with cars. Good thing we've got Adam! I wonder what's wrong?" Mei headed around to the front of the Jeep. Anton and Oliver both had their heads stuck under the hood. Oliver was holding the flashlight.

Adam glanced toward Eve. "We need a cardboard box, something I can flatten. The thermostat was stuck, so I've removed it, but that'll make the engine run too cold." He stood up and made a square with his hands. "Something about this big. I want to cover about half the radiator. That should work long enough to get us into Bozeman."

"I've got something." Mei came back with one of the boxes from her shopping trip. Adam took the lid, flattened the corners and pressed it against the radiator.

"Go ahead and start it. That'll hold the cardboard in place." Oliver got in and started up the motor while Adam topped off the radiator with some of their extra water. He shouted at Oliver over the noisy engine. "You want me to drive it in?"

Oliver shook his head. "We'll be okay. I'll keep an eye

on it. Let's get going. Can you call Anton? I don't have a signal."

"Me either." Adam slammed the hood down. "We can give him a call once we find a room. We're not going much farther tonight."

"It's not fancy, but at least the room looks clean." Oliver held the door open to the one room they'd been able to find at the first motel they came to. Two beds and a small sitting area with a nice bathroom.

"It beats sleeping in the back of the truck." Adam laughed and carried his and Eve's luggage into the room. Mei followed Eve inside.

It was starting. Mei'd gotten out of the Jeep, looked around the darkened parking area and realized she could see almost as well as if it were dawn or early dusk. The moon was almost full tonight, but it wouldn't be up for another hour or so. She'd stood there a moment in what should have been pitch-black night, but wasn't, staring out toward the rugged hills surrounding the motel, listening.

She'd picked up the sound of an owl flying over, the steady whooshing beat of its wings easily discernible. She'd heard a toad hopping across the pavement and managed to grab it and put it into some bushes before it got flattened by someone driving through the lot. Her arms still itched, her skin felt all crawly and weird, and there was a buzzing in her head. A feeling of something about to happen.

"Oliver?"

He turned and smiled at her. "What's up, babe?"

"I think it's happening. I feel really weird. I'm hearing stuff I've never heard before, and I can see in the dark. Do you think maybe I'm ready to shift?"

"Oh, crap." He took Mei in his arms and gave her a quick, hard hug. "Adam? Is there anyplace out there where we can run? I wasn't paying attention when we drove in."

Adam walked out of the bathroom, drying his face with a towel. "There's at least a small patch of forest on the hills behind the motel." He smiled at Mei. "Do you feel like you're ready?"

She nodded, almost afraid to give voice to all the changes going on inside.

"Well, let's go then."

Just then Eve walked back inside. She'd gone back to the truck for her overnight bag. "Go where?"

"Mei's ready to shift." Oliver grinned, and his relief was obvious, but she knew he'd expected it before now. "We're going up the hill behind the motel. You girls might want something more than just sandals. We'll need to hike up a bit and shift once we're out of the lighted area."

Eve looked back down the trail they'd followed up a steep canyon behind the motel. The trail wouldn't have been visible to anyone with mere human sight, but they'd followed it soundlessly for almost half a mile without a flashlight to guide their way.

Mei hadn't stumbled at all. She'd buzzed with an energy all of them felt. Eve couldn't wipe the grin off her face. Her first shift was still so fresh in her mind and now Mei would get to experience the same thing.

If they hadn't found each other, if Eve hadn't gone to Tampa . . . she hated to even think about it. She really needed to listen to Adam and put the past where it belonged . . . in the past. Over and done with and time to move forward. Why, when that made such good sense, was it so hard to do?

The guys stopped in a small, protected meadow completely surrounded by trees and low-growing shrubs. The lights from the motel were barely visible below them, lost in the tangle of leaves and trees.

Mei stood nervously moving from one foot to the other on the uneven ground. Oliver took her by the hands. "You need to take all your clothes off. Just put them in the bag I brought. That'll keep the stickers out of them and hopefully the ticks as well."

Adam laughed. "May I explain that Oliver learned that lesson the hard way."

Oliver glared at him. "You may, as long as you don't describe where the tick decided to pause for a meal."

Mei giggled. "I can imagine, but I'd rather not." She slipped her shirt over her head, stepped out of her shoes and pushed her shorts and panties down her legs. She bundled everything up and stuffed the clothes into Oliver's knapsack.

Eve and the others did the same and Oliver tucked the bag beneath the trunk of a fallen tree. The four of them stood there, naked. Mei looked nervous as all get out, but excited, too. Adam and Oliver had big grins on their faces. Eve felt as nervous as Mei, as excited and happy as the guys. "Adam? Why don't you and Oliver shift first? Mei, concentrate on what they're doing, how they do it. I'll shift with you."

Mei nodded. She was shivering, either from the chill in the air or just plain nerves. She wrapped her arms around her middle and hugged herself tightly.

Adam shifted. Oliver did the same. Eve stared at them for a moment, caught in the beauty, the pure impossibility of two wolves where men had stood. She took a breath and smiled at Mei. "Okay. Are you ready? Did you get the mental image, the process, okay?"

Mei frowned. "I did but . . ." She shrugged. "This is just way too weird. Maybe we need to wait another day. Let me take another pill . . ." Her voice trailed off.

Eve laughed. "Get in my head. Do just as I do. Ready?"

Mei nodded, a short, sharp jerk of her head.

Eve shifted. She immediately looked at Mei. Mei stood there, naked and shivering, still entirely human. She stared at the three wolves and burst into tears.

Eve shifted back. So did the guys. "What happened? Couldn't you feel it?"

Mei nodded, sobbing. "I could. Honest. I was right there in your head and I tried to do everything you did. Nothing happened. The buzzing in my head got louder and my heart sort of skipped a couple beats, but nothing."

Oliver wrapped his arms around her and she cried even harder. He tilted Mei's chin up and forced her to look at him. "Do you want to try it again?"

She nodded.

"Okay, then link with me this time. We've gotten pretty good at this mindtalking thing, haven't we?"

Mei nodded again. Oliver swept his hands up and down her back, comforting her. "Link with me."

Eve and Adam stepped back. Oliver was obviously conversing with Mei telepathically. She nodded, at one point she even smiled. Oliver moved away from her, the air around him shimmered. A wolf sat where Oliver had stood, staring up at Mei.

She cried even harder. "Why can't I do it?"

Oliver shifted back and took Mei in his arms once again. He shook his head. "I don't know, sweetheart. I think that's enough for tonight, though. We'll see Anton tomorrow. We're heading home as soon as Adam gets a new thermostat for the Jeep. Anton will know exactly what to do."

He turned to Adam and Eve, but he kept his arm wrapped tightly around Mei's waist. "Why don't you two go ahead and get in a good run? I'm going to walk Mei back down to the room and fix her a glass of brandy, and then we're going to bed. As close as she is right now, tomorrow I'm sure she'll be ready."

"Sounds good." Adam leaned close and kissed Mei on her tear-dampened cheek. He backed away and shifted. Oliver and Mei slowly put their clothes back on while Adam waited patiently nearby. Mei hugged Eve and turned slowly away. Her shoulders slumped and dejection hung about her. Eve watched them walk down the hill. Mei's pain was a tangible thing, something that lingered even as she and Oliver disappeared from view.

Finally Eve turned away, and became the wolf once more. The moon was rising, sending a silvery glow over the hillside. It would have been a perfect night for Mei's first shift. A perfect time to run beneath a moon that was almost full.

She should have been able to do it. Even Eve could sense the heart of Chanku beating strongly in Mei's chest.

Chanku, and yet not exactly the same. Racing after Adam, Eve wondered what it was about Mei that didn't quite ring true. She thought about it long into their run, until the moon was high in the sky and her sides heaved with exhaustion. But there were no answers. None she could find in her small knowledge of their kind. Finally putting the question aside, she raced after Adam, following her mate through the moonlight.

Mei had stopped crying by the time they walked down the hill and reached their motel room. Oliver didn't expect to see the other two for at least a couple hours. Truth be told, he'd rather be up there on the mountain, racing beneath clear moonlight than down here with questions he couldn't answer.

Of course, he'd rather be running with Mei, both of them on four legs. Why in the hell hadn't she shifted? She had all the signs, she'd taken the nutrients long enough. He'd seen enough new Chanku brought into the fold, so to speak. Jealous, all those years, knowing it was something he'd never do. Woman rarely took more than three or four days. Mei'd been taking the pills for four days now.

He unlocked the door. Head down, Mei stepped into the room. Oliver closed and locked the door behind them.

When he turned around, Mei raised her head. He held his arms wide. Sobbing, she ran into his embrace.

"What's wrong with me? Everything you said was going to happen is happening, but I couldn't do it. I linked with Eve and I saw her start the process, but my body just locked up. The same thing happened when I tried it with you. Am I some kind of freak?"

He couldn't help himself. Oliver burst out laughing. Mei shoved him away and glared at him. She knotted her hands on her hips, her tears disappeared and Oliver fell even more in love with her.

"Sweetheart, listen to yourself." He took a deep breath and tried to swallow back what sounded too much like a case of the giggles. It was almost impossible. "You're standing here complaining because you can't turn into a wolf, and asking me if you're some kind of freak? Sweetie, we're all freaks. You, me, Adam, Eve . . . every one of us. We're impossible. We shouldn't exist, but we do. Relax. You'll be able to shift. Be patient. I had to wait for many years, from the time I first realized I had the potential to become Chanku, until Adam found a way for me to actually cross that barrier."

Mei nodded and hung her head. "Okay, but it better not take me years. I'll try and be patient." She turned and walked away from him when he would have hugged her as tight as he could. "I'm going to go take a shower now. By myself."

Okay. So she was still a little upset. He could handle that. "I'll get mine when you're done." Oliver reached for a beer out of the cold case they'd left in the room, but it hurt that she hadn't wanted him. He let his thoughts drift her way.

And realized he should have been paying better attention. The door had shut behind her, but her mental self-recrimination rang in his mind, clear as a bell.

Why isn't he insisting? Any other time, Oliver would be right behind me, whether I said I wanted him or not. Maybe he doesn't love me anymore because I'm not really like them.

Oliver put the unopened beer back in the case. He tugged his shirt off, slipped out of his shoes and stripped his pants over his legs. Then he followed Mei into the bathroom.

She turned on the water and stepped beneath the spray and wondered if she should leave in the morning and try and find a way back to Tampa. Her body ached and her heart felt like lead in her chest. What a fiasco. She should know better than to believe things were finally going to work. Hadn't her life always been totally fucked?

Tears welled in her eyes again, but it didn't matter. Not while she stood under the cleansing spray where even she couldn't tell she was crying. *Hardly.* Then a tingle ran up her spine and she sensed him before she saw him.

Oliver. When he pulled the curtain back and stepped into the shower behind her, Eve couldn't have stopped her silly grin if she'd tried. When he put his arms around her from behind and drew her close against him, she wanted to cry for joy. Instead, she turned around and kissed him, and felt his heat and strength and the love she never should have doubted.

"I love you, Mei. Not because you can or can't shift into a wolf, not because the sex is fantastic or because you're so beautiful you make me ache. I love you because of who you are. The woman inside who says she loves me back. Everything will be fine. I promise you. Don't ever give up on yourself. And please, don't ever give up on me."

She raised her head and stared at him, knowing Oliver would never lie to her. He looked so damned serious, even with the water beading in his short hair and the sparkle in his gorgeous eyes. She knew her lips still trembled, but she finally managed a smile. "I promise."

And she hoped like hell she was strong enough to keep it.

They'd actually taken a shower without having sex. Oliver hadn't thought that was possible, but Mei hadn't done anything more than kiss him. Then she'd turned around and washed herself, rinsed the soap and conditioner out of her hair and stepped out of the shower before Oliver realized she was going. He managed to rinse the soap off himself and follow her just seconds later, but he needn't have worried.

She'd thrown the blankets back and lay on her side on the clean sheets, propped up on one elbow with her chin resting in her palm. Her bottom leg stretched long and straight, but she'd bent the other at the knee, posing with all her feminine attributes on display.

Her long, black hair hung in tangles over her breasts and curled across one hip, spilling onto the sheets. She licked her lips when she saw him, a slow, sensual sweep of her tongue that moved across her lower lip, then the upper.

Oliver stopped, midstep. The towel he was wrapping around his hips fell to the floor from useless fingers. He made a conscious effort to close his mouth, and was proud of himself for thinking of it. He stood perfectly still while his cock swelled out of its nest of hair and slowly, all on its own, rose up to brush his belly.

Mei's studied, sultry look slipped and she grinned. She looked like a kid checking out the latest candies in the store window, only she was obviously focusing on his only moving part. Then she held up one finger and crooked it, urging him closer, and the child was replaced by the seductress.

As if she pulled an invisible thread, Oliver crossed the

short expanse between the bathroom door and the bed. He leaned over her and drew in a breath, absorbing her scent, the rich flavors of her arousal, the tangy fragrance of Chanku. It was different with Mei, an unusual bouquet of aromas that were seductive, addictive . . . entirely Mei.

And they owned him. Controlled him. Stoked his arousal, led him like an addict to his drug. He needed her. Needed the touch and feel, the taste and scent, the flavors unique to Mei. Oliver crawled slowly up on the bed. He kissed her knee, the smooth flesh of her inner thigh and laved her with his tongue. He traced the line along her hip, leaving kisses on the bony line of her pelvis, the smooth flesh along her flank. Her navel got his attention, a quick swirl of his tongue and a gentle nip beside the neat little indentation. He moved along her ribcage, nipping and kissing each raised line of bone.

She moaned and arched into this mouth when he reached her breast. He took her nipple, the one on the left, and dragged it between his teeth, tugging to the point of pain. He knew when he reached it, knew because she cried out with a sharp little "ah" that stopped him. He licked her then, swirling his tongue around the tip, easing her distress, licking and sucking with as much gentleness as he could.

He found her mouth, licked long the soft swell of her lower lip, nipped at it and dragged a groan from her. Then he found the seam between her lips and traced it with his tongue. At the same time, Oliver opened his mind. Opened to her thoughts, her desires, her physical reactions to his touch. He found her needy and wanting, her sex swelling with arousal, her fluids thick and streaming between her legs.

Smiling to himself, Oliver slipped back along her lean length, positioned himself between her thighs, and prepared to feast. He nipped her inner thigh, traced the seam between leg and groin. Nuzzling the soft flesh between her legs, he spread her legs wide, cupped her buttocks in his palms and lifted her to his mouth.

She was ambrosia to him, her flavors sweet and succulent, her tiny moans and gasps of pleasure the added spice to his meal. He made a feast of her tastes and textures, suckling thickened labia into his mouth, lapping at the salty fluids escaping from her sex.

He ignored her clit and knew it was making her nuts, but he spent an inordinate amount of time lapping at her creamy center, running his fingers along the dark cleft between her buttocks. He found the sensitive tissues of her perineum and traced a line to her ass, ringing the tiny puckered opening with his fingertip.

She groaned and pressed against him and he pushed harder, then retreated. Press, retreat. Press, retreat. Press . . . and he gained a bit of an entrance. Pressing harder, his finger slipped through the tight ring of muscle into the slick passage beyond.

Mei groaned, but she didn't pull away. Instead she pushed against him, her body begging for more. He forced his middle finger deeper and used his thumb to tease her clit. She gasped, cried out and clenched down on him, but he kept up his steady thrust and retreat.

He leaned back down, closer, his tongue working around his own fingers, finding her sweet creamy center, lapping up her juices as if she were a buffet for him alone. She moaned and arched into his mouth. Oliver opened his thoughts, shared her tastes and the ripe texture of her swollen folds. The way she felt against his tongue and lips.

She cried out, then merely cried, her sobs choking her breath, her body shuddering in the throes of climax. Oliver brought her down, slowly, his hands and mouth touching, tasting, tantalizing every nerve ending, every sensitive spot she had.

When her sobs abated and her breathing slowed, Oliver crawled over her body. He kissed her gently, thoroughly.

Then he rolled over and lay beside her. She'd found release. He still throbbed, hot and heavy, his cock begging for her warmth. But she'd rolled to her side and curled into a ball, her body shuddering with her tears, her sense of loss.

She had no idea what she hadn't achieved, tonight. But she felt its loss just the same. Ignoring his own needs, Oliver rolled over and pulled her up against his chest. Warm and sated, she clung to him, her tears dampening his shoulder, her fingers clutching at his arms. He felt her smooth belly against his cock and willed that part of him into quiescence. Another time he would love her. For now, he would hold her. Comfort her. Convince her he loved her because she was Mei, not because she could run like the wind on four legs.

Hours later, Adam slipped through the door with Eve close behind him. Oliver was just coming out of the bathroom when they entered the room. He glanced up at Adam and caught his thoughts.

Is she okay?

I think so. We'll know more after we meet with Anton.

Agreed.

Eve went into the shower. Adam followed her.

Oliver took his place in the chair beside Mei's bed. She slept soundly, almost as if she'd been drugged. He hoped the pills, the nutrients they'd given her without any concern for her health, hadn't harmed her. Hoped she would be okay in the morning. For now, though, he knew he wouldn't sleep. The arousal he'd experienced with Mei had grown. He needed relief, if only by his own hand, but now Eve and Adam were here and privacy was lacking.

There were some things he just didn't do with an audience.

He decided to wait it out. Eventually his erection would go away and he'd be able to catch at least a little sleep.

Eve came out of the shower first, glowing with the tremendous level of need that followed a good run. Adam was right behind her and his libido was obviously in an even higher gear than Eve's, though Oliver knew they'd already had sex at least once in the shower.

Adam glanced at Oliver, sitting quietly beside Mei. *Come with us, my friend. There's no reason to be alone.*

Oliver's cock twitched and he felt a dull ache in his balls. They were certainly interested in Adam's offer. *Are you sure?*

Adam nodded. *Would I ask if I wasn't?*

Guilt enveloped him. Oliver glanced over at Mei. She slept soundly. Would she understand? No matter. Once she shifted, she would have an understanding of pack dynamics impossible at this point in her development. When she shifted, not if.

He joined Adam in the other bed. By the time Eve came out of the shower, Oliver already lay on his back with his legs hooked over Adam's shoulders. Adam filled him, slow, smooth strokes that took him deep inside Oliver. Eve watched for a moment, her fingers sliding between her legs as she caught their rhythm. Finally she leaned over and took Oliver's erect penis in her damp fingers and held the crown between her lips. She tongued the slick head, found the tiny eye and sucked the creamy drop of fluid from his tip.

Oliver groaned, and reached for Eve. He lifted her so that her sleek thighs straddled his face. She tightened her lips around the head of his cock and her tongue stroked the sensitive underside just behind the crown. Her fingers tickled the round curve of his balls and rubbed his sensitive perineum, tickling the taut ring of his sphincter when it stretched upward with Adam's strokes.

Oliver fought for control. Black spots swirled in front of his eyes as Adam's tempo increased, his thrusts grew deeper, harder. Adam's hands tightened around Oliver's legs, lifting him with each pounding penetration. Eve wrapped her fingers around the base of Oliver's cock and sat back to adjust to this new angle, dipping her sex closer to Oliver's face until she practically squatted over him and her swollen labia were right there, a creamy feast just for him.

He dipped his tongue inside and swirled tightly around her protruding clit. She jerked away from the intimate touch against the sensitive bundle of nerves. Oliver wrapped his fingers around her thighs and held her steady, forcing her to endure what she so obviously wanted. His tongue moved in and out of her slick folds, lapping and licking as fast as he could, but he was barely able to keep up with the thick flow of her cream. Her musky, feminine scent filled his nostrils and he drew her deep into his lungs.

The scents and quiet, muffled sounds of their lovemaking, the mad rush of bodies searching for completion as the edge of reason beckoned, enveloped Oliver. He was pure sensation, a part of their love as much as they were his. All three minds opened, images and sensations flowed between them, growing, swelling until they were one single, pulsing tangle of desire, an aching, living, breathing creature of passion.

Yet still, he needed more. They understood, and reacted.

Packmates. A single entity. Aware one of theirs suffered, Adam and Eve knew Oliver needed them, needed the contact of flesh and the lush peaks of passion. Needed the sharp edge of pain, the intensity of sensation verging on torment.

There'd been no question, no complaint. Adam recognized Oliver's need and filled it. Eve recognized Oliver's loneliness and shared as much of herself as she could.

Mei slept on, alone, apart. She was not yet of them, not yet able to understand the true dynamic of the pack. When one was alone, the others joined with him. When one was afraid, they protected. When one needed that most intimate touch, from gentleness to the boundaries of reason, the pack was there.

Some day, hopefully soon, Mei would understand. Oliver had no doubt she would shift. Unfortunately, while he'd cautioned patience, he'd run out of it himself. He wanted her with him, now. Wanted to share with Mei what he had with the other Chanku.

She wasn't ready, and so he welcomed the pain.

Groaning with each powerful thrust as Adam's hips rocked forward to the rhythm of his own personal muse, Oliver let himself fly. Let the sensations take over, let his body's need take control.

Stabbing into Eve with the full length of his tongue, he felt the hot grasp of her mouth around his cock just as Adam pounded into him harder. Deeper. His balls slapped against Oliver's butt and his cock stretched sensitive tissues. His flat belly slammed into Oliver's testicles on each forward thrust as he took him without mercy. With love and the full knowledge of what he did.

Oliver seemed to float above the intense pain in his balls, the burn in his ass each time Adam's cock thrust home. Tormenting and overwhelming, the pain consumed him. He welcomed it. Begged silently for more. Adam complied. He knew what Oliver experienced. What he needed.

The pressure grew. The sense his body reached a limit he'd not crossed before, a line he'd not passed over. Deep, yet necessary. An atonement he must pay before pleasure.

He clamped his lips around Eve's clitoris and squeezed her without mercy. Her body shuddered and her lips parted in a silent scream of release. Her hands squeezed the base of his cock and held back his climax and the pressure grew. Eve shuddered, her thighs trembled and she rolled away from Oliver's mouth, but her fingers still clasped his cock. Adam rocked against him, his fingers digging into Oliver's legs, his cock tearing into his bowel.

He felt Adam's climax in his mind as Adam's body locked up, his cock buried to the hilt inside Oliver, his mouth twisted, a rictus of agony, of pleasure too great to withstand. Eve leaned over and clasped Oliver's cock in her mouth, her fingers loosened their punishing grasp and he exploded, arching up into Eve's mouth, clamping his muscles tightly around Adam's cock.

He felt Adam's cock jerking deep inside him, felt the hot wash of his seed against the ever present condom, but Eve captured Oliver's ejaculate, sucking and swallowing, her fingers gently caressing his balls, her lips soothing his cock. Adam withdrew and headed for the bathroom, Eve licked Oliver's cock clean before she left to join her mate.

Oliver lay there, heart pounding, lungs heaving, body totally wasted. He'd be sore in the morning. He'd never experienced anything so intense in his life. Never wanted this punishing, powerful sex such as they'd shared, but he'd needed it tonight. He'd have to think about that later, the reason he'd wanted the pain.

Oliver heard Eve and Adam coming out of the bathroom and rolled to one side. He looked into Mei's beautiful green eyes, awash with tears. Before he could speak, before he could explain what she'd just witnessed, she turned away. Sighing, Oliver went into the bathroom to wash.

Chapter 9

Mei felt Oliver crawl in beside her but she held perfectly still and pretended to sleep. He'd showered and the scent of soap clung to his body. With her heightened Chanku senses, though, she still smelled Eve and Adam's scent on his skin.

He snuggled up behind her and Mei's head suddenly hurt. Her brain felt like it was going to explode, and she knew Oliver was trying to read her thoughts. She didn't want him in there. Wasn't ready for him to see what was going through her mind. She might not be able to shift, but she'd learned how to block.

Confusion dictated her silence. What could she say? What should she say? She had never witnessed sex like that before. Angry, intense sex. Sex meant to inflict as much pain as pleasure. It had been both disturbing and unbelievably arousing.

She'd felt Oliver's emotional and physical pain and she should have wanted to stop it. Stop Adam from hurting him, stop Eve from tormenting him.

Instead, she'd almost climaxed, just from watching the three of them. She had climaxed, finally, using her hand, fucking herself with the same powerful anger she'd sensed in Oliver. She'd discovered a side to Oliver she'd not expected.

Just as she'd discovered something unexpected about herself. Something she wasn't quite ready to face. Why was Oliver so angry? Why did he think he should be punished? Why did she seem to feel the same?

She searched her memories of all they'd talked about, everything he'd told her about himself, and she could find no reason for him to think he'd done anything wrong. He was a generous lover. Tonight he'd given her such a glorious climax, and then he'd held her, wrapped her in his arms so she could sleep.

He'd thought only of her comfort. Why hadn't she thought of Oliver?

Because you're a selfish, miserable, whining bitch, that's why.

She blinked rapidly, but couldn't stop the tears. She'd thought only of herself, of the fact she'd wanted to change and hadn't. Oliver had told her it might take longer.

He said he'd waited almost ten years. He'd never really explained why or what exactly happened. Was that the source of his anger? What had that man done to him, the man who had bought him when he was little, that would keep Oliver from his true heritage?

Come with me. We need to talk.

Oliver's voice slipped easily into her mind, breaching the barriers she'd thought were so strong. So much for her great mental blocks. Mei rolled over and looked into his eyes, sparkling with banked fires in the darkness.

She nodded. He slipped quietly out of bed. She followed. Oliver handed a pair of jeans and a T-shirt to her and pulled on a pair of his own worn jeans.

He didn't put on a shirt, but the night was warm enough. Mei clenched her fingers to keep from touching the smooth expanse of dark muscles across his chest. When she raised her chin and looked into Oliver's eyes once again, she realized he watched her. He knew exactly what effect his body had on hers.

He knew it, and liked it, even as he used it. A lure. One she followed without question. She probably should have been embarrassed. As disturbed as she'd been by his sex with Adam and Eve, she still felt aroused.

Quietly, not waking the other two from their sleep, Mei and Oliver slipped out of the room. He took her hand and they padded barefoot across the parking lot. Dawn was breaking over the mountains to the east of them and the moon hadn't yet set behind the mountains in the west. The air was crisp and cool and deathly still. The occasional sleepy chirp of a bird seemed to echo through the silence.

Oliver dropped her hand and shoved both of his into his pockets. He bowed his head. "I'm really sorry. So sorry you saw us, Mei. I hope we didn't frighten you. I imagine what we did looked pretty intense."

She clasped her hands over her stomach to keep from reaching out for him. "I don't understand. You're such a gentle lover with me. Tonight, it seemed as if you needed pain. You wanted Adam to hurt you. Eve, too. That wasn't their call, it was yours. Why?"

There was a small grassy picnic area. Oliver led Mei to one of the redwood plank tables and sat beside her on the tabletop, feet dangling. "I'm not really sure. I was upset because you couldn't shift. I mean, after all the lead up, all the excitement when you first started showing signs of the physical changes, it was a hell of a shock when you couldn't. I know you were horribly disappointed. It's my fault. I shouldn't have pushed you."

Mei shrugged. "It's not your fault. I was acting like a spoiled baby. It's something I have to deal with, not you. But Oliver . . ." She took a deep breath and forced herself to ask. "Will you want that from me? Rough sex like that? I don't think I could ever hurt you!"

Oliver smiled and leaned his head against her shoulder.

"No need. Anytime I'm up for a little self-flagellation, I've got Adam." He chuckled quietly. "Damn but my ass hurts! We've never gotten rough before. That was a first." He scooted around on the table to get more comfortable. "Might be a last, too."

Mei laughed, then clapped her hand over her mouth. They weren't all that far from the rooms where people still slept, but she suddenly felt even closer to Oliver. "I'll admit, it was hard to watch you, but I did." She glanced away and felt the warmth creeping up her face. "At first. Then I couldn't make myself look away. I was so surprised, how turned on I got. You guys were scary intense, but I came. With my own hand."

She felt it, even now, the warmth between her legs. The sensitive swelling of her clit against the rough seam of the jeans. No panties. She'd forgotten panties, and suddenly that seam felt amazing. Maddening, but amazing.

But this wasn't about her. It was about finding answers. Mei shuddered, drawing back from her body's screaming need. What in the hell was going on with her? She'd never been this way, never searched for sexual release in every move she made. The muscles in her sex clenched. Dismayed, she felt the gathering of fluids between her legs, the deepening of her arousal.

She took a breath, let it out and tried to center herself. Then she consciously turned her attention away from her needy sex. She focused on Oliver. On him, not the release he could provide. "What happened to you, Oliver? What was it that kept you from being a man? Can you tell me?"

He turned and stared directly into her eyes. It was unnerving, to be studied so closely, but there was no sense he was trying to read her thoughts. Still, Mei felt as if he judged her, weighed her reaction to whatever he might say.

"I was castrated."

Mei's hand covered her mouth before she realized she'd even moved. "But how? Now you're . . . ?"

Oliver nodded. "When I was a baby, maybe a toddler—thank goodness, I don't remember—my testicles were surgically removed so that I'd not grow up to be a threat to my master's daughter. I was nothing more than a plaything for her."

He looked away, toward the mountains. Mei didn't try to see his thoughts. This was private. Much too private to intrude. She should stop him, but she couldn't. She had to know. There was a powerful sense in her that there could be no secrets with this man. None.

Oliver seemed to gather himself. He took her fingers in his hand and played with them for a moment. Still looking down at their joined hands, he continued. "I've told you how I ran away and came to the states, how I went to work in a circus. What I didn't tell you is that I was a eunuch. Until less than a month ago, I was not, technically speaking, a complete man."

"You said Adam fixed you. How in the world could he manage to replace body parts?"

Oliver laughed and shook his head. "All the years I was with Anton, he never once thought of linking with me so I could shift. He tried everything else, but never that. Adam did. At first he linked so I could experience sex. That's how it happened the first time with Eve." He laughed softly, shaking his head as if he still couldn't believe what they'd done. "I sort of borrowed Adam's hard on."

"Now, that is definitely sharing." Mei tried to imagine what it had been like. Her excitement kicked up another notch. She tried to temper it, but her juices flowed and she thought of Oliver, his long, thick cock sliding deep inside Eve.

"Definitely the ultimate in sharing." Oliver rubbed her fingers with his and squeezed her hand. "Eve was able to shift before Adam could. She had a lot of issues to work through and that's why she took off. That's when she headed for Florida. Adam knew he had to let her go, so he concentrated his energy on fixing me."

"I wonder if I was one of Eve's issues?" Mei stared at their clasped hands. "She had no idea I'd be there."

"Possibly. Anton Cheval and Stefan Aragat have an ongoing argument over the importance of circumstance versus fate, or predestination. I think Anton is going to love your story." He turned his head and smiled.

Mei's heart did a little flip. "So how did Adam fix you?"

"He linked with me after he learned to shift. I've always taken the supplement, even before we had pills and just ate the dried grasses ground up in our food. It helped me with my telepathy. Besides, Anton insisted, and the only one who ever gets away with telling Anton *no* is Keisha, his mate. Even with the nutrients, I didn't have the right mental pathways to shift. It's such a visceral act, so intimately linked to our libido, our sexuality . . . Adam got into my head. We bonded, almost as deeply as a mating link. It was terrifying, exhilarating . . ."

Oliver's voice drifted off. Mei thought of the mating bond. Eve and Adam still hadn't bonded, and Eve admitted to being a little afraid of the depth of the link. The loss of privacy, of separateness that accompanied the powerful link. She would have no secrets. Nor would Adam.

And if Mei bonded with Oliver . . . she sighed. Her pathetic life would be an open book.

Oliver leaned over and kissed her. "Anyway, once we formed that link between us, it was like we were one person, not two. It was truly amazing when Adam shifted. My thoughts were so closely aligned with his, I was able to draw on his sexuality and make that first shift. I'll never forget looking down at my body, seeing paws and the thick fur. And balls. I had balls. Adam really hadn't said it might happen, but I actually shifted into an intact male."

Mei slowly shook her head. Such a simple, silly thing after a lifetime of pain. "And they stayed?"

Oliver slid off he table, stood up and tugged her hand.

"Lights just went on in our room. Looks like they're awake." He turned back and kissed Mei. "Yeah. They stayed. I didn't want to shift back to human. I couldn't believe the rush of feeling fully male for the first time in my life. Imagine all those hormones, pouring into my bloodstream. I was willing to stay a wolf rather than give that up. Adam convinced me to shift back."

"What was that like? Turning back into a man and wondering if you'd still have something down there?" Mei tugged on his hand and brought Oliver to a stop. This was too important, too much a part of the man she loved. She needed to see him when he told her.

Oliver smiled and looked away. "Well, the first thing I did was pretty unmanly. I burst into tears. Sat there in the forest, buck naked, holding my dick in my hand and staring at my balls, crying like a baby." He turned slowly back to Mei, and his eyes glittered. "Then I got mad. I was just so pissed that anyone would have done such a terrible thing to a little baby boy. Force him into a life that was incomplete. I think, maybe, that's the anger I was feeling tonight. I wanted you there, sharing this amazing life with me, and you couldn't, and it wasn't through any fault of your own."

Mei looped her hands over his shoulders and kissed him full on the mouth. "It's not your fault, either. It's not anything anyone did to me, not like what happened to you. Don't worry. I will, though. Change, I mean. Soon. I feel it."

Oliver nodded and took her hand once again. When they walked back to the room, Mei thought the anger in him seemed to have melted away. Her arousal, however, pulsed within her body and her mind, powerful and alive. A separate entity, clawing for freedom.

"You weren't exaggerating when you said the house was huge!" Mei leaned forward to get a better look as they took a final turn into the long driveway leading to Anton Cheval's mountain home. It was late afternoon after a long day of driving, but once Adam put the new thermostat in the Jeep, the trip had been entirely uneventful.

Just long. Way too long.

Oliver glanced at her and grinned. It was hard not to be affected by this beautiful place he'd called home for the past ten years. Built entirely of stone and wood, the structure seemed to grow up out of the earth and the forest, an integral, natural part of the rock and trees surrounding it. The house flowed in wings off to both sides and broad decks stretched all around. A wide staircase curved up to an intricately carved front door.

Anton Cheval and his mate Keisha stood on the deck. Stefan Aragat and Alexandria came out the front door just as Oliver pulled the Jeep into a shaded parking area beside the house.

Adam raced up the driveway in Stefan's cherried out pickup with the headlights flashing on and off and the horn honking. Oliver got out of the Jeep and helped tug Mei to her feet just as Adam spun a brody in the gravel driveway and slid to a perfect stop in a shower of small stones, right at the base of the staircase.

He leapt out of the truck and took a deep bow. "Your truck, M'sieur Aragat. Intact. On time. Unmarked . . . and it's almost got a full tank of gas. Happy Birthday!"

Stefan raced down the stairs, arms wide. "My truck!"

Eve crawled out and stretched before shooting a guilty look at Stefan. "Sorry I took it for so long."

"You didn't take it, Eve. I offered it." Anton sent a mock glare at Stefan who was busy rubbing his hands over the smooth hood and practically humming with delight. "Besides, it's not his yet. His birthday isn't for two more days." He walked down the steps and put his arm around Eve's shoulders, gave her a quick kiss on the forehead and shook Adam's hand. "Thank you. I see you got everyone home safely."

"Well, Oliver had a lot to do with it." Adam turned and flashed him a smile and Oliver grabbed Mei's hand. He tugged her across the graveled drive to meet Anton.

"Anton, this is Mei Chen. Mei, Anton Cheval, our pack's leader."

"Hello, Mr. Cheval." She held out her hand, but tilted her chin down, apparently too shy to look at him.

Anton took her proffered hand in his right and tilted her chin up with the fingers of his left. "My name is Anton. We are not formal, here."

Oliver grinned but he didn't say anything. Later, maybe, when Mei felt more comfortable around all these new people. Anton had absolutely no idea how formal he sounded, nor how intimidating he could be. Even now he smiled at Mei, but there was still a frown puckering his expressive brows. Suddenly his eyes went wide and he smiled, broadly. Oliver relaxed a little more. That surprised smile changed Anton's entire appearance from austere and threatening to something he could only describe as beautiful.

Anton was nodding, as if agreeing with himself. "And you, my dear Mei . . . I can see that you are indeed special. Very, very special."

He pulled Mei against him for a quick hug. Then he reached for Oliver and pulled him into a tight embrace. Oliver breathed deep of his mentor's scent and hugged him close. It felt good to be home. Good to have Anton in charge once again.

"You've found a treasure, Oliver. An absolute treasure."

Oliver cupped his hands on Anton's broad shoulders and kissed him. Then he stepped back beside Mei and dropped his arm around her waist. "Eve gets the credit for finding Mei. However, I intend to be the one who keeps her." He tempered his promise with a kiss to her temple.

"I certainly hope so. Anything to keep you home. You have no idea how badly we've missed you." Anton grinned and slapped him on the back.

Keisha called down from the deck. "When Oliver sees the mess you've left in his kitchen, he'll have a much better understanding how badly he was missed." She laughed. "Welcome home, Oliver. And welcome, Mei. Please, come in. I'll be out shortly. The mistress of the manor is calling."

Xandi laughed and turned to follow Keisha as the sound of crying babies filled the air. "From the sound of things, she just awakened the master. We'll be back in a bit."

Oliver glanced at their luggage, piled in the backseat. "We'll get this later. I want Mei to stay with me in the cottage."

Anton paused. "Actually, I'd like both of you to stay in the main house, if you don't mind. At least until Mei gets through her first shift. Is that okay with you?"

Oliver looked to Mei. She shrugged. "Fine with me," she said. "This is a spectacular home. It's really beautiful."

"Thank you. Good." Anton reached for a couple of bags. Oliver grabbed the rest. Eve joined them when they went back to the house, but Adam and Stefan stayed behind. The two of them were still crawling all over the truck.

"Mistress of the manor?" Mei cocked her head and stared at Oliver.

He laughed. Damn it felt good to be home. "Keisha's daughter, Lily Milina. The master is Xandi and Stefan's son, Alex. They're both just a couple months old, and from the sounds I hear, their lungs have continued to develop."

"And they're all like you? Everyone can shift into wolves?"

"Everyone except the babies. They're not old enough."

Anton held the door for them. "I will apologize in advance for the mess I've left you."

"You left a mess?" Oliver stepped into the broad foyer. "I thought Stefan offered to cook."

"Cooking is not Stefan's forte." With that succinct statement, Anton led them into the house.

"Wow. You weren't kidding." Mei stood in the doorway to what had to be the biggest, most gorgeous kitchen she'd ever seen in her life. At least it might have been gorgeous, except for the black smear running up the wall behind the stove, the dishes piled in the sink and all over the kitchen table, and the trash compactor that was too full of garbage to close.

"He certainly wasn't." Oliver shook his head. Mei didn't think he was upset. He looked more like someone trying really hard not to laugh.

"At least it looks like you didn't starve." Oliver pointed at a garbage bag filled with the sort of plastic containers frozen dinners came in.

Anton appeared to be biting his lips and trying not to laugh. Mei glanced at him again and was almost certain of it. Maybe he wasn't as scary as she'd first thought.

"No. We did fine, once we discovered the amazing selection of frozen dinners at the grocery store. That brilliant bit of information came to light after Stefan caught the stove on fire and singed the wall the day you left. I forbade him from using it again." Anton cleared his throat. "The microwave oven is a truly wonderful piece of technology. Much better than a gas stove."

"I wondered about the black spot. Soot, eh?" Oliver folded his arms across his chest. "So, you saved this for me? You expect me to clean up this mess?"

Anton shook his head, chuckling. "No. I expect you to show me how to run the garbage disposal and turn on the dishwasher. A few loads should just about take care of it."

"Roll up your sleeves, boss. You're getting a lesson in kitchen maintenance one-oh-one."

Anton nodded, and the crestfallen look on his face tipped Mei over the edge. Laughing, she found a seat on one of the bar stools that ran the length of a long bar.

Eve joined her a few minutes later. "I had to go see the babies. They are so cute! The guys are still climbing all over the truck. It's going to be a long afternoon of guy talk, and there's no way I'm going to miss watching Anton Cheval do dishes."

Anton glanced over his shoulder. "I heard that. Be careful what you say, sweetheart, or Oliver'll put you to work."

Eve laughed and batted her eyelashes at Anton. Mei just sat and grinned, soaking up the banter, the beautiful surroundings, the sense of family and love that permeated every bit of this place. Plus, Anton Cheval wasn't at all bad on the eyes, even if he was an old guy.

He'd rolled his snow-white shirt sleeves up above his elbows and wrapped a towel around his lean waist. Standing at the sink with soap bubbles everywhere, he looked perfectly at ease washing the dishes. He was also one of the sexiest men Mei had ever seen. He had to be old enough to be her father, but the man was drop-dead gorgeous. He was also smart and funny and it was obvious he loved Oliver like a son.

Or a lover? She hadn't really thought of that, but knowing how the Chanku libido worked and from what Oliver had explained about the dynamics of the pack, they could be lovers. She felt a spike of white-hot arousal course through her veins.

Arousal that had been simmering ever since this morning . . . or had that been last night?

If Oliver and Anton were lovers, would he soon be hers, as well? Mei turned and looked at Eve. Eve smiled and nodded, like she was agreeing. Damn. Mei realized she'd have to block her thoughts a little better. She hoped Anton hadn't picked up on that little slip.

Just then Oliver walked into the room with a stack of

clean dish towels. He smiled at Mei, that dazzling smile that made her feel loved and wanted and unbelievably horny, all at the same time. He leaned over and kissed her, then knelt down in front of one of the cupboards and began stacking the towels inside. Watching Oliver's perfect ass inside those faded, tight jeans took her mind entirely off Anton Cheval.

Anton realized he actually enjoyed doing the dishes. The light banter among his audience was easy enough to follow, and it gave him a perfect opportunity to ramble in and out of everyone's thoughts.

Only Oliver and Stefan truly understood the scope of his mental power. And Keisha, of course, but she knew him even better than he knew himself. The most amazing thing was that she loved him in spite of what she knew.

The Goddess had definitely blessed him when She brought Keisha into his life. But what about Oliver? Would Mei prove to be a blessing or a curse?

Oliver didn't know what was coming. Neither did Mei, but Anton knew she was more than ready to shift. Thank goodness she hadn't figured it out before, when they were still on the road, or Adam and Oliver might have lost her forever in the darkness.

Anton rinsed the plate he'd been scrubbing for a good five minutes. At least it was clean, and he was actually making some headway on the mess they'd left over the past week. After Stefan caught the stove on fire and the dishes and chores somehow began to pile up, Anton decided it might be good for Oliver to know just how much he was needed.

For a lot more than just household chores. At least, though, that was a start. There was a chance, once Mei shifted, Oliver might choose to leave. Of course, it depended on Mei, on her ability to adjust, but Anton couldn't bear the thought of losing Oliver.

Mei was lovely. Beautiful inside and out, a perfect mate for Oliver in so many ways. Not so perfect in another.

If only it weren't such a big *other.*

Eve got up and opened the refrigerator, acting as comfortable in his home as if she'd always been here. She'd actually lived here for less than a week. He wanted Mei to feel that way. Comfortable. At home. Eve grabbed a chilled bottle of white wine and checked the cupboard for glasses.

"What? No clean wineglasses?"

Anton laughed. "Not yet. There's clean crystal in the dining room."

"Nah. These'll do." She grabbed a couple of water glasses and plopped them down on the counter in front of Mei. "And to think I was bragging about what a classy joint this is." She gazed back at Anton with a decided twinkle in her eyes. "I am so disappointed." She poured his really good, extremely expensive Chardonnay into the tall glasses, emptying the bottle when she topped off Mei's.

"Not so disappointed, obviously, that you're leaving me any of that Chardonnay." He flashed her a companionable grin. "However, you're teaching Mei bad habits. Mei, the rest of us would have gone for the crystal, but then we have a lot more class than Eve."

Eve laughed, tipped her filled glass in a salute to Anton, and took a swallow. "You might have the class, but I've got the good wine and the best seat in the house. Great entertainment, by the way." She leaned close to Mei and nudged her shoulder. "Hasn't he got a great ass?"

Mei snorted and almost spewed wine out her nose. Anton threw back his head and laughed. *Thank you, Eve. Maybe now she'll relax.*

You're entirely welcome. She's a nervous wreck. I hope you don't mind my taking advantage of your hospitality. It's not as if I really know you all that well. He felt her laughter in his mind and had to school his features not to

respond. He didn't want Mei to know he and Eve con-
versed.

I mean, we've never slept together. Not once.

*That can be remedied. Once you and Adam bond. Are
you truly ready for him, Eve? I know you weren't when
you left.*

Yes. I am. And thank you. I owe you a lot.

*As I owe you. Do you have any idea what your finding
Mei has done to my bet with Stefan?*

*Ah, the old fate versus coincidence. I imagine you're
ahead.*

Damn straight. And loving every minute.

He turned around. Mei caught his eye. *I know you're
talking about me. Your blocks are too strong for me to
read what you're saying, but don't think, just because I
can't shift or that I'm shy, that I'm stupid.*

"Ah, Mei. You are going to give our Oliver a wonderful
run for his money. Welcome to our pack."

Eve looked from one to the other, obviously aware
she'd missed something. Anton knew he was grinning like
a fool, but Mei smiled serenely and nodded. "Just so you
don't underestimate me. People do that a lot. Oliver doesn't."

"Nor will I, Mei Chen. Nor will I." Unable to stop grinning, Anton turned back to the job at hand. She was growing stronger by the minute. The nutrients had brought Mei's
body fully into her Chanku heritage. Her self-assurance
was as great a sign as was the sense of the beast about her.
He knew her alter ego ran swift and sure, just beneath the
surface.

The mess in the kitchen was almost under control.
Oliver came back with more dishes he'd gathered from the
dining room, stopped beside Mei and kissed her soundly.
He was obviously as anxious as Mei for night to fall and
the dark forest to beckon. Not that they didn't run in daytime, but for a first shift, only the night would do.

Keisha and Xandi should have the babies fed by now. One of them would stay tonight and watch Lily and Alex so the other new mom could join them when they ran. All of them.

Including Mei. Only a few more hours. She rubbed her arms and Anton remembered that feeling, of bones and muscles wanting so badly to leap through the thin barrier of skin. She may be feeling the same things they all had when the nutrients first took effect, but Mei was unique. That much he knew. How unique, how different, Anton wasn't sure. Excitement coursed through his veins. A sense of expectation. It was always like this when a new Chanku shifted for the first time, but in Mei he sensed something beyond anything they'd known. Whatever, in a few more hours, Mei Chen would finally embrace her true heritage.

Chapter 10

"It's beautiful out tonight." Mei smiled at Anton, but her lips trembled. She clung tightly to Oliver's hand and her every move radiated anxiety.

Anton ran his hand over her sleek, black hair. "It's a perfect night for a first shift. Relax, Mei. You are more than ready tonight." He turned away and led them out into the meadow. Generally they'd all just strip down and shift on the big front deck, but he'd chosen the meadow and moonlight for tonight.

Mei needed the ceremony, the trappings of occasion. Anton realized as he walked out into the open area, he needed it as well. His sense of events moving beyond his control was strong tonight. Foreboding followed every move. Expectation drew him onward.

The moon was full, a perfect silver orb hanging high in a velvet sky. The meadow shimmered in quicksilver and shadows and the dark forest surrounded them. They'd gathered many times here, for many different reasons. None as potentially life altering as tonight.

If only he had a better feel for what was to come. Anton glanced at Oliver and caught his friend's eye. Oliver nodded. He too, was remembering other times in this meadow, but from a totally different perspective than Anton's. Where

Anton saw the meadow as a gateway to knowledge, Oliver had to be remembering the many times he'd been excluded from rituals and spells.

Excluded because he was not fully Chanku.

No longer, thanks to Adam. Anton studied the rangy mechanic as he sauntered across the meadow. He seemed to glow in the moonlight and his dark blond hair glimmered with silver fire. There was power in Adam he'd not yet figured out. Power beyond the mere ability to shift. Anton turned his attention back to Oliver and Mei. There was power in Mei as well, but it was foreign to him. *Alien.* Was it her Asian heritage? Hard to tell. He'd never come here before with so many questions.

Knowledge was his power. Anton recognized knowledge as his ultimate strength. For that reason, among others, he was glad Adam and Eve had chosen to stay on in Montana. Though Eve was essentially an open book to him, Anton realized he had much to learn from Adam.

Pulling himself out of the track of worry his mind refused to ignore, Anton glanced back toward the house. Would Keisha or Xandi be the one to stay behind and mind the babies? Selfishly, he hoped it was Xandi who remained.

He'd missed running with his mate, missed the sleek alpha bitch racing beside him, but babies definitely took priority. He looked away from the house and caught Stefan's eye. Stefan grinned and shrugged. Obviously, he hoped Keisha would be the one who watched their young.

Anton tipped him a brief salute. At least one of them would be paired. Adam and Eve arrived at the center of the meadow at the same time as Stefan. Anton noticed a movement on the deck and glanced up just in time to see Keisha close the door behind her, step out on the deck and walk across the grass. Anton's heart pounded thankfully in his chest. He couldn't bring himself to look at Stefan.

He didn't have to. He sensed Stefan's disappointment

and it made him ache. Not enough, though, to ask Keisha to stay behind with Xandi.

Ready to shift, Keisha walked proudly toward them clad only in moonlight. Dark and lush and unbelievably lovely, she took his breath. Rounder and softer now, since giving birth, her breasts were full and they swayed in a hypnotic rhythm with each step she took. Her nipples, luscious and larger than before her pregnancy, glistened. Anton's gut clenched, hot with need. She'd just fed Lily. He wished he'd been there, watching their baby suckle those luscious breasts. He licked his lips and felt foolish. What kind of pervert was jealous of his only daughter?

At least tonight Keisha would run with him. Possibly they would make love . . . two wolves in the forest, the nature of the beast their most powerful connection of all. His cock swelled and his testicles ached. He wished everyone else would just go away and he'd take her here, in the meadow with only the moon as their witness.

"She's asleep and I'm free!" Smiling, Keisha leaned close and kissed him. She smelled of fresh, clean baby and rich mother's milk. Once again, his groin tightened. "It's Xandi's turn to run tonight, but Alex is being a fussbudget and she doesn't want to leave him."

Thank the goddess for small favors. Keisha had absolutely no idea the power she held over him. None. Oblivious to Anton's compelling need, Keisha smiled brightly at Mei. "Are you ready, Mei? This is so exciting!"

Anton practically groaned. If he didn't hurt so much from wanting her, he'd probably laugh out loud.

Mei nodded. Exciting wasn't the word she'd have chosen. *Terrifying. Impossible. Scary as hell. Definitely scary.*

Anton unbuttoned his shirt and the others followed his lead. Within moments, all of them were nude, all of them tall and beautiful and perfect. She couldn't see Oliver. He stood behind her, but every one of them—Eve and Keisha,

Adam, Stefan and Anton—all of them so utterly gorgeous it was unbelievable.

Mei clutched her pale yellow sarong around herself, overwhelmed by the beautiful people surrounding her. Especially the men. Their cocks were hard and curved, crowns flared, shafts thick. She knew her eyes must be bugging out, but she'd never seen so much hard male flesh at one time in her life.

Oliver stepped up behind her and nuzzled her ear. *You can play with as many of them as you want. Later.*

She giggled, and her nervousness slipped away. "Sorry." Mei shrugged and felt totally stupid. Again. "You're all so gorgeous. It's a bit intimidating." She turned around and grinned at Oliver. "But Oliver just said I get to play with you later."

Keisha and Eve both laughed. "He's right, but you're just as beautiful," Eve said. "Don't worry. It's okay, feeling a bit nervous. I was so embarrassed the first time we all got naked together." She glanced shyly at Adam. "In fact, this is the first time I've done this with everyone, with Adam here, too."

Adam stepped up behind her and cupped her shoulders in his palms. He didn't say anything, but the kiss he planted beneath her ear spoke volumes.

Anton slapped his hands together in a quiet clap that immediately drew everyone's attention. "Okay. Listen up. Mei, when you tried to shift before, what did you do?"

She straightened her shoulders, well aware she was, and would continue to be, the center of attention tonight. "Oliver and Adam shifted first. They told me to link with Eve and follow her lead. I had no problem linking, but when I'd try to shift, it was like hitting a brick wall."

Anton nodded. "We're going to try something different. You've had five days of nutrient, more than enough for a woman to make her first shift. I sense the beast in you.

She's strong and alive. She's ready for her freedom. Do you feel her?"

Mei closed her eyes and searched. She didn't have to go far. The power was there, barely banked. She rubbed her hands along her arms. "I do. It's very strange, like another entity inside me. I hadn't noticed that feeling before."

"Good. I want you to forget everything you watched with Eve. Everything you might have seen when Adam and Oliver shifted. You are unique, Mei. You're not Eve, not Oliver. Not me. You need to follow your own path, and find your own form."

They stood around her, a protective circle filled with energy. She'd been alone most of her life, but now Mei felt Oliver's powerful love, Eve's encouragement, Adam's excitement. Keisha, Stefan, and Anton stood together and their joy for her was almost palpable. They felt like family. For the first time in her life, Mei was surrounded by family.

She closed her eyes and raised her face to the moon. There was no warmth in the glow, but she felt the pull, as if her body was the sea and her tide rushed onward to the shore. She found the *other* in her mind.

Chanku.

And it was beautiful, really, in all its amazing simplicity. She understood, finally, why she'd not been able to call the wolf. What a fool! What a silly fool she'd been. So blind to the truth, so trapped on the narrow path she'd assumed was hers to follow.

She'd not understood her own reality. Truly unique, undeniably perfect. Smiling, Mei leaned forward, her body stretched, her entire being shifted, winked out, and changed.

Her broad paws hit the ground, her long thick tail swished the air and she snarled. Then with a single powerful leap, she went over the top of Adam's crouching wolf and raced for the forest.

* * *

"Holy shit. Mei?" Oliver grabbed Anton's arm. "What the fuck was that? What happened to Mei? What is she? A jaguar? Some kind of leopard? What happened? We need to go after her!"

The rest of them stood speechless, staring at the forest. Keisha and Eve held hands, as if clinging to one another for support. Adam paced a moment, still in wolf form, and then shifted back. Stefan merely shook his head in disbelief, then he glanced down at the ground and picked up a tiny metallic coil. He held it in his palm and showed it to Anton.

Mei's IUD.

Totally bemused by the unexpected, Anton took a moment to gather his thoughts. "Not a jaguar, Oliver. I believe she is a snow leopard. Solitary animals. They're quite rare, actually. They come from the same part of the world as our ancestors. Damn. She's beautiful. Absolutely beautiful."

Shaking his head, Adam held up his hands, palms out, in wonder. "Explains why we couldn't help her shift into a wolf."

"That it does." Anton grabbed Oliver's shoulder to steady him. "We need to go after her. She is an unknown. I'm not even sure we can communicate with her in this form, but she could be in danger in unfamiliar country."

No one questioned him. Thankfully, they rarely did. That was a good thing, especially now, when he had absolutely no answers. Anton shifted and raced across the meadow. The others followed, though Oliver quickly passed him, nose to the ground as he followed Mei's scent.

Moonlight barely penetrated the thick forest bordering the meadow, but the musky scent of cat was an easy trace to find. Unique in these woods along the Rocky Mountains, there was nothing like it to confuse the sensitive noses of the pack of wolves following Mei's trail.

* * *

She was powerful and fast, but her body wasn't built for running long distances. She wasn't ready for them to find her yet, either. Not until she'd had a little time to come to terms with this absolutely amazing thing that had happened. Mei slowed to a trot. Fat paws brushed the earth, a long, furred tail balanced her. She followed what was obviously a well-traveled path and the scent of wolf was strong here. She recognized Anton's and Stefan's odors, but she wasn't so sure about the others.

Right now, she wasn't all that sure about much of anything except the fact she wasn't at all like she'd imagined. She'd done exactly as Anton told her. She'd called up the beast within, but she sure as hell hadn't expected this! Mei snarled and the sound seemed to roll up out of her chest. If she could, she'd be laughing right now. Little Mei Chen . . . jungle cat!

Unfortunately, she had no idea what kind of cat that was.

Still, it was amazing. Absolutely amazing. Slipping off the trail and angling downhill, she found a small pool of clear water beneath a steep rock face. Lapping quietly at the water's edge, she tried to assimilate all the differences in this new body. She was powerful. Her muscles rippled beneath her skin, and while she wasn't all that tall, she was long and sleek with a magnificent tail.

Her coat was a mottled pale cream, almost white, with irregular dark brown to black rosettes of color. She ran her long tongue over the front of her left leg and then lifted her paw and licked at the thick pads. She lifted her left foot, turned it over, flexed the paw and watched her claws come out.

She wished she knew what kind of cat she was. She wasn't big enough to be a leopard or fast enough to be a cheetah, and she didn't know any other types. Whatever species, she damned sure wasn't a wolf! No wonder she'd not been able to follow Eve and shift.

It was not her nature to be a wolf. Such a simple explanation, but not really an answer at all.

The sound of animals rushing headlong down the trail caught her attention. *Chanku?* Had they followed her? Well of course they'd follow her, once they got over the shock of her shifting into something totally unexpected. She wasn't ready to face any of them. Not yet. She wanted more time to experience this new body without interference. Glancing around, Mei chanced to look up. A rocky ledge almost eight feet overhead appeared large enough to hold her.

With a powerful thrust of her muscular hind legs, she leapt directly to the ledge, turned and settled down to watch. There was so much to think about. A wolf was one thing, but a cat? She'd never expected anything like this. Nothing could compare to the feel of her muscles, the way they seemed to flow over her bones.

She heard the sound of rustling vegetation, the scurry of tiny creatures through the brush as they ran for their lives. Six wolves moved silently into the tiny glade. They sniffed the ground, whining, tails wagging as they picked up her scent. She tried to listen, but the mental speech in their wolven form was difficult to understand. She watched them and wondered why they didn't look up.

Wondered what she would do if they saw her. She recognized Oliver and her heart stuttered in her chest. How could he love her now? He'd talked of the mating bond, how they would finally link when they mated as wolves.

Well that's not going to happen. Could he possibly love her now? She felt absolutely no attraction to him in this form. Knew she loved him as a human, realized she couldn't as a cat. Pondering the question hurt her head.

She'd rather be hunting. She raised her head and sniffed the air. There was game in the forest. A lot of it. Deer and rabbits, fat squirrels and small mice and voles. She salivated, imagining their taste, picturing her huge paw coming down on some scurrying creature, her razor-sharp claws extending, holding it.

How could she know these things? How could she taste blood on her tongue and know it was deer? How could a young woman from Florida know exactly how to be a spotted cat in the forest?

The wolves lapped water at the pool. Then, one by one, they turned to leave. All but one of them. The largest wolf among them, black and powerful with shimmering amber eyes paced back and forth beneath the ledge. Paced until the last of the pack had melted into the thick undergrowth.

Then the animal turned, raised his muzzle and looked directly into Mei's eyes. The beast shimmered and Anton stood there, his tall, beautifully strong body pale in the moonlight, his face a study of concern and amazement, of curiosity and unimaginable intelligence.

"Come down, Mei. Please. It's time to go back."

I don't want to. I want to run, to hunt. I want to kill.

Anton shook his head. "As I feared. I don't understand you in this form. Do you know what you are, Mei? How special you are?"

She snarled, sat up on her haunches and swept the air with one broad paw, claws extended. Anton merely laughed. She should have been angry that he showed her so little respect, but when she thought about it, it really was funny. She leapt down and landed neatly beside Anton. Then she shifted.

"This was not what I expected." She stood there, hands on her hips and glared at him.

"Oh, Mei." He laughed harder. "You're not what any of us expected! Poor Oliver is beside himself. Come back. Let us try and figure out how one little Chanku among many decided to become a snow leopard. I certainly didn't see this one coming."

She flashed a sideways glance at him and shook her head. "What the hell is a snow leopard?"

"Shift and you'll know. C'mon. It's a long way back and faster on four legs. Follow me." Anton shifted and the black wolf waited patiently at the edge of the trail.

She had a moment's fear. What if she turned into something entirely different this time? She reached for the beast and was suddenly standing behind the wolf on four big paws. She snarled, he growled and they headed back to the house.

Adam called to Eve and veered off the trail. The others were heading back now that Anton had Mei. Adam had other things on his mind, chief among them the rich, musky scent of the female he wanted to take as his mate. Eve nipped his flank and then trotted along beside him. Her pale coat glistened in the silver light, and he felt a sense of destiny too powerful to ignore.

It was their time, tonight. Here, deep in the forest with the moon glinting through the branches and Eve running beside him, her wolven aroma the most powerful aphrodisiac he'd ever experienced. His body tightened, his balls pulled up hard and close between his legs and he knew he must have her. Now. But was Eve ready?

Would she accept him, knowing the depth of the mating bond? The lack of self, the subjugation of will? Everything either of them had ever experienced, every hurt or embarrassment, every achievement, every worry and joy—all of it shared. Was she willing to give up that much of herself?

She'd been terrified of commitment, afraid of losing herself in Adam, and she'd run clear across the country to avoid bonding with him. Now, though, she said she was ready. Willing to give herself completely to another person. In many ways, willing to subjugate her own will to his.

Was he willing to do the same?

He thought of his life, of the successes and failures he'd experienced. The years of loneliness, the years his only true contact with another soul had been the terrifying link to his sister, a woman who was more nightmarish fantasy than reality until just weeks ago. Manda had finally found love. She'd told Adam that Baylor Quinn was the best part of her.

His sister's words stayed with him. When he thought of Eve, Adam knew she was the best of him. The most important thing in his world. He needed her. Wanted her on a level that went deeper than any desire he'd ever known.

Eve paused, one paw lifted. She raised her nose to the gentle breezes and sniffed, then turned and stared at him. Challenged him with her beautiful gray eyes. He felt her thrill of excitement, her need to hunt. Her challenge. She would always challenge him.

He wanted to shout for joy when, like a silent wraith, she slipped off the trail and melted into the shadows. Adam followed, his nose twitching with the smell of game, his cock twitching with need for his bitch.

His heart pounded in his wolven chest and his instincts kept him as silent as Eve, but his human mind rejoiced. They'd ran together as wolves, but never hunted together.

Never made love as wolves. The hunt would raise her desire. The blood of a successful kill would give them something powerful tonight. He followed Eve's lead. Watched the way she carefully placed one paw in front of the other. He copied the low, crouching glide that disguised her profile and allowed both of them to slip through dry brush without sound. They'd moved high on the mountain now, close to the tree line where the air was thin and wind whistled through the dry, midsummer grasses. She moved more quickly than he and the image she showed him, of a large buck feeding in tall grass, urged Adam forward.

Eve circled to the left. Adam took the tack to the right.

The buck raised his head, aware of something, unsure what he sensed. He was an animal in his prime, shoulders heavily muscled, antlers spreading wide and sharp above a broad head. Eve exploded out of the thick brush. She caught the big animal's lower jaw in her powerful fangs and used the weight of her body to take him down.

Adam dove for the animal's throat, avoiding the dangerous antlers, clamping down on both windpipe and jugular. Sharp hooves scored his flank but his powerful jaws quickly ended the animal's fight. Panting, Adam scrambled to his feet. Eve snarled and paced beside the warm body. Her narrowed eyes glinted feverishly and he knew her blood ran hot with the thrill of a fresh kill and her own burgeoning desire.

Adam backed away, deferring to his alpha bitch. Somewhat appeased, she ripped into the animal's soft belly, tearing at skin and muscle with sharp teeth and powerful jaws.

She was terrible and deadly. Vicious and overwhelmingly beautiful. Everything he could possibly want in a mate and more. Adam's body trembled with need for her. Shivered with desire. Hunger gnawed at Adam's gut, but he paced just beyond the body. He'd not challenge her for the kill. Instead, he waited impatiently until Eve had fed, growling and scratching at the blood-soaked dirt beside the body. When he finally moved in to feed, she snarled, but she didn't attack.

The rich scent of fresh blood filled his nostrils. Adam tore at the carcass, gulping great chunks of muscle and tearing flesh from the bones of one haunch. Eve wandered back over to the deer and ate more, but she watched Adam warily. The human part of their minds accepted the nature of the beast. When the kill was fresh, when their blood was hot, both of them knew their wolven instincts could overpower whatever humanity existed.

As it did now.

They'd run far tonight and the area was unfamiliar. Adam's thigh ached where the buck's hoof had slashed him, and the moon was sinking in the sky. It was time. He wanted her. Needed her. If they mated now, she would be his forever, bonded on a level beyond any link either of them had ever known. Linked deeply into his psyche, whether human or wolf. No matter . . . she was Chanku.

She was his.

Eve wandered around behind him and licked his wound. Blood seeped from the tear in his flesh, but the harsh rasp of her tongue over his injury felt good. He lifted his head to watch her.

Just in time to see the flash of silver and hear the loud thud of heavy paws racing toward them. *Grizzly!* Adam spun around as the bear reached the carcass. The animal took a powerful swipe at Adam. He ducked and avoided the blow, but Eve rushed in to protect him, snarling and growling, her jaws wide.

No! Get away! She was no match for the bear. Neither was Adam, but instinct ruled the wolf, and love ruled the man. The bear lunged at Eve. Adam went for the beast's throat. The big male reared up on its haunches and swatted Adam, hard. He rolled away across the grass, scrambling for purchase but unable to regain his footing. Before he could return to attack, Eve charged once again. The bear's paw caught her solidly along one shoulder. He batted her away as if she were nothing but a toy. Eve yipped once before she landed hard against a rocky outcropping almost six feet from the carcass.

She lay there, unmoving, her body sprawled in the rocks like a child's stuffed toy. The bear eyed her for a moment, beady eyes dark and dangerous. Then the smell of fresh blood and the bounty of meat forced his huge head around. Snuffling and growling, the grizzly tore at the dead deer.

Adam crawled to his feet and crept around behind the

bear. He sniffed Eve. She was unconscious. Blood seeped from three long slash marks on her shoulder. It appeared her thick coat had protected her though, and the cuts weren't deep. He couldn't tell how badly she'd been hurt, but he couldn't shift, not until he got her away from the grizzly. A wolf, at least, could fight back. A naked human was powerless against eight hundred pounds of angry bear.

Unable to move her, Adam sent out a call for the pack. In less than a heartbeat, they answered.

Anton caught Adam's message and passed it on to Oliver. He stopped on the trail with Mei beside him and shifted. She did the same, and they waited there for Oliver to return. "Eve's been hurt," he said, as soon as Mei stood before him. "Grizzly attack. Adam's with her. She's unconscious and can't shift. I'm going back. Can you find your way home?"

Mei shook her head. "I'm going with you."

Anton really didn't need a bossy female right now. If it weren't for Mei, he'd be running beside Keisha, not herding this youngster back home. "No," he said. "You need to go back. Oliver's coming to help me."

"I can't understand you," she said. And then she shifted and the snow leopard prowled, pacing back and forth on the narrow trail.

"Oh fuck." Anton sensed Oliver growing closer. He shifted and the wolf waited when Oliver rounded the curve.

Oliver saw Mei and came to a complete stop, but his question was for Anton. *Do you know where they are?*

They're in the west meadow, just at the tree line. Follow me. He took off at a ground-eating lope, one he knew the snow cat couldn't stick with.

But Mei fooled him, and her long stride kept her in pace with both Anton and Oliver. They drew closer, all of them with tongues hanging and sides billowing, until the stench of the grizzly was in their nostrils and their hackles rose. Anton stopped their headlong rush and had them approach downwind.

The bear was lying down, his massive head buried in the deer's innards, twisting this way and that as he stuffed himself on the bloody carcass.

Adam was off to one side, not nearly far enough from the grizzly, but he covered Eve with his body. His relief, when he saw them, was unmistakable, a tangible thing. He raised his head, ears pricked forward, and watched as they worked themselves closer to the spot where he and Eve lay.

Anton and Oliver were almost beside him when the grizzly raised its shaggy head. The bear turned and charged, running faster than anything that size should be able to move. Mei streaked in between Adam and the bear.

Paws flashing, mouth wide, she left a bleeding gash across the bear's muzzle. Surprised by her attack, he spun around and turned his back on the wolves. Adam and Oliver shifted and carefully lifted Eve's inert wolven body and carried her toward the tree line. Anton remained in wolf form in case Mei needed help, but she was amazing, twisting and turning like lightning, slashing and biting, her powerful jaws and razor-sharp claws doing more damage than the bear obviously expected.

Growling, he shook his head and blood flew from his torn snout. He stared out of beady little eyes, watching the leopard as it paced back and forth in front of him. Finally it must have registered with the grizzly that his belly was already full and there was no reason to put up with such a nuisance. He turned and lumbered off, away from the carcass, away from the wolf and the humans and the snarling leopard. Once he was gone, Mei shifted and ran to Eve. "Is she okay? Why hasn't she shifted?"

Oliver wrapped his arms around her. "She's unconscious. She can't shift until she comes around. Are you okay? Goddess, Mei. You were amazing!"

She looked down at the ground and her face flushed, visible even in the fading moonlight. "I'm fine. Oliver? I . . ."

He hugged her close. "Later. When we get home, we'll sort all of this out."

She nodded and turned to look at Anton. He wished he had answers. For now, there were none. "Thank you, Mei. Oliver's right. You are truly amazing. I should have known better than to ask you to stay behind." He touched her shoulder and felt her shaking, and he pulled her into a tight embrace. "You are a very, very brave young woman."

She suffered Anton's hug, but only for a moment before slipping away. "Thank you," she mumbled, glancing back at him only once before going to stand beside Oliver. He took her hand and pulled her close.

Adam squatted down and picked the injured wolf up off the ground. He cradled her in his long arms and held her close to his chest. Oliver and Anton resumed their wolven form. Mei shifted, and the leopard paced alongside the small group, practically invisible with her patterned coat. They formed a small phalanx, better suited to protecting Adam and his burden as creatures of the night.

It was a long walk home. Dawn was breaking when they finally stumbled across the meadow.

Anton touched the sides of Eve's broad wolven head and let his thoughts slide gently into her mind. The spark of life remained, but he sensed it growing dim. Adam paced at the foot of the bed. The others ringed the room, waiting.

He withdrew from Eve's brain and focused on Adam. "She needs medical care. This is beyond me."

Adam whirled around and glared at him. His eyes glittered with the tears he'd not allowed to fall. "What? Do we take her to a fucking vet? She has to shift. No one can treat her like this."

"You can." Anton folded his hands across his chest. "You fix things, Adam."

"I fix cars. I fix machines. I fix mechanical crap where I can just screw in a new part. I can't . . ."

"You fixed me." Oliver stepped forward. As far as Anton knew, only he and Adam, possibly Mei, were aware of Oliver's life as a eunuch. Oliver looked at the others in the room, then turned his attention to Eve. "I was castrated when I was a child." There was an audible gasp from some of the others.

"What the fuck?" Stefan's harsh whisper brought a smile to Oliver's face.

"I never told anyone. Only Anton knew. But I told Adam, and he fixed what was broken. I'm not a eunuch anymore. I'm a man, because of you, Adam."

Adam held his hands out in a helpless gesture that tore at Anton's heart. He glanced at Keisha, standing quietly with Lily in her arms and remembered her story, how she'd been so badly damaged. Yet the combined love of her pack had healed her.

"Adam, you, Oliver, and Eve joined minds to discover more about Mei. You combined your power, not to heal, but to probe her thoughts. Because of that link, I imagine you know Eve's mind better than anyone here. What if you go deep. Let Mei and Oliver share their strength. I can link with the three of you and add more power. Think of yourself as an imaging machine. See if you can find out what's wrong. See if you can fix what's broken."

Mei touched his arm and Adam's head jerked around. "It can't hurt, Adam. We have to do something."

"What if I make her worse?" Adam's voice broke and the tears he'd been holding back finally fell.

Anton smoothed the ruffled fur along Eve's injured shoulder. "You can't make it worse, Adam, but you're the only one among us who might be able to help. Her life force is fading. I don't think she'll survive the night."

*   *   *

They dimmed the lights in the room. Stefan, Keisha, and Xandi had taken the babies and gone to prepare a meal. Adam sat on a stool next to the bed and stroked Eve's back. She lay still as death, the labored sound of her breathing loud in the darkened bedroom.

Adam felt as if he were too far away, so he crawled up on the bed and lay beside her. Anton, Oliver, and Mei gathered behind him and placed their hands on his body. He felt their connection, their warmth and latent power flowing through his shoulder, hip, and thigh.

Mei and Oliver were both familiar and he welcomed their connection. Anton's power pulsed at his hip. He'd never linked with Anton on a physical level, never experienced the spirit beneath the flesh. With strength like that guiding him, Adam realized he might just be able to do what Anton had suggested.

He wrapped his arms around Eve's body and held her close. Her breathing was shallow, her heart fluttering beneath his hands. He focused his thoughts, all his mental energy, and concentrated on Eve's injured brain. At the same time he tried to channel the power emanating from the warm hands holding him.

Slowly, carefully, he entered her mind, aware that Anton Cheval followed, a silent shadow of thought. There was injury here, a vast pooling of blood beneath her skull. The pressure kept her from consciousness. If he could help her shift, would the changing patterns of her skull and her brain remove the pressure?

Or, would the change merely kill her?

Slowly, Adam withdrew. The others watched him, waiting. Trusting his skill.

He had no skill. None, damn it all. He was a mechanic, not a doctor. He . . .

"What do you think?"

Adam snapped around at Anton's soft question. "I think you're all crazy if you expect me to—"

Anton held up his hand. "I was with you. I saw the injury. I agree with your idea. If we can help her shift, it could remove much of the damage."

"It could also fuckin' kill her." Adam's hand shook. Damn, but he loved her so, and she was slipping away. Leaving him, bit by bit, her life force growing weaker with each beat of her heart.

"Doing nothing will kill her." Anton's soft voice cut through Adam's anger. He was absolutely right. "You saw the extent of the bleeding," he said. "So did I. Can you link with her, even though she's not conscious? Can you help her shift without waking?"

Adam nodded. "I think so. I'll need all of you." He lowered his head. "We need to do it now. While she still has the strength to complete the shift. I think I know a way to control that part of her brain."

He lay back down and wrapped his arms around Eve's inert wolven form. He felt the warmth of his packmates' hands. Felt their power when he slipped deeper into Eve's mind and found that tiny gland near her brainstem that controlled their ability to shift.

He searched for her, for any living, conscious part of Eve, and found a spark. There wasn't much, but it was enough. He drew more on his friends, felt Oliver's hands tremble against his thigh, felt Mei's fingers dig into his shoulder.

Only Anton's hands were steady, and his power was a constant, throbbing pressure in Adam's head, but he used the power and moved slowly inside Eve. He wasn't sure what he did, only that it somehow felt right. Wasn't sure if he'd helped the woman he loved or damaged her beyond repair. He let the power flow, felt the heat and energy from Oliver, Mei, and Anton as it burned through his system, flowed along his nerves and veins, found its outlet in Eve.

The bestial body pressed close to his seemed to disappear and reform. He was almost afraid to open his eyes, but the warm flesh he held wrapped in his arms was no longer coated in fur.

Her heart beat stronger, her mind seemed clearer.

But she lay there, still and silent, unconscious. Eyes closed, breathing shallow and fast, and Adam had no idea how to help.

Chapter 11

"She's breathing better, her pulse is strong and regular." Anton brushed Adam's tangled hair back from his eyes. "Sleep, my friend. Both of you need to rest. I'll be back later, but for now, sleep. We'll see if anything changes over the next couple hours."

Adam nodded. "I don't know . . . do you think we should take her to the hospital? Maybe now that she's human . . ." His voice trailed off into a whisper.

"She isn't, really. None of us is human and I don't know what their medicine would do to her brain. Broken bones are one thing, but an injury to the brain is something else. Our brains are not human and I'm afraid their treatments could harm more than help us. The doctor who treated Keisha and Xandi during their pregnancies is the only one who knows our true nature, and he's gone for a month. Adam, I truly believe you are Eve's best hope. Stay with her. Call me when she awakens, or when you've had enough rest to go back in. I will be here quickly and lend whatever strength I can."

Adam nodded and lay back down beside Eve. Anton slipped quietly out of the room, but he worried about Mei and Oliver as well as Eve. The two had gone to Oliver's cottage to sleep, but the easy love between them had been irrevocably changed tonight. He wondered how Oliver would cope, knowing he could never bond with the woman he loved.

Stefan and Xandi had gone to their wing. Anton needed Keisha. His body ached for her. His heart cried. He'd felt too much grief tonight, experienced too much heartache. Keisha would understand. She always knew exactly what he needed.

She waited just outside their room. *Lily is asleep. The monitor is with Xandi and Stefan, should she awaken. Come, my love. You promised me a run in the forest. If Adam calls, we won't be far.*

Anton's exhaustion slipped from his shoulders like an unneeded cloak. He stripped out of the jeans he'd thrown on earlier and took Keisha's hand. Together they went out onto the deck, shifted and raced for the forest.

So different in daytime. The sounds of the night, all muted rustlings and sharp cries had been replaced by birdsong and the rich smell of sun-warmed grass. The resinous scent of pine and fir, of spruce and cedar filled the air, and sunlight spattered the narrow trail with bursts of brilliant color.

Keisha raced just ahead, her long legs leading them deeper into the forest. She swerved on to a smaller, narrower trail and Anton followed. He recognized the trail, one he'd not followed for many months. Keisha burst out of the darkness of the deep woods and into sunlight, with Anton right on her tail.

The old mill pond sparkled in the late morning sunlight. Anton and Keisha both stopped at the water's edge, lapped the cool water with heads low and front legs bowed. Then they shifted. The air was filled with the buzz of cicadas. A pair of mallard ducks swam lazily on the far side of the pond. Anton took Keisha's hand in his, and a sense of peace surrounded them.

"Do you think Eve will survive?" Keisha watched the ducks but Anton felt her heartache.

"I do. Adam will allow nothing less."

"Do you really believe he has the power to heal her?" Keisha turned and pinned him with her brilliant amber gaze.

"If he can believe in himself, yes. I don't think there is much that Adam Wolf can't do."

Keisha frowned. "Is he more powerful than you?"

Anton chuckled, leaned close and kissed her. "No, my love. He is not more powerful than me. His skills are different, though. I believe his ability to heal is something we can learn from him. Once he understands it better himself."

"Why Eve?" Keisha turned her head to stare at the water, but her question hung on the morning air.

"Why not?"

Keisha spun around. "What do you mean, why not? You act as if none of us has any control over our futures. I'm beginning to hope Stefan's right, that it's all coincidence. I don't want to think we're fated for some of the horrible things that happen. I don't want to believe in a destiny we can't change."

Anton wrapped his arms around Keisha and drew her close. "My love, it's a cliché, but bad things happen to good people. I don't believe our destiny is set in stone, but I do believe that good things can come from the bad. You were attacked, you shifted without realizing your own power, and you killed. I found you because of the horrible things that happened to you. If they hadn't happened, I would be living half a life. I wouldn't have you, I wouldn't have our lovely daughter." He shuddered as the reality of what could have been washed over him. He might as well be dead, if not for Keisha and their child.

He kissed her, hard and fast. "My love, there is nothing

without you. Nothing. Was it fate that I found the newspaper with the article about you? Or mere coincidence
that your voice would come to me, so many hundreds of
miles away? I don't know. I only know that you are my
life, the source of my power, the one who gives me a reason to take one breath after another."

There were tears in her eyes when she kissed him.
Anton pulled her close. Her breasts were full and firm, her
belly slightly rounded from the birth of their daughter. She
was more beautiful now than when he first saw her, yet
even then she had captured his heart. His mind whirled
with thoughts of Lily's birth, when their plane had gone
down and Keisha's early labor had terrified him.

But members of the pack had come in time, their
daughter was born healthy and whole, and Keisha had
been the strongest one of them all. He wondered if she had
any idea of her own power.

Her lips moved over his, soft and full and promising so
much more. She kissed his neck, his collarbone, trailed
along his chest and knelt in front of him. She stroked his
erection with cool, slender fingers, cupped his heavy sac in
her palm and leaned close to suckle the broad head of his
cock between her lips.

He groaned, unmanned by her wet mouth, her warm
tongue, the sharp rasp of teeth over his shaft. He loved the
contrast. Her coffee-colored skin against his pale flesh, the
soft slide of her lips over the marble strength of his cock.
He felt his knees tremble and the taut coil of heat that
raced from his spine to his balls took him right to the edge.

Gasping for breath, Anton cupped her face in his palms
and eased her away. Her lips slipped over the crown of his
cock with a soft *pop*. As she pulled away, her tongue came
out and she licked the very tip.

"I want you," he said, and his voice sounded rough in
his own ears. "I need you more than air, more than life.

You are my life." His breath was unsteady, his heart raced. The cool air moving across his damp cock tightened all the muscles in his groin.

Keisha looked up at him and smiled. Then she leaned close and licked the tiny drop from the tip of his cock, circled her tongue in the weeping eye and kissed him.

Anton laughed. "Oh, shit. Are you trying to kill me?"

She winked. Before he could react, Keisha shifted.

Anton's heart stuttered in his chest. He'd wanted this last night. Wanted the wolf, the hot, hard thrusting sex of two animals mating. Needed the mindless release that left his body sated and his mind clear. He shifted and pawed her shoulder. Keisha yipped, spun around and nipped his flank. When he lunged for her, she took off, running full tilt, back into the forest.

She was smaller and lighter. Her feet fairly flew over the packed earth, and leaves and pine needles scattered in her wake. She didn't run to escape him. No, she challenged him. Tested his strength and speed, his power, his love and his desire.

When Anton finally cornered Keisha in a small glade with a rocky berm rising behind her, both of them were winded, sides heaving, tongues hanging. He raked her shoulder with his paw and caught the thick fir at the back of her neck in his teeth.

She turned as if to challenge him, but he held her tightly, wrapping his front legs around her shoulders, holding the back of her neck in his jaws. He thrust hard and fast, jabbing into her sex, his back paws slipping and digging at the soft earth, his wolven penis sliding deep inside Keisha's slick heat. She snarled and tried to twist away, but the hard knot at the base of his cock slipped inside, locking them together.

As their bodies meshed, Anton felt Keisha's thoughts swirling deep inside his mind. He opened to her, felt the strength of their link, the power behind the mating bond. The fine line between Keisha and Anton melded, wavered, became one single entity.

He was the bitch, welcoming the heavier weight of the male, the thickness of his cock thrusting deep inside her channel. The solid knot slipped through and her muscles trapped him, only he felt as if his clenching muscles held them close . . . and it was Anton's cock that was trapped . . . but he was Keisha, and she was Anton and they were one. A single creature, its multifaceted body trapped in the lush power of orgasm, mind fragmented and rebuilt into a single thought, a single voice. A singular, powerful love.

They toppled to the soft grass together, bodies still tied, sides heaving, limbs shaking. And Anton finally had the answer. He knew how Adam could help Eve.

Adam stood just outside Eve's room and glared at Anton. "No. That's sick. It's just flat-out wrong."

"You can reach her. You can heal her if you bond. Make love to her, link with her . . ."

Nausea roiled through Adam's gut. Anger at Anton, at the entire situation. He *fixed* things, damn it. Why the hell couldn't he fix Eve? "She's unconscious. Sex with her like this, no matter the intention, would be the same as rape. I can't believe you'd even suggest it. Damn it, Anton . . ." He turned away, scared, disgusted, frustrated. She was still unconscious. He couldn't stand it, couldn't imagine how he would go on if Eve died. Finally Adam pulled his anger under control. Barely. "Besides, we can't bond as humans. We bond as wolves, right?"

Anton grabbed his arm and spun him around. Adam had never seen him angry, never witnessed the steely strength in Anton's eyes, the pure physical power in his grasp. He looked down at his arm, at the spot where Anton grasped him so tight he wondered if the bones might crack.

Anton followed the direction of Adam's gaze. He shuddered, shook his head and turned Adam loose. He took a deep breath, let it out. Visibly sought control. "I'm sorry. You're right. I know you're right, but we have to save her. You're the only one who can do it." He turned away and his shoulders slumped. The power seemed to have gone out of him, along with his anger. "I need a shower. I'll check back with you later."

Adam watched as Anton walked slowly down the long hallway. His thoughts were a jumbled mess. Anton Cheval was his mentor, teacher to all of them. Seeing him like that, hopeless, powerless, frightened Adam more than he wanted to admit.

Shit, if Anton was giving up hope . . . No. Eve needed his strength, and if she couldn't get if from the pack leader, she'd have to get it from Adam. He turned and went back into Eve's room, shed his pants and crawled into bed beside her. She lay perfectly quiet, perfectly beautiful. If he hadn't seen the injury beneath her skull, he would have thought she merely slept. Curious, he wondered if she had healed at all over the last few hours.

He pulled Eve against his chest and stroked her hair. Alone, without Mei and Oliver, without Anton's added strength, he wasn't sure he could go as deep inside her mind as he'd gone a few hours ago. He let his eyes fall shut, focused his thoughts and pressed his lips against Eve's temple.

Adam?

Her mental voice was weak, but it was there! "Eve!" He caught himself, kissed her softly, used his mind. *Eve. Wake up, sweetheart. Can you wake up?*

I've been trying. I can feel you beside me but it's as if there's a huge weight on my head, as if something is holding me here in the dark.

You've been injured. I think your head hit the rocks when the bear swatted you aside. Anton thinks that if we make love, if we link during climax, the strength of the bond might be enough to bring you back.

If that's so, why haven't you tried?

He wasn't sure if he wanted to laugh or cry. Damn, if it worked, he owed Anton an apology. *I was afraid it would make you hate me, having sex with you without your knowledge. It felt like rape, like what you were running away from.*

He heard Eve's gentle laughter in his mind. *Oh, Adam. We never just have sex. You make love to me. It's not the same, my love. Don't you know that by now?*

He smiled and brushed his lips across her temple. Her eyes flickered, but they didn't open. *I should have figured it out, sweetie. I'm just a slow learner, I guess.*

Once again she laughed, but it was silent, deep inside her injured mind. He kissed her lips and felt her sigh in his heart, but she didn't kiss him back. He moved lower and took her nipple between his lips and gently tugged. The soft areola slowly tightened and her nipple puckered into a taut nub. His throat ached and his eyes burned with unshed tears. Even unconscious, her body reacted.

He kissed his way along her ribs, ran his tongue around the soft swell of her belly and dipped into her navel. He kissed the line between thigh and groin and rubbed his chin in the soft curls covering her pubic mound. Carefully, so as not to hurt her, he spread her legs apart and nestled himself between her thighs.

Is this okay? Are you . . .

Don't stop. I feel . . .

She sounded sleepy, as if mindtalking exhausted her, but when he nuzzled the damp folds between her legs, he felt her juices begin to flow. Slowly, with infinite care, Adam made love to her with his mouth. He missed the silly banter, the soft sighs, the clutching fingers that always tangled in his long hair. He missed the way her body writhed to get closer to his searching tongue, but he wallowed in her taste and her feminine scent, suckled at the sweetly swollen labia protecting her sex. When he circled her clitoris with his tongue, he felt a ripple run through her abdomen.

She was wet and ready for him, but still Adam paused. He knelt between her thighs and the thick crown of his penis rode in the creamy fluids between her legs. "I love you, Eve. Come back." He watched her face, praying for a blink, a smile. Nothing.

"Damn you, Anton Cheval. I hope to hell you're right." He lifted her hips in his hands, to the angle Eve would have taken if she were able. His cock slipped between her folds and he felt the hot sheath of her channel clasping him. Pulling him forward or trying to keep him out?

He wasn't sure. He thrust harder and finally connected with the mouth of her womb. She lay completely still. Tears ran down his face and blinded him, but that was a good thing. Making love all alone was the loneliest thing he'd ever done.

Adam slowly withdrew, then thrust forward again, and with this deepest penetration, he tried to connect with Eve. He felt her, a pale copy of the vibrant woman who loved him so powerfully, who gave so much more than she took. *If you're there, Eve, you have to help me. I can't do this alone. Link with me. Let me know what you're feeling. Tell me how I can help.*

More, Adam. Harder. Make me part of you.

He grabbed Eve's comatose body and lifted her as he sat back on his heels. She loved to make love this way, her legs wrapped around his waist, the weight of her body forcing him deep inside. He rested her head against his shoulder, held her arms around his waist and pressed hard and deep. He felt her thoughts and knew she tried to link, and he used his own mind to bridge the gap.

Close, so very close, but her body had yet to respond. Adam slipped a hand between them and found the small prepuce protecting her clit. Slippery with her cream, it was beginning to swell, rising out of its little hood. He touched her, stroked her gently, felt the juices flow between them.

Her nipples grazed his chest, twin peaks of taut flesh. Her hips seemed to sway just a bit closer, the muscles in her vagina clamped down on his cock. Her eyes were still closed, but there was a soft, sensual curve to her lips. Once again he searched for her thoughts, tried to make the connection. A shudder ran through Eve. He felt her hands moving over his back, felt renewed strength in her legs.

Then it happened. The link he'd prayed for, wished for. His cock pressed against her cervix and he felt it, felt the pressure deep inside, only as Eve would know. Her arousal grew and it swirled through Adam. His nipples ached, his clit throbbed, his inner muscles clenched against the thick, hot penis invading her flesh.

The link grew stronger, the sensations increased. Eve's climax neared. Adam struggled to control his own release. He leaned over and drew Eve's left nipple into his mouth. Her heart beat a rapid tattoo against his lips, her skin was flushed with sweat and a rosy blush.

He tilted his hips, drove inside her—harder, deeper, penetrating as far as their bodies allowed. Eve arched against him, her lips parted, her mind opened to his every thought, every need.

Adam slipped inside her mind even as his cock claimed her body. The injury was visible, there with her jumbled thoughts and powerful emotions. He gathered up the blood cells that had leaked from the injury to her skull, absorbed them into himself in a link that was as physical as it was emotional. He took Eve's pain, her injuries, the tiny clots and damaged tissues and left only healthy cells behind.

He wasn't even sure how it happened, or what he had done to make her right. He only knew that he had done all he possibly could. Panting and blowing as if he'd just run a mile, Adam slowly withdrew from Eve's thoughts, from her brain. He kept their bodies linked. Carefully, he lay Eve back down in the rumpled sheets and balanced his weight on his elbows. His cock still rested inside her warmth and he felt the steady throb and pulse of her waning climax.

"Open your eyes, my lovely Eve. Open them for me."

He watched and waited, praying for her response. His heart felt as if it would beat right out of his chest. His throat burned and tightened, his voice was a harsh whisper. "I love you, Eve. It's not fair to make me wait like this. Open your eyes. Please sweetheart. For me?"

Her lashes fluttered, stopped. Fluttered again. Slowly, as if coming out of a long sleep, Eve opened her eyes. She blinked. Closed them. Opened again. Reached up with her left hand and touched the tears rolling down his face. "Adam? Are you okay?"

There were no words—he couldn't speak. Couldn't have said a word if his life depended on it. Nodding in disbelief, in thanks, Adam clenched his jaw against the cry trapped in his throat. He cupped her face in his hands, kissed her lips and emotion overtook him. Finally, he lowered his face to her warm breasts, and wept.

Oliver awakened alone in his bed. The shades were still drawn and the cottage quiet. He sent out a searching thought, but couldn't find Mei. She'd come back here with him, made love with him, but they'd still not talked about her shift.

He needed to talk. Had to find out if she was willing to find a way to make this work. Bending over, he picked a pair of cotton boxers up off the floor and slipped them on. Then he padded out into the main room to look for Mei.

There was no sign of her. He headed toward the bathroom and opened the door. A snow leopard sat on the counter, staring at herself in the mirror.

"Holy shit, Mei. You scared the crap out of me!"

Laughing, Oliver went to stand beside her. She snarled, but there was no threat in the sound. She leaned close and sniffed him, and the loud chuffing noise she made seemed to cover all sorts of emotions. She watched him with her big, green eyes, but it was strange, not being able to understand her thoughts.

She turned away and looked back at herself in the mirror. Oliver studied her reflection, as well as his own. She was beautiful, her pale coat decorated in a blend of gray and dark brown rosettes and her eyes, while mostly green, looked almost blue beneath the bright light here in the bathroom.

Damn how he loved her, but making this work seemed completely impossible. He was Chanku, a wolven shapeshifter, finally, after a lifetime of hoping one day to find his true nature.

He'd always wanted to find love, as well, and he'd found it with Mei. Unfortunately, her nature and his were about as incompatible as anything he could imagine. Even Anton had never heard of anyone turning into a cat. They were always wolves. Only wolves.

Except Mei.

He reached out and touched her fur, rubbing his fingers through the thick coat. It felt like silk to him. Her long, thick tail hung down from the counter where she sat. In the thick of battle, when she'd attacked that bear without any fear for her own safety, he'd watched how she used her tail, how it helped to balance her leaps and control her twists and turns.

She was a perfect snow leopard. Beautiful, strong, and very brave. And he was totally wrong for her mate. "Mei, what the fuck are we going to do? I love you."

She shifted, right there on the counter. Her image shimmered and suddenly she sat there like a child, knees drawn up against her chest and her long, black hair falling all around her and pooling in silken swirls on the cold tile counter. She tilted her head and her hair shimmered under the bright light. "I can't understand you very well when I'm the leopard. The language is . . . I dunno." She sighed. "Yet you can understand human speech when you're a wolf. I mean, so can I, but not as well as you do. Why is that?"

He shook his head. "I don't know. It's all new, all a big question." He took her hands in his and turned her around so that her legs hung over the edge of the tile counter. They dangled, long and inviting. "All I said is that I love you."

Mei blinked and two big tears spilled out beneath her lashes. "I love you, too, but what are we going to do? You guys all talk about that important mating bond, but you do it when you're wolves." She tried to laugh and it came out as a sob. "That ain't gonna happen. We can't even communicate."

"We do just fine when we're human." He leaned close and licked one salty tear off her cheek.

Mei bit her lips and sniffed back more tears. Then she spread her knees wider and he stepped between them. They'd both been too keyed up to sleep after leaving Eve's bedside. Their powerful Chanku libidos led them into bed, but for the first time since they'd met, the sex between them was unsatisfactory. Mei had climaxed and burst into tears. Oliver hadn't found his release. He'd pulled out as soon as Mei's body shuddered and her emotions gave way.

The counter was the perfect height. Mei's smooth skin felt like satin. Her soft nether lips glistened with moisture. Oliver leaned close and blew gently against the tiny hood protecting her clit. He saw her muscles clench and release, and her clitoris seemed to swell beyond its collar. He touched the very tip of her clit, then softly laved it with his tongue.

Mei leaned back and thrust her hips forward. Slowly, Oliver knelt on the soft rug in front of the sink and carefully spread Mei's legs apart. Her scent was spicy, different from what he remembered, and he knew the first shift had forever altered her flavors.

She might be a cat and he a wolf, but her taste made his groin tighten and his heart raise its tempo. He licked between her folds, driving his tongue deep inside her slippery channel. The taste drew him and he moaned against her sex and lapped her cream as if she offered him ambrosia.

Mei whimpered, a small, tight sound deep in her throat. "You're making me crazy." She grabbed at his arms and tried to drag him up, but he held on to her thighs and worked her wet folds with teeth and tongue and lips. She was strong and her legs locked behind his shoulders, but he held her squirming body in place and ravaged her sensitive tissues.

He sensed her climax, felt her arousal spike and witnessed the kaleidoscope of colors flashing behind her eyes. They were both Chanku and both spoke the same language, a dialect of sensation and arousal, of overwhelming desire and a lush craving for more. Oliver suckled her clit between his lips and thrust three fingers deep in her sex.

Mei screamed. She arched her back, her legs clamped down, her hands pulled at his arms, his shoulders, clawed his back. He fucked her with his hand, laved her with his tongue, and loved her with all his heart. Her body shuddered with each stroke of his tongue, and her inner muscles clamped tightly around his fingers.

When he finally pulled away, Oliver held his hand up to his lips and licked them clean of her juices, sucking each of his fingers into his mouth while she watched with wide and wary eyes. His balls ached, those orbs he'd wished for all his life. They reminded him how much he'd gained . . . and how much he had to lose. His cock tented the front of his boxers. Holding Mei's gaze with his own, he slipped the baggy shorts down over his legs.

He'd never been so big or felt so hard. His cock was

WOLF TALES VI / 207

heavy with blood. Usually it rose to touch his belly when he was aroused, but tonight it jutted out, perpendicular to his body, aimed for Mei's soft center. The veins crossed his shaft, pulsing with life. A tiny drop of white bubbled at the dark tip.

Mei reached out, slowly, and ran her finger across the crown, then just as slowly raised her fingertip to her mouth. She sucked and her eyes closed. Oliver felt her pleasure, tasted the salty flavor of his own fluids. He waited. Mei scooted forward, grasped the thickened shaft and rubbed him across her damp folds.

A shock ricocheted from penis to balls and back down his cock. Oliver groaned, clenched his buttocks and thrust forward. Her fingers circled him, but it took both her hands to hold him. She dragged one of her palms through the fluids between her legs and used her own juices to lubricate his shaft. She did the same with her other hand. Then she slowly stroked him, sliding the soft skin over what had to be the hardest boner he'd ever had.

Oliver groaned again and fell into Mei's rhythm, free-falling into her warmth, her desire, her magic touch. Pumping his hips slowly, he fucked her hands, fighting for control while she squeezed and teased his greedy flesh. Her shields were up and he couldn't read her thoughts, but from the lazy smile on her face he knew she loved what she did to him.

He thrust forward once more and found himself entering her creamy center. Her hands caught his hips and she pulled him forward, deeper. He slid into her tight sheath, past the rippling muscles, past the smooth lips of her pussy, deep inside her channel until he felt the hard mouth of her womb. His balls rested against her hot perineum and the cold tile counter. The mixed sensations, heat and warmth and tight, clasping muscles, and cold, hard ceramic tile almost took him over the top.

"You're trying to kill me, aren't you?" He placed his hands flat down on the tile and thrust forward a little bit more. Mei moaned.

"Never. God, Oliver. Do that again."

He did. And again, until he was plunging into her like a pile driver. He wrapped his fingers around her butt and held on tight to keep her from sliding across the cool tile. Her legs wrapped tighter around his waist and she opened her thoughts once again, opened to desire, to all the love he poured into her.

And she gave it back, tenfold. Mei's need, her fears, her excitement over her shift, and her anger that she'd become something different, something that might keep her away from the only man she'd ever loved.

Oliver knew he was that man. Knew he loved Mei every bit as much. He felt her sex clamp down on his cock, felt her squeezing him and holding him deep inside. He threw back his head and howled and the thick streams of his ejaculate filled her as he pumped his life force deep inside.

And when they were done, when he leaned over Mei with his breath coming in short, sharp gasps, he saw his seed flowing from her sex. Pooling on the tile between her legs, nothing more than a thick, creamy fluid she had no use for.

They couldn't bond. Couldn't mate in their feral forms. They were both Chanku, but the mating bond was impossible.

He loved her, admired her. Needed her. But would love alone be enough to overcome an obstacle none of them had ever faced? He'd been willing to leave his pack and stay with Mei if it turned out she couldn't shift.

The question now was, would Mei be willing to stay with Oliver? Would love be enough to overcome their totally different natures?

He leaned forward and kissed Mei and her taste and

scent held him like a vise. There had to be a way. There was always a way.

He raised his head, to ask her, to tell her how much he loved her. Suddenly Anton's voice echoed in his head. Mei's eye's went wide. They both heard the message at the same time.

Eve's awake. She's okay. Adam brought her back.

Chapter 12

"I remember charging the grizzly and thinking, you know, girl . . . this might not be your smartest move." Eve laughed, then shook her head. "After that, nothing. I don't even remember getting hit." She rubbed her hand over the bandage on her shoulder and smiled at Adam.

Stefan, for once, actually seemed to be in a serious mood. "You were damned lucky you weren't killed."

Eve nodded. "I know. Even luckier I had Adam." She laughed again and winked at Stefan. "I always knew he was a good mechanic. I had no idea his talents included brain surgery."

"Neither did I." Adam squeezed her hand. "I never would have attempted it if Anton hadn't threatened me."

Anton walked out from the kitchen with a fresh bottle of wine. "That was not a threat," he said. "Merely a suggestion I fully expected you to follow." He poured himself a glass and held it up to Adam as a toast. "When Adam and I met, he told me he could fix things. I've learned to take him at his word. Here's to our resident repairman. A man with a most unusual and amazing talent."

The others raised their glasses. Adam dipped his head in acknowledgement. Then he sat back, even closer to Eve and wrapped his arm around her shoulders. He listened to the ebb and flow of voices as everyone talked about Eve's injury and Mei's unusual shift. They'd gathered here on the shady side of the deck, sipping at wine and munching on crackers and cheese as if Eve's life hadn't been in the balance only hours before.

As if Mei hadn't shocked everyone with her unusual shift. But that, of course, was the reason the entire pack was here. To celebrate the women. To talk about Mei and remind her she was one of them, no matter what. To see for themselves that Eve was all right. To let her know how much they loved her, how glad they were she'd survived.

Adam understood why Oliver stayed so close to Mei. He felt the same protective urges with Eve. He couldn't take his hands off her, needed reassurance she was okay, proof her terrible injuries had completely healed. He shuddered, remembering his fear when he first looked inside her brain and saw the damage, and he'd wondered if he would ever hold Eve in his arms again.

Would his fear have been even stronger, had they already bonded? Or would it have been less? He couldn't imagine anything worse, but there was no doubt in Adam's mind that they would bond as soon as Eve felt strong enough. He couldn't wait to take her into the woods, just the two of them. Two wolves in the forest, mating in a ritual as old and primal as anything either of them would ever experience.

He glanced once more at Oliver and Mei. That was something his friends would never know, that mystical connection of two bestial minds connecting on a level more primitive, more intense than their mere human minds could ever know. If only there was some way to help them.

He tried to imagine what that connection was like, the powerful link even stronger than what he'd felt when he healed Eve this morning.

I healed her. Shit. He still couldn't wrap his head

around that one. He was a mechanic, damn it all, not a doctor, but he'd done the equivalent of brain surgery when he'd removed the clot. Was there something going on in him even he didn't understand?

Did he have abilities he'd never recognized? Adam glanced down at his hands. They were scarred and stained, the nails chipped and broken from years of working on mechanical things. A mechanic's hands. Not a doctor's.

But what he did didn't take clean hands or manicured fingernails. It took the ability to fix what was broken.

He'd always had a talent for seeing what was wrong. He could diagnose any problem in just about any kind of machine, and if he couldn't find the right part to repair it, he'd build his own. He wasn't sure how he knew what to do. He just did.

Did he do that for Oliver? *Build* him new parts? Ollie's balls were definitely new. Adam tried to reconstruct that fateful night when he'd helped Oliver shift for the first time. He had no idea what he'd done, but he knew what he had wanted to happen, beyond the mere act of helping Oliver change from human to wolf.

The same way he'd known what needed fixing when he got inside Eve's mind. Eve had been broken. So had Oliver.

He glanced again at Mei. She wasn't broken. She was just different. There was nothing there he could fix, but damn it, he wished he could. She and Oliver sat close together, hands tightly clasped, eyes downcast. He sensed their deep sorrow and knew they had to be absolutely miserable. What would it be like, knowing you could never fully bond with the one you loved?

He felt Eve's warm body beside him and wanted that bond with her now, more than ever. As soon as she felt strong enough.

Mei was as strong and healthy as she could be. So was Oliver. Without something broken, there really was nothing to fix, but if there was a way to help, he'd do it in a heartbeat. Adam looked away. Damn, it hurt not to help them, but their problem was beyond him.

Not necessarily.

Adam jerked his chin up and stared across the deck. Anton Cheval smiled at him. Adam shook his head. *Are you nuts?*

Not at all. Look what you did for Eve. The way you healed Oliver . . . find a way to help them. You can, you know.

I don't know how. They're not broken. They're two separate species.

Are they? Anton cocked one dark eyebrow.

He's a wolf. She's a fucking snow leopard. Frustration made him angry. Damn, he'd help if he could. There was just no way.

You'll figure it out. Anton flashed a grin that dared Adam to argue.

He glowered at the wizard a moment and then forced himself to relax. Anton loved questions without answers. Adam preferred answers. He hugged Eve. She was his answer to everything, but they'd still not bonded. He needed her, now more than ever. He'd come so close to losing her. Too close.

Eve snuggled against his chest and looked up at him. *Later.*

The seductive promise in her eyes hit him right in the groin. He tried to make light of it, whimpered pathetically and looked at her with crossed eyes.

Eve laughed.

Are you serious? Are you strong enough?

Definitely. She nuzzled her face against his arm. *Tonight. Preferably somewhere without bears. We can skip the hunt, too.*

Adam laughed and hugged her close. The others glanced up from their conversations. He'd forgotten they were still the center of attention. Eve blushed. Adam merely checked his watch, then sighed and let his mind wander ahead. Tonight couldn't get here soon enough.

"Mei? Do you mind?"

Anton's voice jolted Adam out of his momentary euphoria. He glanced over at Anton and frowned. What the hell was he up to, now? The wizard had gotten up from his chair. He stood in front of Mei with his hand out. She hesitated a moment and then reached for him. He pulled her to her feet. "Will you come with me for a moment?"

Oliver began to rise. Anton shook his head. "Please. I want to talk to Mei by herself for a moment. Won't you trust me with the woman you love?"

"I trust you with my life." Oliver sat back down. "But that doesn't mean I like the idea of you taking Mei off by herself."

"I promise to return her to you unharmed." Anton laughed and tugged Mei's hand. She followed him into the house, but Adam noticed she glanced over her shoulder more than once, watching Oliver.

What in the hell was Anton up to now?

Anton led her inside the house, through the foyer and down the long hallway. Mei didn't have a clue where he was taking her. She tried to tug her hand free of his grasp. Anton immediately released his grip. "I'm sorry. I don't want to frighten you, Mei. Please relax. I'm really quite harmless."

"Said the spider to the fly." Mei cocked one eyebrow in Anton's direction and he burst out laughing. She hated the fact he was so attractive when he laughed, and she wondered if that was her damned Chanku libido acting up. Oliver hadn't been kidding when he said sexual attraction took on a whole new meaning once a person went through their first shift.

"We're going to my study. It's quiet, and far enough

from Oliver that his powerful male curiosity won't get in the way of what I hope to find out from you."

"What exactly is that, Anton?" She planted her feet and stared at him. She was tired of feeling as if she'd done something wrong. Tired of the condescending looks and all the theories about why she was different. She'd always been different. Always been a loner, so it wasn't like it was all that big a deal. Hell, it wasn't her fault she'd turned into a leopard instead of a wolf. Why did everyone act like it was such a bad thing?

Anton shook his head. "It's not a bad thing at all, and yes, I can see everything you're thinking." He held up his hands in apology. "I'm sorry. I don't mean to snoop, but you do wear your emotions and your thoughts on your sleeve. And Mei, before you get angry because I know what's going on in that amazing mind of yours, I want to say you have every right for your anger and your confusion—but not your mistrust of me or any of the others. We have only your best interests at heart."

She stared at him a moment. His thoughts were totally unreadable. Now that really pissed her off. At least with Oliver she could see into his head as well as he looked into hers. "So you're saying I can trust you, and I'm supposed to believe you?"

Anton smiled at her. He really was absolutely gorgeous when he smiled. His usually austere face lit up, his eyes sparkled and there was such a wonderful sense of mischief about him. "Well, in most matters, yes." He leaned over and kissed her lightly on the lips. "I will even promise not to try and seduce you—for now. It wouldn't be fair without Oliver here to defend your honor."

He opened the door to the study and ushered Mei inside before she could come up with any kind of answer. The man threw her totally off balance. She'd never been in this room before, but the house was so massive she knew

216 / Kate Douglas

there was a lot of it she hadn't had time to explore. It was dark and cool inside. Books lined the shelves and the rich aroma of what had to be either pipe or cigars added a light perfume.

She wondered if Oliver had ever been invited in here, or if he'd merely served Anton and Stefan and then quietly departed. All those years, alone, apart from the pack he wanted so desperately to join. She glanced over her shoulder at Anton. Was he reading her thoughts now? Did he know why she refused to hold him in such high esteem? The others seemed to think he was all-powerful, but he'd failed the truest friend he could ever have.

"I know." Anton bowed his head, accepting her unspoken anger. "In many, many ways I failed him, even though I loved Oliver from the very beginning." He reached into a glass cabinet and brought out a bottle of cognac, poured two small glasses and handed one to Mei. "I had no idea he'd been mutilated as a child, though I sensed there was something different about him. Later, once I discovered my own shapeshifting background, I sensed he was Chanku as well, but the nutrients had no effect."

"So you made him a servant? One step up from the slave he'd been? How generous of you." She took a sip of her cognac and coughed. It burned! She'd never tasted anything like it.

"It wasn't like that, Mei. He asked if he could work for me when I left the circus. He was ready to move on as well. Oliver is a much more organized individual than I will ever be. He took on the role of my personal assistant of his own choice. That was the job he wanted, in the beginning. Before we knew anything at all about Chanku." Anton leaned against the heavy oak table and crossed his feet at the ankles. Mei took a seat in one of the big, leather wingback chairs.

"He told me he'd met you in the circus."

Anton smiled and nodded. "A lifetime ago. Before I

took my magic act to the stage, I worked in a small circus. We wintered in Florida, and that's where I met Oliver. He was a beautiful young man. I was not yet aware I was Chanku. We became friends."

"Were you lovers?"

"We might have been, had he been interested. I have never been concerned with my, or anyone else's, sexual orientation. I loved fucking, whatever my partner—or partners'—sex. I'd never met a man without any libido at all. Oliver had no interest in me sexually, but he wanted my friendship." Anton sipped his cognac and stared out the window. "I had no friends before Oliver. None. I am not an easy man to know."

"Duh. That's because you're scary." Or he had been, before this wonderful glass of cognac. She took another sip. False courage? No matter. It appeared to be working.

Anton laughed. "Ah, to everyone but you, my brave little snow leopard. You show no fear of me at all! When I left the circus to take my magic act on the stage, Oliver went with me. I helped him gain his citizenship. He honored me by taking my name." He smiled at Mei. "I never expected children, but then I never, in my wildest dreams, expected to find a woman like Keisha. Oliver was my friend, my son, my closest confidant. Sometimes he was my father. He cared for me, and I for him. We still do, both of us, care for one another."

Mei stared into her glass, wondering where this conversation would lead. "It's his way," she said. "Oliver cares for people the way Adam fixes things. With all his heart."

"That he does. He stayed with me through my years onstage in Las Vegas and in Hollywood. I was very successful. I made a lot of money and invested it well. Before long, I had enough to move on with my life and do what I really wanted. I quit performing to study necromancy and went from the bright lights on stage to the dark corridors of museums and universities. I spent my time reading ancient tomes in travels across Europe. Oliver traveled with me and he took over the role of my caretaker. If not for him, I'd probably have starved and ended up naked on a street corner, so caught up was I in my research."

Anton's laugh sounded unusually self-conscious. "I would forget to eat, forget to bathe. I was very single-minded in my pursuit of the skills of wizardry."

Mei stared at him. "Is that what necromancy is? That's crazy! You're telling me you wanted to be a sorcerer?"

Anton laughed and held his glass up in a toast. "Don't jest. Never disbelieve something you don't understand. The more I studied, the more I understood, and the more I believed. There is magic in this world, Mei. That's how I discovered my heritage. Our heritage. I learned about the Chanku through references in ancient scrolls and old legends, and in doing so, I discovered what had been missing in my life. Once I shifted, I also realized something that made absolutely no sense, in the overall scheme of things. The one man I was closest to appeared to share the same genetic abilities as I did. What were the odds of that?"

Mei watched him carefully. As he talked, Anton's cool and formal manner seemed to fade. Animated now, he smiled and gestured. "I learned all I could of Chanku history. I had already formed my own theory that the ability to shift had been lost due to some unknown ingredient in the diet, since they could no longer shift once they left their ancestral homeland. I was drawn to a group of grasses native to the Himalayan steppe and nowhere else. I collected a wide variety of plants, dried them, and ate some every day. Even so, you can't imagine the emotions I experienced when I suddenly realized I had the ability to become a wolf."

"Were you expecting it to happen?" Mei thought of her own expectations, and what a shock it had been to suddenly be something other.

"Oh yes. I knew the Chanku became wolves, but in the

back of my mind existed a huge reservoir of doubt. What if this was just fantasy? How could I be sure? But shortly after I began ingesting the grasses, I felt the changes in my body begin and knew I was no longer entirely human. My eyesight, my hearing, my perception of sound and sight. It was all changing. When I finally shifted, the sense of relief was amazing, but something else happened as well. That's when I realized, with my enhanced perception, that Oliver could be just like me."

"Did you tell him about it?"

"No." He rolled his eyes in a terribly non-Anton gesture. "Can you just see trying to explain that one? He knew I was studying necromancy, but had no idea what I had learned. I'd kept my information about the Chanku entirely secret from him. Instead, I added the nutrients to his food, fully expecting him to join me as a wolf. He would be the first of my new pack. I had it all planned out, only it didn't work the way I expected. Oliver gained telepathic abilities almost at once, but was unable to shift. By then we had become close enough, he'd told me about his horrible childhood. I realized his emasculation had cost him that part of his heritage. He'd been cheated out of something he'd never missed. Now he missed it. Terribly. And it was my fault."

"You must have felt really horrible." At least she hoped he had. Anton appeared to have a habit of disregarding those around him.

He nodded. "Unfortunately, you're quite right. Keisha is trying to cure me of my shortcomings." He smiled.

"Is it working?"

This time Anton shrugged and his sheepish expression made her laugh. "Not very well."

"Well, now that we have that out in the open . . ." Mei sipped her cognac. She wondered if Anton realized how open he was being with her. He so rarely talked about his private life, or his own shortcomings. "What about Stefan?" She'd been curious about him. Stefan appeared to have so many different sides, from clown to thoughtful mate and father, to loyal friend. "How did he end up here?"

"Ah, Stefan. Stefan Aragat was a famous magician. His star was rising as mine was falling, but then I was pursuing other knowledge that took me out of the public eye. It was during a time when Oliver had returned to Barbados, hoping to discover something more of his own history, and I was alone. Stefan came to me. He begged me to teach him what I knew of necromancy. We were young, so full of ourselves and cocky as hell, but I was his mentor and I relished the role.

"As soon as Stefan came to my home, I sensed he, too, must be like me and I decided to find out. I never thought of the dangers of what I was doing when I added the nutrients to his food without telling him. I figured he would suddenly find out he could become a wolf and I would tell him all about my wonderful discovery. He would then, of course, revere my brilliance."

The self mockery in his voice stripped away the humor and left Anton looking bereft. He swallowed, seemed to gather himself, and his eyes glittered when he looked at Mei.

"You think I'm an egotistical pain in the ass, don't you?" He laughed. "Don't worry, my dear. You're not alone. It's my nature. I figure as long as Keisha can put up with me and still love me, that's all that matters. However, Stefan was many times worse. He was determined to beat me at my own game, to be the better magician, the more powerful wizard. Now we understand the dynamics of two alpha males, but then we had no idea how to make it work. We argued shortly after I began giving him the nutrients. I demanded an apology. He refused. I cursed him." Anton paused and took a deep breath.

"I cursed him, and he shifted. Only the shift was partial

because he hadn't had enough of the grasses for his body to completely change from human to Chanku. He crouched there in shock, half wolf, half man. Terrified, furious, but more frightened than anything. I tried to explain what had happened. He would have none of it and ordered me to change him back." Anton laughed. "He ordered me, with a voice twisted and almost impossible to understand, and I was such an arrogant bastard, I refused. I didn't have the courage to tell him I had no idea *how* to change him, and I didn't know enough yet to realize he merely needed more of the nutrient to complete his shift. I demanded his apology. I was his master and he had wronged me. Hell, I accused him of hubris, yet no one was more guilty of it than I."

Mei thought of the easy camaraderie between Stefan and Anton, their obvious love for one another. It was impossible to imagine how much they must have hated one another then.

"Not hate." Anton held up his hand. "I know. Stop snooping." He laughed and took another sip of his cognac. "I arranged for a driver to come and get him. He had paws and there was no way he could drive. Completely disguised, he managed to get to his home in Oregon without the media catching wind of his changed condition. I arranged for Oliver to go to work for him, to keep an eye on Stefan for me. I felt guilt, but not so much that I worried about making him better. In my mind, he deserved what had happened. What I didn't realize at the time was how much of my anger and dislike was a result of the true emotion I felt for Stefan. I loved him. Passionately, but I didn't understand my own convoluted feelings, nor was I aware of the impact the grasses had on the libido. The arousal, the desire I felt for Stefan, manifested itself as anger, an emotion I understood much better."

Mei stared into her glass, thinking of all she had learned. Wondering how it applied to her. "How did you end up . . ." She flipped her hand, searching for the words. "Here, where you're obviously the best of friends."

"Alexandria was the key. She fell in love with Stefan while he was still partially a beast. That spurred him to come here, to apologize and ask me to change him back. That's when we finally discovered, with Alexandria's less than subtle prodding, that he and I loved each other. Desired each other. I also discovered that this lovely woman was just like me and Stefan. I gave both of them the nutrient, and both of them shifted within the week."

"And what of Oliver."

"He was here waiting when Stefan arrived. Stefan finally understood that I'd not abandoned him, that I'd sent Oliver to watch over him. I just hadn't learned enough about our species to help him. The thing is, Mei, Alexandria found Stefan . . . actually, he found her when he rescued her in a blinding snowstorm. Oliver found me. Stefan came to me. We were somehow drawn to one another, and I believe it has to do with our Chanku genes. Eve left a man she loves to return to Florida for no special reason, but she found you. Adam was hitchhiking when Oliver drove past him. The truck broke down right in front of a man who fixes things, one who is also Chanku. The stories go on and on and on, for every single one of us. Somehow, we all find one another. I believe in fate, Mei. Stefan and I tease one another with our silly 'coincidence versus destiny' argument, but there's no denying the unbelievable sequence of events that have brought all of us together."

"Except all of you are Chanku wolves, and I'm a snow leopard. Explain that." Her glass was empty and she set it down, harder than she'd intended. It clattered loudly on the table beside her chair. Anton immediately added more of the dark, golden liquid. He stayed there, standing over her.

"I can't explain it, which is why I brought you here, why I've told you some of our history. I want you to trust me enough to let me inside your head. Not a mating bond, but a link every bit as deep as that you feel with Oliver. I'm asking you to share my bed. Just you and me. You will learn things about me I've shared with no one else but my mate. Keisha understands and agrees. I hope to learn things from you that will teach me more about all of us."

Anton stepped away and set the decanter on his desk. He turned around and leaned against the edge again, as if he'd not just thrown her for an emotional loop. "I have not spoken to Oliver because I wanted your permission, first. If you agree, you can discuss this alone with him, or I will go with you. It's up to you. Mei, I want to know if the beast we become is due to our nature, or if it's merely the way our brain perceives the change. Do we all have the ability to become more than one creature? Can you also become a wolf, Oliver a leopard? Can you both become horses or birds? Can any of us choose the creature we become, or is it somehow hardwired into our brain? I don't know, but I want to find out. I have to, and you are the key. With your permission, we may be able to learn more about ourselves than we ever have in the past. To do this, you have to trust me."

Mei blinked. Trust had never come easy, but she'd never loved before, either. She loved Oliver. Anton held out the hope she and the man she loved might somehow be able to mate, to become a bonded pair. All Anton asked was to take her to bed and have wild monkey sex—and fuck with her brain at the same time.

No problem. Right? Could she do it? Maybe, if Oliver agreed. It wasn't as if Anton didn't turn her on, even if he was an old guy. No, just the opposite. She found him extremely sexy, and Oliver had been right. She could think of sex with Anton without guilt.

Oliver had explained the changes that happened once they started taking the nutrients, how the brain seemed to completely rewire itself. He'd explained the lack of jealousy among packmates, how sex was an important part of the pack's interaction. She'd thought he was kidding, but the day they all climbed into bed together in that motel had certainly opened her eyes. They'd made love to her with the same purpose, though. They wanted to get inside her mind, and she'd agreed. She'd been excited seeing Oliver and Eve together, she'd loved Adam's touch, loved the sense of sharing.

That's what it was, after all. Sharing. Bodies, thoughts, needs . . . desires. Anton wanted even more. He wanted to share knowledge she didn't even know she possessed.

Knowledge that might allow her to bond with Oliver. Mei glanced at the cognac beside her, picked up the glass, and found it surprisingly easy, now, to swallow it down in one gulp.

Who was she to stand in the way of education? She stared at Anton a moment longer, more curious than she would have believed about his reaction. More interested than she probably should be about his plan. If she wasn't Chanku she'd think this was the worst pick-up line she'd ever heard, and she'd heard a lot of them.

But she was and it wasn't, and Anton watched her with those glittering amber eyes, the eyes of the alpha wolf, and silently demanded her acquiescence. He was not a man to beg, though she imagined he would, if that was the only way to get her into his bed. If the only reason had been for sex, she would have turned him down immediately, Chanku or not. Even if he begged.

Of course, it wasn't about sex at all. Sex was merely the means to an end, a pathway to knowledge. Odd, how it all made perfect sense to her, now. She spun the empty glass between her fingers, then looked up, expecting to see a smug expression on Anton's face. Instead, he looked unusually sympathetic.

She nodded. "Okay. I'll do whatever you ask, Anton.

So long as Keisha is okay with it, because I really love your mate. And only if Oliver agrees."

"Thank you." Such simple words for such a strange, complex situation. He gazed into the distance a moment, then held out his hand. "Oliver knows. We will hear his decision in a moment."

Then he took Mei's hand and led her back outside to the deck.

Oliver looked up when the door opened. Mei stepped out first, but it was Anton's vivid gaze that caught him. Oliver's heart stuttered in his chest. If he and Mei had already bonded, he'd not think twice of her sharing Anton's bed, but he couldn't ignore the taint of fear he felt, of the pack's ultimate alpha male bedding the woman he loved.

Yet it was the only chance of Oliver ever bonding with Mei. There was no choice other than to agree, but it wouldn't be easy, knowing they were making love, their minds linking at a level beyond anything Oliver and Mei had shared. Anton was capable of so much more than Oliver! Would it change Mei's feelings for him? Would she turn to Anton afterwards, preferring him to a lesser member of the pack?

He stood up and put his hands on Mei's shoulders. "I love you. Whatever you and Anton discover, remember I will always love you, even if it means . . ."

Mei's finger touched his lips. "Nothing negative. Anton will find the answers he needs. I love you, too." She leaned close and kissed him, and they might have been the only two people on the deck. Then Mei turned away and led Anton back inside. Oliver felt as if his heart might explode.

He loved them both. No matter what, he would always love them both.

"Oliver?"

He jerked around at the gentle touch of fingers on his

shoulder. Keisha stood behind him, smiling. Before he could speak, another set of fingers trailed in a slow, sexy dance across his back. He whipped around the other direction. "Xandi!"

Alexandria smiled. "Stefan's watching the babies. Eve and Adam just shifted and headed for the forest. I imagine they'll be gone awhile. We thought you might like to join us."

"Join you?" Why had his brain suddenly stopped functioning? It might have something to do with Xandi's scent or Keisha's warm fingers slipping beneath his loose T-shirt.

"She loves you, Oliver." Keisha found his nipple. She circled it with one perfectly manicured nail. He felt the shock all the way to his balls. "She's young and more beautiful than any woman has a right to be, but she loves you, not Anton. If she didn't, I wouldn't be standing here so calmly, hoping to seduce you." She laughed and plucked at his nipple, pinching just to the point of pain. He almost whimpered.

"Come with us. Now that we know the reason why you ignored all our invitations for so long, Xandi and I figure we have a lot of time to make up for."

"Plus, it'll keep you from sitting here thinking about Mei and Anton." Xandi leaned close and kissed him. Her lips were smooth and warm and Oliver couldn't help but kiss her back. Her tongue breached the seam of his mouth and quickly teased, and then she backed away. "I'd like to think the two of us are capable of taking your mind off one adorable little leopard."

He felt the heat in his chest expand, and it wasn't arousal so much as love. It burst out of him in laughter, the kind that healed, that made one whole. "I imagine you're right." He held his arms out, elbows cocked. Xandi slipped a hand around one, Keisha around the other. Then they led him into the house, heading in the opposite direction from the one Anton and Mei had taken.

Chapter 13

Mei's shyness evaporated the minute Anton led her into one of the guest rooms and closed the door. She wasn't certain how it happened, but all the misgivings she'd had, all the self-confidence she'd always lacked, seemed to float away. Instead, she felt a sense of her own power as a woman and her strength as a snow leopard.

She might be different from the rest of the pack, but she was no less. She was as strong, as intelligent, as beautiful.

"Yes, you are. More beautiful than even you imagine."

Anton stood on the far side of the bed. He removed his shirt, slowly unbuttoning it as he watched her with a feral gleam in his eyes. Mei slipped her own cotton top over her head.

Anton kicked his shoes off and reached for the zipper to his slacks. Mei realized she'd never seen him in shorts or even wearing a shirt that didn't button. "You're not a T-shirt and shorts kind of guy, are you?"

He laughed and shook his head. "Keisha's been trying to get me to relax my style habits. It hasn't worked." He stepped out of his pants and folded them neatly over the chair. His knit boxers didn't come close to disguising the size of his erection or the fullness of his sac.

Mei slipped out of her short skirt and stood there in her

panties. This felt so bizarre, stripping down in front of a man she barely knew, knowing she was about to get completely naked with him, have sex with him. Even more bizarre was the hot flow of fluids between her legs, the awareness of her labia swelling, her clit rising out of its prepuce.

She didn't do this. Ever. At least she didn't used to do this, but now it seemed right. Oliver said her brain was different now, her sex drive paramount, her needs more intense.

"He was right."

Mei rolled her eyes. "Are you always in my brain?"

"Most of the time. It's a fascinating brain to visit. I'm looking forward to the secrets I expect to find."

She parked her hands on her hips and thrust her breasts forward. "If that line's supposed to turn me on, it's not working."

Anton threw back his head and laughed. "Ah, Mei. I have much better methods than using a line on you." He stripped his shorts down his long legs and her mouth went dry.

Oliver was an average-sized man with a good-sized package. Anton was scary. In a good way. She licked her lips and stared, unabashed. Anton held his hand out to her. "Time for me to see if my methods work."

Still wearing her panties, Mei took Anton's hand and let him pull her onto the bed, but she lay on her side, propped up on one elbow, and stared at him. "Oliver said Chanku don't age as fast as regular humans. How old are you?"

Anton stopped, as if taken aback by her question. "I'm fifty-three."

"You barely look thirty. Is Stefan older than you?"

"No. He's younger, but the gray in his hair might make him look older." He sat on the side of the bed. Mei felt the heat from his body. Her sensitive Chanku nostrils caught the faint musky scent she recognized as aroused male. "He'll be forty-five tomorrow. It's his birthday."

"Oh, yeah. The truck." Mei drew a little design on the bedspread with her finger. "I'm twenty-seven. Does that bother you?"

"Should it?"

She shook her head and suddenly felt tired and confused. "I don't know. This is all new to me. Not just the fact I can turn into an animal, but the change in my senses, the way things smell, the way I see stuff. My perception of things is different. My needs."

"That's the biggest change. Arousal becomes a constant. Desire affects every decision we make, every thought we have. I desire you. Equally, I desire Oliver and Stefan, Xandi and Keisha. Adam and Eve. My body craves the sensual contact, the sexual release, and the connection that comes with that release. For Chanku, an orgasm isn't merely the body convulsing in pleasure. It's the mind wrapped in sensation, the heart beating in sync with one partner, or two . . . or more. It's the link during orgasm that's addictive. We never have enough. Never."

His voice was low and sexy, but it was his mind that seduced. Words of pleasure tickled and aroused her body, while something deeper, visceral, tantalized and seduced her mind.

He was linking with her, already sharing his thoughts and his own arousal, and her body responded. Oliver had said Anton's abilities were beyond description. She believed him, now. Not only the man's ability to read her thoughts, but to plant thoughts of his own.

He fantasized and shared the images. His tongue between her legs, his fingers plunging into her sex, his cock slowly filling her as his tongue made slow, leisurely love to her mouth. Caught in his mental foreplay, Mei suddenly realized he knelt between her legs and had already removed her panties. It was no longer his fantasy that filled her. Now it was his tongue, lapping at her swollen labia, tasting the juices flowing so copiously.

She lay back and moaned and her fingers clutched at the bedspread. Anton had told her this was about her pleasure, her desires, and she took without guilt, lost in sensation, her body centered on the tongue laving her sensitive tissues.

The fantasies continued as he poured them into her open mind. His tongue speared her deep, lapping from ass to clit and she spread her legs, only vaguely aware of the fur roughened shoulders between her thighs, the cold, wet nose pressing against her clitoris.

She would have opened her eyes, but the fantasy held her in its grasp. She was the leopard, but it was a wolf that pleasured her, and that couldn't be. No, she was a woman. A slim, dark-haired woman and the paws that held her still definitely belonged to a wolf.

She felt her natural blocks crumble as her arousal grew, felt the subtle pressure of another mind, unlike hers, traveling deep within her brain, flowing along her synapses and tracing the coils and loops within the gray matter that controlled the woman. The tongue speared deeper, licked harder. Her desire was a flower, opening to meet each sensual touch.

At the edge of a great abyss, the tongue deserted her, the paws disappeared, a thick shaft nestled in the sensitive valley between her thighs and slowly forced its way between her labia.

She felt the pressure again, felt the subtle intrusion of another mind, the not so subtle intrusion of thick, hard cock. He shared with her then, and she knew what Anton felt, how her vaginal walls clamped down on the velvety surface of his shaft and the way her muscles rippled along his length.

Muscles pulling him in, holding him deep inside. When he touched the mouth of her womb, she knew what he felt.

When he withdrew to thrust yet again, Mei whimpered with the pleasure Anton experienced, and she arched her hips to take him deeper. When her tissues stretched to hold his great size, she took pleasure in the tight clasp around his erection, and all the while he was there, in her head, in her thoughts.

Harder, faster, her fingers tangled in the blankets, her body a receptacle for pleasure. Hips lifting to meet each solid thrust, muscles rippling and convulsing around him, she teetered there, a scream caught in her throat, a million images flooding her mind.

She saw Anton. Knew him as she knew no other man. She wanted this with Oliver, this pure sharing, the sense of connection she'd never experienced with another person. Anton saw everything, the secrets she'd kept, the desires she'd hidden. Saw and accepted. There was no judgment in him, no criticism or censure.

Only love. Pure, uncomplicated love, totally without reservation. She knew he loved. Her. Oliver. All of them, and she saw that love like the scattered images in a kaleidoscope, all shape and form and color, repeated over and over again, growing in scope and size until the colors were her entire existence. Higher, sharper, she screamed with the sweet pain of orgasm roiling through her body like sunlight spilling over a dark plain. Her climax, when it finally subsided, left her shaken, filled with a bittersweet knowledge that she was, and would always be, closer to this man than the one she truly wanted.

Anton was her first. He would always be the first to have taken her beyond life as she knew it. He had taken her into the vast universe of her own mind and at the same time, had freely shared all the knowledge in his.

He was brilliant and she would never understand half of what he knew, but she respected his honesty, his generosity, his openness. He'd opened himself to her, warts and all. Mei turned and smiled at him. He lay there beside

232 / *Kate Douglas*

her with a frown on his beautiful face. She knew him now for what he was. Not a perfect man, not by any means. Not always as self-assured as he appeared. Frightened, sometimes, of what he didn't know, what he would never fully understand.

He was flawed in many ways, but always struggling to be better. He loved his wife and daughter more than life itself, loved the members of his pack, loved Mei.

"Thank you," she said. "Your secret's out."

He rolled his head to one side and smiled. She watched as a tiny bead of sweat rolled from his hairline across his temple. "Which one? I have . . . had, more than most."

She fought an impulse to taste the salt of his sweat. It wasn't her right to reach for more intimacy. "You're not perfect. You make mistakes, just like the rest of us. You want to do better, but sometimes your ego gets in the way, and if Keisha didn't occasionally slap a little common sense into you, you'd be totally insufferable."

He rolled to his back and laughed. "That about nails it. Thank you, Mei. You're as lovely on the inside as you are on the outside and I find your honesty extremely refreshing. Oliver is a lucky man to have found you."

She hesitated to ask the one question they'd both avoided. But wasn't that the reason they were here together in this bed, both of them still recovering from an orgasm of almost frightening proportions?

"I know more than I did," he said, answering her unspoken question. "Still not enough, but I think that will come as I sort through the knowledge I've gained. This much I know—you, Mei the woman, are by nature a solitary creature. So is the snow leopard. You have a natural grace that is feline, a feisty disposition more feline than lupine. Is it because you are a snow leopard when you shift, or do you shift and become the leopard because it more closely matches your nature? I don't know, but I have a lot more information now than I did."

Damn. Mei flopped back down. "Then you can't make me a wolf? Can't turn Oliver into a leopard?"

"Not yet, but don't give up." He rolled away and went into the small bath. Mei heard water running. He returned with a damp washcloth and handed it to her. "I'd offer to do this for you, but I don't want to push my luck."

She laughed and carefully wiped his seed from between her legs. He took the washcloth and threw it into the hamper. "Do you have anyone do housekeeping here?" she asked. She'd never really thought about the logistics. "This place is huge."

"When it was only the five of us and Oliver still just Oliver, he handled almost everything. Now we share the chores. I think tomorrow's a laundry day." He flipped the top down on the hamper. "We can't very well hire a house-keeper. Too hard to explain the occasional shifts from human to wolf, and the constantly changing bed partners. Better to do the chores ourselves."

Mei nodded and crawled out of bed. She dressed herself while Anton did the same. It was strange, talking about mundane things like housekeeping and laundry with a man with whom she'd just shared such an amazingly inti-mate act. She felt off-kilter. Out of balance. She wanted to shift. She knew Oliver always talked about wanting to be-come the wolf and run, but her snow leopard self wanted to hunt and eat and find a sunny spot on a flat rock and bask.

So different, by nature.

Wolves and leopards. So completely different.

Adam loped along the beaten path with Eve to his left and behind. He'd wanted to give her the lead, but she'd deferred. He knew this country better than she.

Didn't she realize he wanted to watch her perfect gray tail and follow her scent? Tongue lolling, he led her deeper into the cool depths of the forest before finally veering off

the track and winding through thick brambles and even
thicker willows.

I hope you're not getting us lost.

I could only be so lucky. He loved the sound of laughter
in her voice. When they'd first met just a month ago, that
laughter hadn't been as light. She'd not been at all flirtatious, too recently traumatized by her assault. Now Adam
felt as if he was finally getting to know the real Eve. She
was even more perfect than the lady he'd fallen in love
with.

Here. What do you think?

She almost ran into him when he stopped at the edge of
a small, flower-studded glade. Water trickled through
green grass and bright yellow wildflowers to a small pool
at the base of a rocky cliff. Thick ferns grew at the water's
edge, even now in the depth of summer. It was shaded and
cool here, with sun breaking through in dimples of light.

Eve sat. She turned and looked at him in wolven amazement. *This is gorgeous! It's perfect.*

Today is our wedding, Eve. It has to be perfect.

She blinked. *I hadn't thought of it like that, but you're
right. Adam, I love you so!*

There really were no words to express his feelings, but
the need in him rose, powerful enough it was almost a separate entity. His vision glazed for a moment and he felt as
if his muscles swelled along with his cock.

He brushed Eve's shoulder lightly with one front paw.
She stood up, turned and looked over her shoulder and her
thick plume of a tail waved. Like a flag to a bull, it called
him. Adam felt the growl low in his throat, felt the rush of
blood through his body.

Eve was his. His mate. A worthy adversary as well as
someone to protect, to love. The feelings engulfed him—
human as well as wolf. This time he raked her shoulder
with his claws and bit at the thick ruff of fur around her
neck. She snarled, an invitation.

He mounted her quickly, as if he'd mated in this form before. His cock pierced her hot sex on his first jabbing thrust. Eve yipped and tried to pull away, but the thick knot at the base of his wolven penis slipped easily between her vaginal lips, swelling and holding her tight against him. His forelegs gripped her shoulders, his rear paws scored the soft, damp earth as he struggled for purchase.

It was different, this bestial mating. Utterly different than what he knew as a human. The mental link practically slammed into him. Adam forced himself out of the sensual, physical act of sex with his mate to the bond itself, to the mental joining that was nothing at all like he expected.

Eve stopped struggling as their bodies tied. They both panted and Adam felt her muscles clenching and releasing, but all the physical sensation seemed to slip away as he entered her thoughts.

For a brief moment, confusion reigned. He was Eve and the cock inside him was huge and throbbing against his channel, and the weight of the powerful male holding him in place was as frightening as it was exciting. Their minds blended, melded, one into the other and the meadow sort of drifted away.

Replaced by memories. Loneliness as a child, moving from one foster home to another, befriending Mei, moving again and on into adulthood. Homelessness, an aching need to belong and a series of abusive relationships, one after the other, culminating in the one where Anton and Stefan had stepped in to rescue her.

No wonder she'd been afraid of commitment. Suddenly everything about Eve made perfect sense. She was brave and strong, a survivor every bit as tough as his beloved sister, Manda.

He felt Eve in his mind, felt her gentle touch and curious searching and he opened to her. Gave her his past, his present . . . and without any hesitation at all, promised her his future.

* * *

The intensity of mating as a wolf was in and of itself the most amazing experience Eve could recall. She felt Adam on a level beyond human sensation, felt the hard, jabbing thrust of an alien cock, only it was right and proper, that long, sharp thing entering this body. So was the solid bulge of muscle that swelled inside her channel and locked them tightly together.

She let her human mind go and slipped entirely into the wolf. In that moment, that perfect flash of animal intuition, everything suddenly made sense. She'd had reason to doubt her readiness before, reason to leave on her own search for identity. She finally understood the purpose in everything she'd done, every act that led to this moment, this man, this wolf.

All that was Adam flooded her mind. His past, his present, the man he was, the man he was destined to be. A destiny he would never have found without Eve beside him.

He'd come down off her back, twisted to one side, and stood at an angle to her body, yet the link remained—the tie that bound them physically, the mental link that held them even tighter. She gazed into those perfect amber eyes and finally understood the meaning of pure, inescapable love.

And when she tumbled to the ground, it was the woman who lay beside the man.

His cock slipped out of her during the shift, but he had to hold her, had to feel that sleek body next to his, smell her sweetly distinctive scent that had become as necessary to him as breathing. She'd known he was going to shift. The link was that intuitive, that powerful.

When he looked into her beautiful gray eyes, it was almost as if he saw himself looking back, so much a part of one another had they become.

"You're thinking of the same thing I am."

She nodded and pressed her face against his chest, inhaling as if she couldn't get enough of his scent. Then she laughed. "We're going to have to get used to this, but I love it. Our minds feel connected, even when we're not consciously trying to communicate. It's amazing. We have to figure out a way for Oliver and Mei to experience this."

"I know. If they can somehow bond, even it if's just once in animal form, I think the connection will remain no matter what they eventually choose to be."

"Then you believe there's a choice?"

"I'm not sure. I'm thinking Anton may have learned something from Mei. I don't feel as hopeless as I did."

"I don't feel as alone." Eve raised up on her arms and rolled over to cover him. She managed to capture his cock between her legs. He felt his balls contract and his cock swelled even more.

"I don't feel as if I'll ever be alone again," she said, kissing him. Her lips were smooth and warm, moving over his mouth and leaving nothing but pure sensation in their wake.

He thrust his hips and caught her, perfectly. She moved just enough, tilted just right and he slid inside.

Home, he thought. And in his mind, Adam heard Eve's echo.

Home.

Anton tugged Mei's hand and led her out to the back deck overlooking the meadow. Eve and Adam trotted across the thick grass through the long shadows of evening. They ran in perfect sync and the sense of their link was powerful. Anton nodded. He'd suspected something special in these two.

It satisfied him immensely to know he'd been right.

Mei tilted her head and grinned at him. "I just saw what you were thinking! Your thoughts have always been blocked to me. You do have a healthy ego, don't you?"

Anton growled low in his throat. This little one was special, as well. "I was afraid of that. Common courtesy would suggest you keep any information you glean entirely private."

She laughed and hugged him. "I'll think about it. Where's Oliver?"

"I think Keisha and Xandi decided to keep him busy while you and I were . . ."

"Oh."

Her eyes twinkled. That was a good sign. He was afraid of jealousy. So far that hadn't been an issue among them, but it had been a terrible problem for the San Francisco pack. Mei was beautiful. Sensual, intelligent, funny . . . he wanted her bonded with Oliver, the sooner the better.

Anton remembered when one of the San Francisco males turned rogue and attacked a female before she'd bonded. Mei was essentially still free to mate with any male she chose. He didn't want to see the kind of problems with this pack that Lucien Stone had been forced to deal with.

The men here were all good people. Honorable, self-assured men with integrity. Sometimes, though, the beast was more powerful than the man, especially where a receptive bitch was involved. Thankfully, all had turned out well for Jacob Trent and Lucien Stone and his wife, Tia, but it had caused the first rift among any of the Chanku.

He hoped it was the last.

Adam shifted when he reached the deck. He held out his hand and Eve sort of flowed from wolf to woman and took his hand. They both glowed with the kind of contentment that came from within.

Anton heard Mei's quiet sigh beside him. She wanted this. Wanted to know the same thing with Oliver.

"Where is everyone?" Eve grabbed a multihued sarong off the railing and wrapped it around herself. Adam slipped on a pair of shorts.

Anton glanced down at his dark slacks and grinned. Mei was right. He really wasn't the shorts type, but he'd left his shirt off. Keisha loved the sight of him in dark slacks without a shirt. He sent out a silent searching thought.

We're coming. Oliver's on his way. Xandi and I are changing the babies. Stefan's taking a shower. Did all go as you'd hoped?

Almost. The answers are elusive, but I know we'll find them.

Of course you will. I'll be out in a minute.

Of course you will. Amazing, how Keisha never doubted him. He wished he were as confident himself. No wonder he loved her.

"Mei?" Oliver stepped out onto the deck. He'd showered and dressed, but Anton sensed both Xandi and Keisha's scent about him. He looked relaxed, though a bit hesitant.

Mei ran into his arms and the two of them embraced as if they'd been apart for months. Oliver raised his head and looked at him over Mei's shoulder. "Did you . . . ?"

"Some ideas, but not answers."

Adam interrupted. "We will find answers, Ollie. No doubt in my mind. Or Eve's. Now we know what a bonding link is really like, we . . ."

"You bonded?" Xandi walked through the door with her son tied into a multicolored sling across her chest. He slept soundly, close to her body.

Adam nodded. "That we did."

She kissed both of them. Anton leaned back against the railing and watched the dynamics. The congratulations from Keisha and Stefan when he finally showed up, Mei's and Oliver's more subdued best wishes. The sense of love and support in this small pack was amazing. And powerful.

The answer came to him, a flash of light as if the Goddess herself had etched instructions into stone. He went into the house and grabbed a couple of bottles of chilled champagne and a tray of crystal flutes. Keisha followed him and took a large candle-studded chocolate cake out of the pantry.

"Stefan's birthday." He shook his head. "In all the excitement, I completely forgot."

Keisha kissed him as she walked past and headed outside. "That's why you need me. I never forget."

That's not the only reason I need you. There are too many to count.

Keisha smiled. The door closed quietly behind her. Anton stood there a moment, counting his blessings. He would never forget the emptiness before she came into his life and it took him a moment to bring his suddenly chaotic emotions under control.

"No you don't, Stefan Aragat." Keisha slapped Stefan's hand away from the cake just as Anton stepped out on the deck. "That's for after dinner. You are merely to admire it for now. I want you to know I baked it myself, without Oliver's help."

Stefan managed to swipe one finger through the frosting. He licked it off, moaning in exaggerated pleasure. "I thought everyone forgot me."

"Forget you? Not even if I tried. And believe me, there are days when I try real, real hard." Xandi laughed, but she kissed him soundly.

Anton poured the champagne and served glasses to everyone. He raised his in a toast. "First of all, happy birthday to my dear friend and packmate, Stefan, who has not been forgotten, no matter how unappreciated he might feel. May you have many more, and may you always enjoy the ride."

Stefan held his glass up and grinned. "I intend to, in my absolutely gorgeous new old truck. Thank you, my friend. At my age, I'd just as soon forget the celebration and merely rake in the goodies. Eve, thank you for bringing it back in one piece."

Eve held her glass out and tapped Stefan's, but she winked at Anton. He held his glass high once again.

"To Adam and Eve, who have joined our pack even as they've joined one another. We wish you much happiness, and hopefully, many children."

"Not yet. Please! I just caught her!" Adam slung an arm around Eve and kissed her soundly. The others burst out laughing.

Everyone except Mei and Oliver. Anton turned to them and held his glass up once again. "To Mei and Oliver. May you also experience the beauty of the mating bond, sooner, rather than later. I think we know how to fix your little problem."

"Little?" Oliver clinked his glass to Anton's.

"How?" Mei clutched Oliver's arm.

"It's your nature, Mei, to be the solitary leopard. You, Oliver, are the more social wolf, but you are both Chanku. Both shapeshifters. Once Chanku have bonded, the link remains intact." He grinned. "I think it has a lifetime warranty."

Adam grumbled. "Damned well better!"

"As I was saying . . ." Anton took a sip of his champagne. "We so easily accept our ability to become another creature, yet none of us knows how it happens. I can't film it, can't see the actual change, we can't even describe it ourselves. It's as if we wink out as a human and wink in as a wolf." He smiled at Mei. "Or, as in Mei's case, a snow leopard."

"Thanks for noticing." Her dry comment brought laughter. Anton was glad she could find something to joke about.

"There is magic around us. I don't know if we are creatures of magic or some purely physical mechanism, but I feel magic in the air we breathe, in everything we do. It is especially powerful in our sex lives. We can harness that power. Make it work for us."

"Like we did when you rescued Ulrich Mason." Stefan smiled and turned to Adam, Eve, and Mei. "We used sex magic to power our minds. Working together, we sent Anton's consciousness clear across the country. He entered a raven and was able to look around the place where Ulrich's kidnappers held him prisoner."

"How does that apply to us?" Oliver looked discouraged, but Mei grabbed his arm.

"We move my consciousness into the body of a wolf. Is that what you're suggesting?"

"Exactly."

"Now?"

Anton laughed. "No. I'll need time to prepare, as will you. I want you to practice slipping in and out of another's mind. One of the women will have to agree to be your host. Whoever that is, will have to learn to transfer as well."

Eve held up her hand, like a little kid in class, calling on the teacher. "I'll do it." She turned to Mei. "When Adam and I bonded, our first thought was that you and Oliver needed to feel the same joy we felt, the same connection."

"There's a risk, Eve." Anton flicked his gaze from Mei to Eve and back to Mei. "If the link fails during the bond, I have no idea what it could do to your mind. You might end up trapped in the leopard's body. Mei could be caught in your wolven body. It's going to take some planning, some training, and probably a lot of abstinence from all of us."

"Damn. I forgot about that part of the rescue." Stefan's mournful voice broke the tension.

"Did I say Stefan doesn't do celibacy very well?" Anton spoke to all of them, but his words were for Oliver and Mei. "That's part of this form of magic. Whoever takes part in the ritual needs to remain celibate for at least a few days. Not much for humans, miserable for Chanku, but it builds the power. We merely need to harness it. There's risk, but I've discovered there's always a risk when we love. We risk rejection, the loss of our mate, the destruction of our individuality, which can so easily be lost in our love for another. Think about it, be sure it's worth the danger. If so, we should be able to give it a shot on the night of the next full moon."

Oliver wrapped his arm around Mei's waist and squeezed. "I love you," he said, only it was so much more than a simple declaration.

Mei gazed toward the east, where the waning moon rose over the crest of the mountains towering behind them. One more month. She could wait a month for the promise of a lifetime with this man. She'd known Oliver a mere week, yet there was no doubt in her mind. She would risk anything to make him hers. To share the bond each of the others here had found with their mate.

Her solitude had never mattered less, nor had her sense of family ever been more powerful. "Thank you, Eve. I will gladly accept your offer."

Eve held her hand out and clasped Mei's. "Thank you, for trusting me. C'mon, Adam. We're cooking dinner tonight. It's got to be special for the birthday boy."

Stefan raised his hand. "Do I get a choice of menu?"

"No." As if speaking in one voice, Adam and Eve answered together, looked at each other and laughed. Within moments, all of them had slipped away. Adam and his mate to cook. Anton and Keisha to bathe Lily. Stefan and Xandi to spend time with Alex.

Mei and Oliver sat alone on the deck.

She'd never felt such peace, but there was a bittersweet sense of loss, as well. "I'll never be able to make love in my true form. Not unless we find a male snow leopard willing to host your mind for awhile."

Suddenly Oliver threw back his head and laughed. "What do you really know of leopards Mei? Other than how to be one?"

She shrugged. "Not much, really. Anton said he's ordered a book for me so I can learn more about them."

Still chuckling, Oliver squeezed her tight. "One little tidbit that might not be in your book. You know how wolves tie during sex? The male's cock swells inside the female and holds them together?"

She nodded. "I know. Keisha told me all about it."

"It's different in leopards. In most members of the cat family."

"Oh?" She frowned. "How different?"

"A small thing, really. Lots of small things. They have barbs."

"Barbs? Where?"

"Sharp little barbs on their cocks. They don't tie with the female. They sort of get hooked up. Literally. Hurts a lot, I bet."

Mei felt her crotch muscles clench. "Ouch. Anton's idea is looking better all the time." She slanted a look at Oliver and saw the humor in his eyes, felt her laughter bubbling up and out until it spilled forth, uninhibited and free. Then she punched Oliver in the arm.

"It's true! I swear it!" He laughed and doubled over, twisting away from her punches.

Then, when she could barely breath through her giggles, Oliver picked her up and carried her back into the house, through the great room, into the foyer and out the front door. She kicked and laughed and tried very hard not to get away.

Adam and Eve looked up from their work in the kitchen as they passed. "You guys gonna be here for dinner?" Adam snorted. Eve merely laughed.

"Save us some leftovers, and wish Stefan a happy birthday from us," Oliver said. He shoved the front door open with his hip. Carried Mei down the stairs, across the gravel driveway and up the steps to his cottage. "Open the door, wench."

Giggling, Mei opened the door. Oliver carried her inside and shut the door with his hip, but when he let her legs slip along his and she stood in front of him, her laughter died.

Mei looped her arms over his shoulders. She was just about Oliver's height, and she loved the fact they were eye to eye, lip to lip. "We're actually different species, you know. A leopard and a wolf."

"We're different races, too. Asian and black. It's not an issue, either."

Mei kissed him. "For that matter, we're different sexes."

"That's the best difference of all." He slipped her knit top over her head. "The very best difference." He tugged her short skirt down her legs, left her panties lying in the foyer. Then he lifted Mei once more and carried her down the hall to their room.